REIGN OF FEAR

GLEDÉ BROWNE KABONGO

BrowneStar
Media

BrowneStar
Media
www.brownestarmedia.com

REIGN OF FEAR
Copyright 2023 @ Glede Browne Kabongo

ISBN: 978-1-7333253-0-1

To Donat, my anchor in the storm

PART I
LONDON SURPRISE

CHAPTER 1

ABBIE

I T'S BEEN FIFTEEN years since she wished me bad luck.

Despite the passage of time, there's no mistake. *It's her.* Kristina Hayward. I recognize the smooth olive skin and raven-black hair, now expensively styled. Her abundance of confidence has not diminished over time.

Kristina's nerve-jangling last words spill from deep within my subconscious. *I knew you were conniving from the moment I met you. I won't soon forget this, Abbie. I won't.*

Wealthy guests, businesspeople, and tourists float around the reception area. Others follow bellhops pushing carts piled high with designer luggage up to their opulent rooms. It would be so easy to go unnoticed. Lose myself in the busy lobby of London's Savoy Hotel.

However, the situation calls for the direct approach. I won't cower in a corner like some pariah who wants to disappear into the woodwork.

She concludes her business at the front desk and heads in my direction. I shove the tourist guide into my Lana Marks alligator purse and then approach with caution.

"Kristina Haywood?"

A spark of recognition floods her face. It's followed by

a cold, cynical expression. She says, "It's Saxena now. Abbie Cooper, what brings you to London?"

"I'm here on business. You?"

"London is home. Leaving the States was the best decision I ever made."

"That's great. You must really love it here, then."

An awkward silence prickles the air despite the noisy lobby. But it quickly evaporates when my daughter Alexis arrives with her brothers Blake and Lucas in tow.

After Alexis plops down in an armchair, she says, "Mom, we'll starve to death if Dad doesn't come down soon. He's still on a call. I'm seriously about to die from hunger."

The boys back her up by nodding and grumbling.

Kristina watches the exchange, clearly bursting with curiosity. I introduce her to my kids. Lucas almost glares at her, as though he'd discovered she'd done something awful. He says hello after I give him the side eye.

"Kids, this is Mrs. Saxena. We knew each other in college."

"Oh, so you went to Yale," Alexis chimes in. "You must know my dad too."

"Your dad?" Kristina frowns in confusion.

Alexis saves me from an explanation I didn't want to provide. She says, "Finally. Now can we please get to the restaurant?"

Kristina gawks at my husband who just joined us. With vibrant hazel eyes and a lean physique, Ty looks handsome, even in semi-casual outfit. He's decked out in a tailored navy-blue blazer, crisp white dress shirt, and high-end khakis.

"Hello, Kristina." He gives her a firm handshake. "It's been a long time. Good to see you."

"You look wonderful, Ty. Haven't changed a bit," she gushes.

4

The kids seem curious and forget their earlier griping. Alexis says, "This is like a college reunion, isn't it, Mom? We should invite Mrs. Saxena to dinner with us."

"I'm sure Mrs. Saxena has plans of her own. We can't hijack her evening, now can we?"

"I guess not," Alexis says, disappointed.

Ty, the world's nicest Mr. Nice Guy, invites Kristina and her husband to join us for dinner next time they're in the States. Does he not understand I want to get as far away from this woman as possible? I certainly don't want her in our home.

"That's kind of you, Ty," Kristina says, grinning big and wide. "I'd love to catch up on old times."

"We must get going, Kristina," I interrupt. "Our kids will start World War III if they aren't fed soon. Do look us up if you're ever back in the States."

We say goodbye to Kristina and head to dinner. After Ty's lecture tomorrow, we'll fly home. Only then will I relax, secure in the knowledge that Kristina lives a continent away from us.

CHAPTER 2

KRISTINA

KRISTINA INHALED HER fourth cocktail, a powerful concoction of gin, vodka, and Chardonnay.

Her friend Seamus leaned forward so she could hear him above the noise of the bar, which was quickly filling up around them.

"Slow down, Kristina. You never drink this much alcohol."

"Don't tell me what to do. I get enough of that from Callum."

"I'm just watching out for you. What happened?"

Kristina held up her empty cocktail glass, signaling she needed another.

"Not until you tell me what's going on," he insisted.

"I ran into my ex and his perfect wife and their perfect children."

"So what?"

Kristina raked back her thick, dark hair and let out a dramatic breath. She hadn't expected her insides to twist into painful knots. Or the feelings of envy that rose up inside her.

Why did she react at all? Seeing that Ty and Abbie had not one but three kids and seemed happily married came as an unwelcome surprise. Were they happily married, though? Kristina knew better than most that outward appearances were deceiving.

"We dated in college. A future was possible. Until *she* came along and ruined everything."

"She, meaning his wife?"

"Yes."

Kristina believed the moment in time her life intersected with Ty's and Abbie's changed everything. They were so young. Abbie, only nineteen at the time, possessed a confidence and grace Kristina secretly envied. Until she realized Abbie was also conniving and clever in a deceptively subtle way.

"Go on," Seamus encouraged. "What happened at university?"

The truth, petty as it was, Kristina had hoped they would crash and burn when she noticed the exquisite diamond on Abbie's long, elegant finger. Both Ty and Kristina had been seniors. Ty had planned to attend medical school that fall. Abbie had only been a sophomore.

Oh, how Kristina had wanted to rip the sparkler off Abbie's hand that day. Carve the words *Lying weasel* across Ty's handsome face.

Instead, a defeated Kristina walked away so Ty could have what he desired most: Abbie.

Kristina shrugged. "He chose her. His loss."

"And don't you forget it," Seamus said with an encouraging smile.

Kristina felt sorry for herself. From the look on Seamus's face, he pitied her. She didn't want anyone's pity, though. She came to the Savoy to plot her exit strategy.

With its spectacular views of the River Thames, mix of old-world elegance, and modern-day amenities, Kristina already booked a suite. She looked forward to some pampering while she planned her future. One that didn't include Callum Saxena, his controlling ways, or his millions.

When her phone chimed with an incoming text, Kristina

fished it out of her purse. She looked at the screen, frowned, and returned the phone. The device chimed several more times, but she ignored it. The text messages came from Callum, wanting to know where she was.

"Callum?" Seamus asked.

"The one and only."

"Are you going to answer him?"

"No. I'm not in the mood for his nasty temper and constant criticism."

Seamus said, "Won't he worry? Perhaps you should give him a call, let him know that you're okay."

"I'd rather walk through the Sahara naked."

Seamus and Kristina had been friends since they met at Oxford. Seamus dropped out after his first year—to the chagrin of his parents—and joined the army. The two kept in touch. Kristina counted Seamus amongst a handful of trustworthy friends. She couldn't tell him how truly awful Callum was, however.

"You can't avoid him all evening," Seamus said.

"I can, and I will. I've booked a suite here for the next few days. The change of scenery may offer some fresh perspective on how to get rid of things that are holding me back."

Seamus raised a curious brow. "Meaning what?"

"I'm tired of the charade. The illusion that Callum and I are a great power couple pretending to be happy. When in reality…" She paused.

"Go on," Seamus implored. "What were you about to say?"

"Never mind. You won't understand."

"Try me," Seamus said. "All marriages face problems. That's what my married friends tell me anyway."

Seamus, like the others in Kristina's small circle, believed she lived a charmed life. But keeping up appearances had become exhausting, a chore.

At first, the relationship with Callum was exciting. The whirlwind romance. A world of wealth and glamor, unlike anything she had experienced before. It had all been intoxicating. Until it wasn't.

As a middle-class American girl from the Chicago suburbs who moved to England to study at Oxford, Kristina had found everything about Callum, ten years her senior, charming. He treated her like a fairytale princess.

But Kristina miscalculated. She didn't look deep enough. She hadn't paid attention to the red flags or had dismissed them all together.

"Callum is mean, manipulative, and controlling," she told Seamus. "Don't be fooled by his wealth or charm. And don't ever get on his bad side."

Seamus said, "I had no idea. Tell me the truth, Kristina. Are you in danger? Are you afraid of Callum?"

Kristina's eyes welled up, surprising the jaded cynic she cultivated over the years. Seamus had always been a shoulder to cry on—gentle, protective, and never demanded anything of her. She had no doubt, with the proper motivation, Seamus could easily take out Callum and solve her problems.

But revenge was more to Kristina's liking, not murder for hire. Time away would provide the perfect opportunity to plot precisely when and how she would make Callum Saxena pay for treating her poorly.

"I'm leaving," she said abruptly. "Let's join up next week."

Kristina didn't wait for his response. She left the bar, half-blinded by tears she tried to hold back. She bumped into a patron who yelled that she should bloody well look where she was going.

SHE ORDERED ROOM service for dinner. Kristina didn't want to see or speak to anyone or risk running into Ty Rambally and his family again. The evening wouldn't go to waste, however. She grabbed her laptop off the desk, plopped down on the gorgeous floral antique sofa, and booted up.

Ty made his dream come true, not that it surprised Kristina. The results from her Internet search revealed he was a cardiothoracic surgeon at Massachusetts General Hospital in Boston. MGH made the list as one of the top hospitals in the U.S. and top ten in the world.

Her ex was also on the faculty of Harvard Medical School. Only in his mid-thirties, Ty was quite accomplished. He came to London as part of a keynote lecture series from experts in the field of cardiothoracic surgery. University College London sponsored the event.

Kristina wanted to power down her laptop and focus on the delectable dinner room service had delivered. Instead, curiosity got the better of her. She ran a quick search on Abbie.

Upon discovering Abbie was a well-respected neuropsychologist and Harvard instructor who also worked closely with researchers at the Center for NeuroTechnology and NeuroRecovery at MGH, Kristina's appetite for food disappeared.

She placed the laptop back on the desk and walked toward the window, staring out at the view of the River Thames—her heart burdened by swirling emotions she couldn't understand.

CHAPTER 3

ABBIE

TY AND I escape to the private balcony of our suite and drink in the nighttime version of the London skyline. We admire panoramic views of the Tower Bridge, Millennium Wheel, and boats scattered all over the River Thames.

Sitting at a small, round table with a lantern at the center, we dig into the mascarpone cheesecake we ordered for dessert.

"So, what do you think?" I ask.

"About what?"

"Kristina, silly."

"Not much to say. Kristina obviously made her life here."

"Things certainly got awkward over dinner. Alexis wanting to know why Kristina went gaga over Dad. I don't think we've heard the last on the subject."

"Alexis was being Alexis."

"Maybe. Still, it doesn't make sense," I say, frowning.

"What doesn't?" Ty digs the fork into his cheesecake.

"Kristina claims moving to London was the best decision she ever made. And there was the way she quickly corrected me when I called her by her maiden name. It's Saxena now," I say in an exaggerated British accent. "But when you arrived in the lobby, well, our daughter explained it best."

The fork stops midway to his mouth. Ty gives me one of his infamous, world's-biggest-skeptic looks. "You're reading too much into the conversation."

"Am I? Your presence affected Kristina. Alexis picked up on it, and she's only twelve."

Ty places the fork down on to the dessert plate. "What's this about, Cooper? Did seeing Kristina stir up old memories? Are you feeling guilty after all these years?"

"Why would I?"

He shrugs. "I don't know. We became engaged a week after I broke up with Kristina. You exchanged harsh words."

"We did. And the moment Kristina stomped out of that restaurant, she became irrelevant."

I poke at my cheesecake with the fork but can't muster the enthusiasm to indulge. The decadent dessert lost its appeal.

"It took years and a traumatic event to admit our feelings for each other." I absently twirl a lock of loose hair, peering over at the boats on the river. "I wasn't about to sideline our future because you had a fling with Kristina. There's no guilt here."

Making peace with my past hasn't been easy. Though I've grown by leaps and bounds, there's always some bit of the past left over, reminding me I can never fully shake it.

It's the small bit that keeps me up at night, praying my son Lucas never becomes like his biological father: a psychopath. The moment in time Kristina and I crossed paths is insignificant by comparison.

Ty says, "Glad to hear you're not dwelling on the past. We have enough on our plates in the present."

The cheesecake finally makes it to Ty's mouth, and he chews confidently, as though the Kristina issue is settled. I'm not so sure, however.

"Your ex salivating over you in front of our children is

hardly irrelevant. Be careful, Ty. I didn't like the way her eyes lingered on you, nor her body language."

"Perhaps Kristina found the encounter awkward as well."

"I doubt it. Lucas gave her the death stare."

"That's because he doesn't like strangers."

"Or maybe Kristina still pines for you. The relationship ended abruptly. She didn't see it coming."

"We're talking fifteen years ago, Cooper. Everybody has moved on, including Kristina."

"We both know *moving on* isn't that easy for some people. We almost lost our son because Zach Rossdale refused to move on. He held a grudge for ten years."

"The two situations are different." Ty uses the fork to separate the remaining cheesecake into bite-sized pieces.

"Are they? Kristina moved halfway around the world after graduation with simmering resentment over our engagement. She told me she would never forget. It wasn't a compliment."

Ty reaches across the table and squeezes my hand. "Running into Kristina was a coincidence. Let's leave it at that."

We head back to the room to settle in for the night. My cell phone pings on the nightstand before I can slip under the covers. I hesitate to answer. Ty senses my hesitation and asks, "Who is it?"

I peek at the screen. "It's Christian."

"Let it go to voicemail."

The phone continues ringing. "It could be an emergency."

"He can't call you every time he's in crisis. Let him handle his own problems for once."

"I'll keep the conversation brief."

I sit on the bed and answer. "Is everything okay?"

Christian says he wanted to reach me before I left work for the day. I explain we're in London. When he realizes there's a five-hour time difference, he apologizes.

After I convince Christian to tell me what's wrong, he explains that he and Alan clashed again earlier in the day. He's out of ideas on how to handle his father's controlling ways. Christian is even beginning to question whether he has a future at Levitron-Blair, a global media behemoth with assets spanning streaming, television, film, gaming, publishing, and ecommerce.

"I don't think it's anything to worry about. Alan is having a hard time giving up control. It won't be long now until you take over as chairman and CEO. Don't make any life-altering decisions because you and your dad had a fight."

After I hang up from Christian, I slide under the covers and rest my head on Ty's chest.

"Was it necessary to call you about that? You're not his babysitter, Cooper."

"I'm trying to be a supportive friend. Christian has come through for us on more than one occasion."

"And how long is he going to milk that?"

"That's not fair, Ty. Christian doesn't have anyone he can talk to about these issues. Not anyone he truly trusts."

"Right, right, I forgot. My wife is the only person on the planet he can bare his soul to. The only one who can fix him. It's not your job to fix him."

"Don't say that."

Ty props up on one elbow to look me square in the face. "You can't take on any additional stress, Cooper. Tell Christian to find a therapist in New York."

"I'm not his therapist. I'm a friend who has training as a therapist. This helps me too, you know."

"How are Christian's problems helping you?"

"Taking on the leadership of a massive global conglomerate like LB is scary enough without Alan undermining Christian's confidence. It's a tightrope, mentally. My support helps me flex a different set of muscles—the mental and behavioral health aspects of my training as a clinical psychologist."

My current work focuses on assessing and evaluating cognitive and brain disorders related to conditions such as epilepsy, traumatic brain injury, or developmental and learning disabilities. That expertise required post-doctoral training in neuropsychology. Helping Christian takes me back to my clinical psychology roots.

Ty continues, "If Christian is truly a friend, he should recognize dumping his problems on you is unfair. Just be careful."

"What are you saying?"

Ty kisses me on the cheek. "Let's get some sleep. Big day ahead tomorrow."

CHAPTER 4

―•◦•―

TY

THE ROOM ERUPTED in applause after Ty wrapped up his lecture on Advances in Transcatheter Aortic Valve Replacement at University College London. He thanked the enthusiastic audience. When the moderator indicated the time for Q&A, a lively back-and-forth commenced.

The moderator cut off questions at the twenty-minute mark. After leaving the stage, Ty was accosted by a round of congratulations and fanfare over his presentation. Questions regarding when his latest research would appear in the *Journal of Thoracic and Cardiovascular Surgery* slowed his exit from the room.

Through the crowd, Ty spotted someone waving and smiling in his direction. Kristina. What an odd place for her to show. Ty didn't want to make assumptions though. He knew next to nothing about Kristina's life in London, and there could be a perfectly legitimate reason why she was inside a lecture hall filled with medical doctors.

Ty eased through the crowd with a simple plan in mind: say hello to Kristina and head back to the hotel to join the family for an early lunch.

"You're Mr. Popularity. Can't say it surprises me." Kristina's frost-white smile dazzled, complementing her tanned olive skin and white pantsuit.

Ty slung his leather backpack over his shoulder. "Are you looking into cardiothoracic medicine?" He hoped she didn't take offense. Asking why she was at his lecture would be rude. He didn't own the campus, and it was a free country after all.

"No, I'll leave the feats of genius to you," she said. "I was visiting a friend in the building. When I spotted the sign for your lecture, I couldn't believe it. You became a cardiothoracic surgeon like you always planned. Congratulations, Ty."

Sometime later, Ty sat across from Kristina at Café in the Gardens, a central London coffee shop located inside beautiful Russel Square Park. It was a perfect day in late May with clear skies, the breeze a teasing shimmer in the air, fluttering the tree leaves. When Kristina asked him to have coffee with her, there was an urgency in her voice that overrode the urge to turn her down.

"Thanks for coming. Sorry if it's a bit awkward."

"Why did you want to see me, Kristina?" He saw no point in drawing out the meeting.

"When I learned you were lecturing at the university, I made a split-second decision. I didn't think about what I wanted to say. Only that I had to see you before you slipped away again."

Ty leaned forward, cradling his coffee cup. "I'm not sure I understand where you're going with this."

Kristina tapped an expensively manicured fingernail against her coffee container. "I often wondered whether we walked away too soon. You gave me a taste of what it felt like to be cherished, and then you snatched it away. Like a puff of smoke, one moment we were, and the next, we weren't."

Ty bit his lips. His suit jacket felt too hot, so he removed it and placed it at the back of his chair. When he'd broken up with Kristina, he thought honesty was the best approach.

I'm not the man for you, Kristina. It's time I stopped lying to myself about my feelings for Cooper. It would be pointless to continue our relationship. I won't string you along.

"Kristina, I'm sorry I never gave you the chance to express your feelings. Perhaps I was an insensitive jerk back then. Please forgive me. But we've all since moved on, so why you are rehashing the past?"

"Will you let me say my piece now?" she asked.

Ty gestured for her to proceed. "For weeks afterward, I buried my pain over the breakup. When I moved to London after graduation, the distance helped. I didn't have to see you and be reminded that you chose her."

Ty leaned back in his chair and studied Kristina. She claimed she wanted to say her piece because he never gave her the chance. But was that the only reason she invited him to have coffee?

And now that he thought about it, was their meeting outside his lecture purely coincidence? Did Kristina really come by to visit a friend, or did she make an appearance for the sole purpose of getting him alone? To what end, though?

"I don't know what you want from me. We happened a lifetime ago. People change and grow."

"You were special to me, Ty. I was heartbroken when we split. And the miscarriage shattered my heart into a million little pieces."

Leaning forward, he asked, "What miscarriage?"

Ty felt a sudden need to sit down, even though he was already seated. Despite an abundance of sunlight and warm temperatures, a cold wave crashed into his chest, and for a moment, he couldn't breathe.

Kristina said, "I didn't pay attention until it was too late. With graduation approaching, nursing a broken heart, and preparing to move to England, I had a lot going on. I miscarried our baby at seven weeks."

Ty focused his attention on a flock of pigeons competing for scraps of a croissant that had fallen off the table of an elderly couple. Words froze on his tongue. A good thing because his brain had not yet formulated an appropriate response. A baby. *His* baby.

After taking in slow, deep breaths, Ty said, "I'm so sorry you suffered alone." Apologizing out loud made him feel like a louse. He had let her down and his unborn child too. "Why didn't you tell me when it happened?"

"It was better to make a clean break. That's what you wanted, right? Telling you wouldn't have changed anything. It couldn't bring our baby back."

Still, he would have supported her, although Ty had no clue how he would have dealt with the news back then.

After clearing his throat, he said, "Thank you for telling me. Did you have any support at all when it first happened?"

Kristina waived him off. "No. Just me and my determination to continue with my life, my plans. I put my grief aside to focus on the future. It didn't hit me until after I had moved to England and settled in."

She further explained. One day while sitting in a café, a couple walked in. The woman was pregnant, close to giving birth. Kristina became so distraught that the owner of the café called her a taxi to take her home. Once home, she couldn't stop crying.

"For years afterward, I couldn't stand the sight of pregnant women or babies. I avoided baby showers," she finished.

Ty didn't know what to do or say. The heaviness of the revelation clung to the air, making the silence that followed awkward. He conducted his life with integrity and believed ending his relationship with Kristina instead of leading her on had been the right thing to do.

But there were unintended consequences. Although Kristina didn't inform him of the pregnancy, he felt as though he abandoned her when she needed him most.

Kristina snapped him out of his musings when she asked, "Are you happy, Ty? I mean, truly happy. I always wanted that for you."

"Really?"

"Yes, of course. I'll admit Abbie isn't my favorite person, but if she makes you happy, that's great. Does she?"

Kristina was never one to hold back. Ty had liked that about her, yet he found the question intrusive. From the get-go, Kristina and Cooper disliked each other.

"Kristina, if you're asking whether I regret marrying Cooper because we had a rocky start, the answer is no. I've loved her since we were teenagers, but life always got in the way."

"Are you saying you were destined as a couple?"

"I'm saying she's the love of my life and my best friend."

Ty couldn't imagine going through life with anyone but Cooper. It was rough in the beginning, and there were times they each feared they wouldn't make it. Ty owed that woman everything, especially his career. But Cooper had always been a fighter, and their family stayed intact, in no small part to her dedication and determination.

She stayed home for a decade, raising their three children practically by herself while he went through medical school, residency, and specialty training. Cooper never complained and always pushed him to be the best.

Kristina pursed her lips into a fine line as she fiddled with her necklace. "Well then, I'm glad you're happy. It's important. There's nothing worse than being saddled with someone out of obligation."

"What is that supposed to mean?" Ty asked.

Kristina went silent. Then she said, "Nothing. You and your wife are making it work. A lot of people would have given up."

Keeping his temper in check, Ty pressed Kristina. She'd already given him an earful. Now was not the time to hold back.

"So this is the real reason you wanted to see me? To ask about my marriage?"

"Admit the truth, Ty. You and Abbie would not be married if she wasn't raped during her sophomore year at Yale. That's why you proposed out of the blue. You found out she was pregnant as a result of the assault. Abbie knew you would never allow her to raise the baby on her own. Lucas was her bait, and it worked brilliantly."

Red-hot rage rippled through Ty, the pounding in his ears getting louder by the second. She confirmed his suspicion. Kristina wanted to meet for coffee to spew her venom.

"Is your hatred for Cooper so all-consuming that fifteen years later you would use her trauma to fuel your bitterness? Your anger that I chose her instead of you?"

"Testy, aren't we? Have I hit a nerve, Ty?"

"Not at all," he said, straightening his spine. "You lured me here under the pretense of closure. I felt I owed you the chance. Instead, it was simply a ploy to get in your last digs at my wife. That's not cool, Kristina."

"The truth hurts, doesn't it?" She wanted to say more, but Ty silenced her with a wave of his hand.

"You're still grappling with reality, so let me spell it out one last time. I've loved Cooper since high school. My heart belonged to her then, as it does now. Interpret that however you choose. Perhaps you should focus on your own marriage instead of living in the past."

Ty stomped off, startling a group of pigeons who fled from his path. He had grave reservations about this coffee meeting with Kristina. He should have followed his instincts. Who did she think she was anyway, berating him like some little kid? The audacity.

The ambush served as confirmation he made the right decision all those years ago, not that he had doubts. Back then, Kristina demonstrated a possessive, manipulative streak, another reason Ty had walked away. Was her confession that she suffered a miscarriage a total fabrication? Was she playing him?

Ty believed people were capable of change. But Kristina's jaunt down memory lane and unfettered hostility toward Cooper said otherwise.

Tendrils of unease and distrust spiraled up from the pit of his stomach and lodged in his chest. Kristina's appearance at his lecture was no coincidence.

CHAPTER 5

KRISTINA

T HE IDEA OF dealing with Callum filled Kristina with a burning dread. The flash of irritation on his face when she walked through the door told her it would be a rough evening.

"Where were you? I've been trying to reach you for hours," he said.

"At work. Got pulled into a last-minute meeting."

"You're lying. I called your secretary. Sammi said you left earlier in the day."

Damn it! In her haste to make it to Ty's lecture, Kristina forgot to ask Sammi to cover for her in case Callum called.

"So what?" she asked defiantly. "I had things to do." Kristina walked toward the living room and dropped her keys on the coffee table at the center.

"Things to do, such as? Whenever you're vague, it's an indication you're up to something."

Callum was lucky she even made it home to their luxury apartment in the Knightsbridge section of London. The five-bedroom triplex with its L-shaped grand staircase, floor-to-ceiling wood paneling, coffered ceilings, and open seating had taken her breath away. Now, she loathed coming home to the place that once brought her so much joy.

Callum had thought nothing of plopping down a few million pounds to acquire the property because Kristina loved it. In the beginning, she imagined raising their children here. A home filled with love and laughter, birthday and holiday parties, and sleepovers. But those dreams quickly faded, much like the promises Callum made on their wedding day.

"You don't think much of me, so why are we still married, Callum?"

Kristina ambled over to the small sofa with navy-blue and yellow throw pillows near the window and sat. It was her favorite spot in the massive room outfitted with hardwood floors, high-end furniture in warm colors, expensive paintings on the wall, and a gorgeous crystal chandelier dangling from the ceiling. She picked up one of the decorative pillows and cradled it in her lap. It was getting dark out, but it didn't matter.

"Not that again," Callum said. He followed her to the sofa and stood directly in front of her, a move meant to intimidate her. Kristina was numb to the tactic, though. "You haven't brought up ending our marriage in a while, so something must have triggered you, am I right?"

It would bring her immense satisfaction to taunt Callum that seeing a certain someone had sparked something in her she thought long dead. Callum considered himself quite the catch and caught him she had. Now, Kristina wanted to throw him back into the toxic pond from which he came.

"You think you're so clever, don't you?" she asked, contempt ringing in her voice. "You know nothing, clueless as always."

"Oh wait, let me take a guess," he said, tapping his head. Callum parked himself on the arm of the sofa. "Does your foul mood have anything to do with a certain American surgeon?"

Kristina flinched, confirming his assertion. A fiendish smile played across his lips. He said, "The ice queen is melting. It's a bloody miracle. I never thought I'd see it. This calls for a drink."

Callum left and returned with a bottle of the expensive scotch he loved so much, not bothering to pour himself a glass. He drank straight from the bottle. Kristina cringed inwardly. Her husband was out for blood.

"You're wondering how I know?" Callum eased next to her this time. Kristina edged away from him, putting as much distance as she could between them on a sofa built for two. "I've known about your obsession with him for years. The photo you keep hidden at the bottom of your underwear drawer. That hurts my feelings, darling. I'm quite jealous. He's a handsome bloke and a surgeon to boot."

Kristina said nothing. She wouldn't give Callum the satisfaction.

"Shall I go on?" he said. He took another swig of scotch. Kristina never understood how he could down the drink so easily. She tried it once and hated the taste and the burning sensation.

Callum continued, "You were so desperate to reunite with your ex, you got careless. I found a flyer for his lecture stuck in the sofa. When you didn't come home the other night, I suspected you had gone to the Savoy. On a hunch, I called my mate Harry to find out if they had any guests registered with the surname Rambally, and voila."

He looked pleased with himself, as if he should be rewarded for his brilliant detective work. Spying on her was nothing new. Callum started spying when Kristina first asked him for a divorce. Convinced she was having an affair, he occasionally had her followed and once placed a tracker on her car and tried to unlock her phone.

"You're so predictable," she scoffed. "I'm sick of your controlling ways. Sick of you throwing your mistresses in my face. Sick of your put-downs. I'm just plain sick of you, Callum."

Kristina met Callum Saxena ten years ago at a party hosted by the owner of the healthcare marketing firm she worked for at the time. Handsome, charming, intelligent and worldly, she liked him immediately. They talked all night and got on well, bonding over their Indian culture and heritage. Kristina's mother and both of Callum's parents had immigrated from different regions of India to the U.S. and UK respectively.

It wasn't until a few days after their initial meeting that Kristina discovered Callum was the son of Manik Saxena, founder and CEO of Saxena Holdings. They owned everything from consumer-packaged goods companies to investment services and real estate.

Callum got more than he bargained for when he married Kristina, one of the reasons the marriage failed. He wanted a beautiful, well-educated wife who could hold her own in any setting. A wife who knew about world affairs, business, politics and spoke at least one foreign language.

And of course Callum wanted a woman who would give him children. With dual degrees in global affairs and economics from Yale, a master's from Oxford, and fluency in French and German, Kristina fit the bill.

Kristina, in turn, wanted stability, a family, and a successful career. Callum claimed family meant everything to him. He convinced her they shared the same goals. When he proposed on a trip to Switzerland, Kristina believed all her dreams had come true.

Instead of the man of her dreams, she got saddled with a controlling, manipulative narcissist.

"I checked out your doctor friend," Callum said. "If you're entertaining fantasies about reuniting, don't waste your time."

"What in the world makes you think I would share my private thoughts with you?"

"I can read you like a book. You ambushed the poor man at his lecture, hoping he still had feelings for you. When you discovered he didn't, you came home pouting. What a shame," Callum mocked.

Admitting the accuracy of his statement was out of the question. She came on too strong, offended Ty, and he got defensive. Kristina believed in going after what she wanted. Take no prisoners and absolutely no apologies. Her husband never suspected she used that strategy to reel him in. Too bad Callum was false advertising.

"Now who's the one making up fantasies?" she asked.

"Oh darling, do have some dignity. The man is happily married." Callum's phone buzzed. He fished it out of his pocket, glanced at the screen, and then placed it back in his pocket.

Returning his gaze to Kristina, he said, "The good doctor landed himself an exquisite wife, didn't he? I would shag her in a heartbeat. Did you know she's a doctor as well, a neuropsychologist?"

Callum reached for his scotch and took another swig. He continued, "And she gave him three lovely children. If I were a gambling man, I would say the odds of Ty Rambally leaving his wife for you are, um, let's see. Zero. Yes, sounds about right."

Spiteful little weasel! Callum relished feeding her insecurities. What better way to get Kristina riled up than comparing her to a woman she loathed? Abbie was gorgeous. Kristina could admit that. But she didn't care for Callum needling her about it.

She was exhausted from trying to make the marriage work. Callum's taunting only made her more determined than ever to get back into Ty's good graces.

"Why, Callum, I had no idea you so admired Ty. Of course, it makes perfect sense. Ty is ten times the man you will ever be. He's kind, talented, and brilliant. In other words, *darling*, he's everything you're not."

The big vein at the base of Callum's neck pulsated. Kristina pressed on. "You know, Ty mentioned how much he regretted the way things ended between us. He apologized, said he was an insensitive jerk. Then he declared how proud of me he was for taking on the world and doing so with style and grace."

"You're a liar." Callum pointed a finger at her.

"Am I now? Did you eavesdrop on our private conversation?"

Kristina grinned inwardly. Callum was getting worked up. He stood, jaw clenched, hands turned to fists at his sides.

He said, "Then tell me this. If you were so wonderful, why is he married to Abbie and not you?"

"She tricked him."

"Come on, that's a pathetic excuse. You were a jilted lover. Ty found someone better and married her. Plus, she gave him children. A department in which you've fallen woefully short."

Kristina shot back, "Well, of course she gave him children. Ty doesn't shoot blanks."

Callum's face flushed with rage. His nostril's flared like a rhino about to charge.

"I'm afraid the problem has nothing to do with me. You see, dear wife, I had myself checked out three years ago. I have no problem in that department." Callum stood and paced, pretending to give his next words careful consideration. "You claimed you could deliver, and so far, you've come up empty. No pitter patter of little feet."

She ignored his sarcasm. "I've been more than patient, Callum. No more stalling. Let's move forward and end this farce we call a marriage."

"Whatever will our friends say?" Callum pressed a hand against his chest for dramatic effect. "Shall I tell them you left me for a married father of three who lives in America? A man who tossed you aside like a used dish rag for the woman he's currently married to? Oh, the scandal it will cause in our circle. Muffy Dandridge will have enough gossip to keep her going for years to come."

Like you give a damn. Callum didn't want the marriage any more than Kristina did. Refusing her a divorce was his way of controlling her, keeping her prisoner. Well, she would break out of his gilded cage, one way or another.

"Let's end this now while we can still be civil to each other," she suggested.

"I will do no such thing, Kristina, dear. If and when I decide our marriage no longer serves my purposes, don't worry, you'll be the first to know."

Eight years was a long time. That was how long they'd been married. Kristina could honestly say only two of those years were good.

By year three, they had been trying to get pregnant for over a year. That was when Callum had himself checked out, as he said. Kristina had known all about his doctor visit but hadn't said a word. It surprised her he chose this moment to bring up the subject.

Kristina endured a litany of thinly veiled insults from Callum's parents, sisters, and aunts who believed she was barren. They had gone so far as to suggest Callum find another wife, one who could bear his children.

The comments didn't bother Kristina in the least. She believed her time would be best spent exacting revenge. It was the great equalizer after all.

CHAPTER 6

May 22

Words can't explain what it meant seeing you again. I almost had an out-of-body experience. No, I'm not exaggerating. You never fully understood the effect you had... have... on me, Ty. Time stood still in the lobby of the Savoy. You haven't changed. Well, that's not true. You're even more handsome than I remembered. And still the sexiest man I've ever seen. How is that possible?

You're upset with me because of what I said during our coffee meet, aren't you? Were my words too harsh? I didn't mean to hurt your feelings. Would you forgive me if I apologized? You know how difficult it is for me to apologize. I say what I say and that's it. But if apologizing will right things between us, I will. I would do anything for you, Ty. Don't you know that?

It makes no difference to me how many years we've been apart. My feelings for you never changed, and when I saw you, the floodgates opened. My heart swelled like a massive tidal wave. It overwhelmed me. Does that make me silly, ridiculous, foolish, all of the above?

The look on your face when I told you I miscarried spoke volumes. You cared. It pained you that I had suffered alone. You wished you could have been there to help me through, to mourn our loss together. Because that's the kind of man you are—considerate, protective, loving. Despite your parting words, you were angry by then, I was sincere when I asked if you were happy. You deserve to be a thousand percent happy and should accept nothing less.

CHAPTER 7

ABBIE

W E RETURNED FROM London two days ago, and I'm still jetlagged. It's a sunny Saturday afternoon, and we're visiting my parents in Castleview, a suburb thirty minutes southeast of Lexington, where we live.

Visiting the home I grew up in never gets old. It's just Mom and Dad now in this beautiful colonial with an Oxford blue exterior and white shutters, set back from a quiet street lined with hundred-year-old oak trees.

With five grandchildren, and possibly more on the way once my brother Miles and his fiancée Layla tie the knot, Mom and Dad have no intention of moving to a smaller property.

I slide the door to the deck shut and take a seat across from my mother, the indomitable Shelby Cooper. The nine-foot, adjustable patio umbrella casts shade over the table, protecting us from the blazing afternoon sun attempting to bake us under its relentless rays.

In her late fifties, Mom barely registers her age except for a few random strands of gray sprinkled in her pixie wedge hairstyle.

She says, "What's going on? You said it's about the London trip?"

"Yes. Bizarre story. I'm still trying to wrap my head around it."

When Ty returned from his lecture the day before we flew home, I sensed something was off. His mood was subdued, answers to my questions either cryptic or monosyllabic. I chalked it up to fatigue because there are days he functions on fumes.

"We ran into Ty's ex from our college days at the Savoy. It was awkward at first but ended on a pleasant note."

"That doesn't sound so bad."

"Not at all. Until Kristina asked to see Ty alone. And he went."

"Why?" my mother blurts out.

"Kristina said she needed closure. Ty ended their relationship abruptly. If you ask me, it was a ploy to pry into our lives."

"So, you're worried," Mom says. "You wouldn't mention it if you weren't."

"I don't know what to think. Kristina was captivated by Ty. Even Alexis noticed her reaction. Anyway, I warned Ty, who thought I was exaggerating. Yet, less than twenty-four hours later, she convinced him to meet up for coffee."

"And he told you all of this after you came home?"

"Yes. I'm afraid there's more."

"I figured there would be. Go on."

"Kristina claimed she suffered a miscarriage. Ty's baby."

Mom guffaws and rolls her eyes. When Ty dropped the bombshell, my distrust morphed into white-hot fury when he also mentioned Kristina's outrageous attack on me and our marriage.

"What does this woman want from your husband?" Mom asks. "Do you even believe her story?"

"I have my doubts. But on the other hand, it's not something I want to take lightly. A miscarriage is a big deal."

"What was Kristina like back in the day?"

"Manipulative, possessive, jealous. I never liked her and

33

never trusted her. When Ty ended their relationship, the real Kristina came out swinging. She cursed me out, said I used my trauma to trap Ty into marrying me and we wouldn't last."

"What?" Mom gapes at me, incredulous. "She said that to you?"

"She didn't hold back. Acted as though Ty was her possession."

"I don't like the sound of this woman, Abbie," Mom says, shaking her head. "She manipulated my son-in-law into meeting her and unloaded all of this on him. Fifteen years after the fact."

"I can't figure out why she's still bitter after so many years. She's married. We all moved on with our lives."

Mom drums her fingers on the table, a quizzical expression forming on her face.

"What?" I ask.

"Sounds like her marriage isn't going well and seeing you and Ty together triggered her in some way, brought back painful memories. Along with a truckload of regret."

"Why do you think that?"

"If Kristina was over Ty and happily married, we would not be sitting here having this discussion. If she believes you stole Ty from her, and her actions both then and now support that theory, she could be dangerous."

"What? Mom that's crazy."

"Have you forgotten, Abbie? This is not our family's first brush with an unhinged woman driven by jealousy and obsession." Mom is serious now, her tone somber. "Kristina is not harmless. You've seen first-hand the kind of damage women like her can cause."

A cold shaft of fear spreads throughout my body, clawing at every nerve. Mom is right. I had a front-row seat to the reign of terror her so-called, now-deceased best friend inflicted. We didn't see it coming, and it nearly annihilated our family. This situation is different, however. Kristina fired a warning shot, letting us know that fifteen years did nothing to diminish her bitterness and resentment.

"What should I do?" I ask.

"Watch your back. Question everything when it comes to Kristina."

"She lives in London. What could she possibly do to me?"

"Is that a serious question? You think distance is a barrier to someone with an agenda? You know better, Abbie."

"It's not fair, Mom. For the past few years, life has been peaceful." I ignore the taste of hysteria blooming in my mouth. "Now you're saying another crisis is on the horizon?"

Mom reaches over and clasps my hand with hers. "Life's never fair, sweetie. Some people have trouble with boundaries. Whether or not the meeting in the hotel lobby was accidental, we now know for certain the coffee meet-up with Ty was not. Kristina wanted to see if there are cracks in your marriage she can exploit."

"So you're convinced this isn't over, that the coffee meet-up is only the beginning?"

Mom looks me dead in the eyes and says, "You have good instincts. What are they telling you?"

"We haven't seen nor heard the last of Kristina," I say, with cool detachment, a stark contrast to my warm, sweaty palms that have nothing to do with the warm temperatures.

"Are you and Ty okay?" Mom asks.

"Of course. Why are you asking?"

"You're both juggling a lot. Especially you."

"We're good. I mean, yes, it's getting more difficult to carve out time as a couple. But we're trying. Ty floated the idea of a second honeymoon in a tropical paradise."

"Make it happen," Mom says. "The kids aren't babies

anymore. It's time to refocus on your relationship. Don't get complacent, Abbie."

Mom's intensity takes me by surprise. Should I take notes? My parents have been married thirty-five years. Despite the many ups and downs, they still behave like newlyweds.

"I'm not complacent. It's just hard to get away. The only reason we made it to London is because the lecture had been scheduled months in advance and we took advantage of the opportunity."

"With the kids in tow," she says. "When did you spend time together, just you and Ty? I bet Kristina spent more alone time with your husband than you did during the entire trip."

Ah. Mom always nails it. I'm thirty-three, and she still knows me like the back of her hands. During the trip, we took the kids everywhere with us. And before that, on the few occasions Mom had time to watch the kids so Ty and I could have some alone time, all plans for romance went out the window because we ended up collapsing from exhaustion.

Before I can respond to my mother's question, Alexis slides the door open and Ty steps onto the deck, carrying a fruity drink with umbrellas in each hand.

He places the drinks on the table and says, "For my favorite ladies." Then he whispers, "But don't tell Alexis I said you're my favorites."

"I heard that, Daddy," Alexis says. We all chuckle. Alexis is a spoiled-rotten Daddy's girl.

I take a couple of sips of my drink. My mother stands and scoops up hers.

"Where are you going?" I ask.

"Oh, didn't I tell you? Your father and I are taking the kids to Lee's. They're spending the night."

Ty glances at me, puzzled. No one informed us the kids

would be heading to my brother's house.

Mom says, "Not to worry, they'll be fine. They can't wait to spend time with their cousins."

"What about you and Dad?"

"Oh, we're not coming back until tomorrow, sweetie. Sorry to leave you and Ty all by your lonesome." Then she winks at us and heads into the house.

Turning to me, Ty says, 'Did your mother just..."

"Yes, she did. Not subtle at all."

"I like the way she thinks."

"Me too. She's the best."

CHAPTER 8

KRISTINA

ALL IT TOOK was a little ingenuity, a whole lot of moxie, and an abundance of patience. In just three weeks, she crafted the perfect plan to rid herself of her failing marriage and go after what she really wanted. There would be resistance along the way, but that was beside the point.

It was her turn in the long line at terminal E of Boston's Logan International Airport. A stone-faced immigration officer with a buzz cut asked for her passport. She handed it to him, and after he examined it and was satisfied, he said, "Welcome home, Kristina."

"Glad to be home."

She breezed past the streams of people waiting for family and friends to emerge from the long immigration lines. Having traveled all over the world, Kristina was no stranger to some of the world's largest and busiest airports. Dubai, Tokyo, and Beijing came to mind, but there was something special about being on American soil after a decade and a half.

After securing an Uber via ground transportation, the driver got chatty. "What brings you to Boston?" he asked.

"I'm up for a job at MGH," Kristina said.

"That's great. My wife works there as a medical interpreter.

What job are you interviewing for?"

"Assistant Director of Development. I'll be managing the MGH Fund employee campaign. Well, I will after I land the job."

"That's a big job. The campaign raises over a million dollars annually." The driver escaped the late afternoon sun and dipped into the Ted Williams Tunnel, taking them under Boston Harbor. Traffic was heavy. Kristina felt claustrophobic but said nothing to that effect.

Instead, she focused on the driver's comment. "I'm more than capable of handling the campaign." A bold statement, but the word *can't* didn't exist in Kristina's vocabulary.

The interview came together much faster than she anticipated, to her delight. Kristina didn't need a job, not for a while anyway, but on a whim, she cruised the hospital's jobs page. Luck was on her side. It had been a sign, one she couldn't ignore.

A listing for the assistant director of development role popped up less than five minutes into her search. The description was lengthy, and she almost missed it—the two lines that sealed her determination to get the job.

The assistant director's responsibilities included staffing co-chairs for the campaign, co-chairs made up of senior level administrators and physicians. One physician in particular came to mind.

She sent in her resume and reached out to her former college roommate who had a few high-level contacts at MGH. Kristina secured two video interviews. During the interviews, she sneakily hinted she would be in Boston in the near future and available to meet face-to-face. That wasn't true, but they had no way of knowing.

"Good luck with the interview. I hope you get the job," the driver said.

"Thank you."

She didn't need luck. Kristina was too perfect for the role. She more than adequately met or exceeded all the requirements. Her stellar resume couldn't be ignored: a master's from Oxford in Global Health Science and Epidemiology, experience on the marketing and non-profit sides of healthcare, and significant fundraising experience. In fact, Kristina was so confident the role was hers, she never bothered crafting a Plan B.

Upon arrival at her suite at the Mandarin Oriental Hotel, she went to work right away. She banged out an email to two realtors she researched beforehand to find an apartment quickly. Although the Boston real estate market was tight, with astronomical prices, money was no object. Despite his countless flaws, Callum had always been generous with his wallet. Kristina's monthly allowance exceeded what many people made in an entire year.

If Boston proper didn't work—and by Boston proper, she meant Back Bay, Beacon Hill, downtown, or South End—she would consider getting a place in the suburbs.

After unpacking, Kristina showered and carefully laid out her outfit for the final interview. A fitted Carolina Herrera double-breasted blazer in navy blue with matching pencil skirt. Her accessories included a double strand pearl necklace and matching earrings. A pair of leather Ferragamo pumps with stiletto heels rounded out her wardrobe.

She wasn't always so confident, tough, and willing to go to any lengths to get what she deserved. Her mother had unwittingly taught a young Kristina that women who were too nice and accommodating ended up as doormats. No one learned that bitter lesson more than Aasvi Hayward.

Kristina never forgave her mother for being weak, for allowing Kristina's father, Matthew Hayward, to use her and then discard her when he no longer needed her. Because her mother worked hard and sacrificed to help her dad get his trucking company off the ground—especially when banks repeatedly turned him down for a loan to start his business—her parents' marriage should have lasted, stood the test of time.

Instead, the marriage fell victim to a tired, worn cliché. Once Hayward Trucking became a multi-million-dollar business, her father left her mother for a younger woman.

To add insult to injury, Matthew Hayward turned his back on Kristina and her brother Cameron as though they were radioactive waste. No phone calls or visits for birthdays or special occasions.

No showing up for Cam's baseball or soccer games. No applause, or "Go, Kristina" at the top of his lungs during her mathlete days, or "I'm so proud of you for getting into Yale." No walking her down the aisle at her wedding to Callum. What she got was stone-cold, contemptuous silence.

It's never too late to right a wrong, Kristina thought, turning her attention to picking out the right makeup. People believed dwelling on the past could eat a person alive. She subscribed to a different philosophy. The past was an excellent teacher. And she had always been an excellent student.

She wasn't like her sweet, kind-hearted mother who refused to fight back. Her prideful mother refused the divorce settlement, believing that accepting one dime was akin to accepting payment to go away.

Unlike her mother, though, Kristina would take everything owed to her. With fifteen years' worth of interest.

CHAPTER 9

—◆◇◆—

ABBIE

I T'S BEEN A busy morning of back-to-back patients, topped off by a consult with the lead clinical investigator on a drug trial that could have implications for a couple of my patients suffering from traumatic brain injuries.

My stomach growls. I should head out to get lunch, but I'm drowning in an ocean of evaluations and new patient diagnoses. I'll keep going for a while in this small office I've made cozy with potted plants, framed artwork on the walls, and a small bookcase.

When someone raps on the door, I invite them in without looking up from my computer screen.

"MGH is working you too hard. It's lunchtime, and you're still tapping away at your keyboard," the familiar voice says. My visitor strolls into the office with his signature, confident, purposeful stride.

His wheat-blond hair is coiffed to perfection. Dressed in a slim-fitting, Italian silk and cotton-blend jacket and matching dark-gray pants, he's a throwback to the stylish leading men of old black-and-white Hollywood films.

"Christian. What a surprise." I get to my feet and usher him into the office with a hug.

I gesture for him to take the seat across from me and then sit behind my desk.

"What are you doing here?"

"I'm in town for the day on some business. Thought I would stop by to see you. Sorry for the intrusion. I know how busy you are. But it's been a while since we've seen each other. How are you?"

"I'm great."

"Are you sure?" He leans in, concern streaked across his face.

Am I exuding some strange, anxious vibe? Since returning from London, I've been unable to banish Kristina from my thoughts, despite knowing an ocean and continent separate us. I blame my mother for making me paranoid, forcing me to admit we may not have heard the last of Kristina. I pray Mom's wrong.

"Don't I look fine?"

"You always look stunning," he says, assessing my wardrobe and approving with a slight nod of the head. "But something's bothering you. I come to you with my problems all the time. You can talk to me about anything, anything at all, and it will stay between us."

"Stop worrying so much. I'm fine." I straighten a stack of files on my desk to put some distance between his prying gaze and my racing thoughts.

"You can confide in me, Abbie," he says, his voice composed and soothing. "Whatever it is, lay it on me."

"Are you and Alan okay?" I ask, ignoring his plea.

"When it comes to my father, there is no such thing as *okay*."

"What do you mean?"

"Dad is desperately trying to impose his will on me. He recently undermined me on an acquisition. Everything was under control and running smoothly, but he just had to insert himself into the negotiations. I was livid." Christian's nostrils flare as though it was Alan sitting there instead of me.

"Alan can't run Levitron-Blair forever. He must relinquish control at some point."

"The way things are going, that day will never come, and frankly, Abbie, I don't know how much more I can take."

I pluck a pen from the custom pen holder that spells out my name and twirl it around my fingers. I say, "What do you mean? Are you considering quitting?"

"I've thought about it."

His confession surprises me. Christian has been groomed from birth to lead Levitron-Blair.

I spin around in my swivel chair several times, trying to decipher what this could mean for my friend and his future.

"So you don't want this anymore? There's no one else, Christian. You're it. The future of LB is literally in your hands."

"I bought into the legacy narrative. A Wheeler has always run LB, since the company's founding almost eighty years ago. But what if there's something else I'm meant to do?"

"Only you can answer that question. Assuming leadership of LB is not a role you can be ambivalent about. So if you think there's something else out there for you, you should find out. And quickly."

"Do you think I have what it takes to run LB successfully, take it to a new level?"

"What does your gut tell you?"

"If I could get him to back off, things will work out. The panic attacks would go away. I could devote myself to the job at hand instead of always looking over my shoulder, trying to shake my father's shadow."

"Panic attacks? You never mentioned panic attacks. When did they start?"

He waves off my concern. "It's nothing for you to worry about. I'm fine."

If it's nothing to worry about, why did he mention it? In addition to the pressure of assuming leadership of Levitron-Blair, there is pressure of another kind weighing on Christian. His parents and half of New York want to know when he'll get married and settle down.

I ask, "How are things between you and Ms. Von de Heide? According to *Page Six*, you were both spotted, and I quote, 'canoodling' on the beaches of Saint Tropez. Photos accompanied the article."

"*Page Six*, Abbie? Since when do you read the gossip pages?"

"How else am I supposed to keep tabs on you and your bad-boy antics?" I dead pan.

A sheepish grin spreads across his face. He turns away from my gaze, embarrassed.

I say, "You have a reputation with the ladies. Just watch yourself. You don't want it to fall off."

Christian looks back at me, eyes wide, horrified. "Abbie. I can't believe that came out of your mouth."

"What?" I ask innocently. "Let's be honest. You get around."

Christian has been dating cosmetics heiress Samantha Reed Von de Heide on and off over the last three years. Sam stands to inherit billions but struck out on her own by launching a luxury and lifestyle brand that includes beauty products and home décor. Her business operates in thirty countries. According to her website, she's equal parts philanthropist and entrepreneur.

New York high society has been buzzing about the inevitable nuptials, merging two mega fortunes, and Christian and Sam becoming the power couple to end all power couples.

"You and Sam have been together for years. Why haven't

you popped the question?" I ask cheekily.

He won't look me in the eye and instead focuses on one of the plotted plants in the corner of the room.

"What is it, Christian?"

Refocusing his gaze on me, he says, "Sam and I get along great. She's easy-going, and we have fun together. She doesn't make unreasonable demands and has her own successful career."

"But?"

"I need more than that."

"How much more?"

Christian rubs his chin. There's a tenseness radiating from him, though he most likely doesn't realize his body language is giving off the uncertainty vibe.

"Someone who can help me gain clarity when I need it. Someone who understands and can handle the intense pressure of my job, which will only get worse if I take over as CEO."

"And what else?" I ask. He's holding back, the real reason he won't commit to Sam.

After a long, contemplative pause, he says, "You and I have a powerful connection, Abbie. It never waned in all the years we've known each other. In fact, the opposite happened. Our connection grew stronger. I guess I'm still chasing that high—a high I've never been able to replicate with any other woman."

For the second time since he arrived, Christian takes me by surprise. I lean back in my chair to put some distance between myself and this latest revelation.

"Christian, I thought we put that issue behind us. You said you were okay with us being good friends and that you understood there could be nothing more between us."

"And I meant every word of it."

"I'm confused. You said you won't propose to your girlfriend because you don't have the same connection with her that we do. Yet, you understand and respect the rules that govern our friendship. Did I get that right?"

As a therapist, I know how important connections are in relationships. It's often the glue that holds everything together.

"There has to be some connection with Sam. If it wasn't working, you would have walked away. What about the family you say you want? We've had that discussion many times."

"I'm not sure she's the one," he says bluntly.

"Come on, Christian. You've dated enough women to know, don't you think? If Sam isn't the one, who is?"

He says nothing. I wait him out, but he remains tight-lipped. After a long stretch of silence, he says, "Tell me what's going on with you."

"Where did you get the idea that something's going on?"

"I sensed it when we spoke last, while you were in London last week. I will take it as a personal insult if you keep insisting everything is fine. You're worried about something. Why is that?" Christian pins me with a determined stare that says he won't back down until I spill my guts.

"Since you won't let this go, I'll show you how silly it is to worry. We ran into Ty's ex during the London trip." I provide a quick background and rundown of our encounter with Kristina in the lobby of the Savoy hotel.

"Anyway, she was shocked to see us together and that we had a family. Then we all went about our business. Now we're back home, and Kristina is in London with her husband."

I lean back in my chair, convinced Christian will be satisfied with my explanation and let the matter drop.

He says, "Running into an ex can be uncomfortable, especially if things ended on a sour note. It sounds like that's exactly what happened. Why was this woman shocked to see you and Ty together, Abbie?"

I let out a deep frustrated sigh. This line of questioning is only feeding my paranoia about Kristina. No good can come from dredging up the past for Christian's benefit. For one, he'll try to fix it. For another, that's between my husband and me. There's no need to involve a third party.

"It's nothing, Christian. I knew Kristina when she and Ty dated. Then Ty broke up with her and proposed to me. She was angry and confrontational, said we wouldn't last. I guess it surprised her we *did* last, fifteen years and counting. Anyway, it's a non-issue. I all but forgot about the incident."

"Have you?" he asks brazenly. "There's more to the story. Why won't you tell me?"

"I'm starving. Let's get lunch," I say and then stand to prove how serious I am about getting food. Christian doesn't budge.

"You suspect this woman might be trouble, don't you?"

PART II
LET THE GAMES BEGIN

CHAPTER 10

KRISTINA

K RISTINA'S GAZE DRIFTED to the striking couple across the street from the Bristol Gardens restaurant. Their body language radiated a closeness, the kind of familiarity that resulted from a long association. Perhaps even intimacy. The woman threw her head back and laughed at something the man said. They each clutched the restaurant's signature takeout bag.

The woman was black, tall, and sleek in a purple sheath dress that stopped just above the knees, her svelte figure accentuated by impossibly long legs Kristina thought only runway models and gazelles possessed. Then recognition flooded her brain. Abbie!

However, the man fawning all over Abbie was not her husband. The man resembled a blond Calvin Klein model and reeked of wealth and privilege. Who was he? How did he and Abbie know each other?

Kristina opened her purse, retrieved her cell phone, and snapped a few photos before Abbie and the man started moving again. *You're being very naughty, Mrs. Rambally*, Kristina thought. She recalled her conversation with Ty in London. *The love of my life*, he had said of Abbie.

Based on what she just witnessed, Ty might be in for a

rude awakening. What was Abbie thinking? The woman had the perfect husband—smart, successful, handsome, a man who adored her—and instead of appreciating him, she was out in public flirting with the human version of a Ken doll.

Something about that man made Kristina curious beyond wanting to uncover his connection to Abbie. She had never seen him before, yet something about him looked and felt familiar. Several cars went speeding by, blocking her view.

When she glanced across the street once more, Abbie and her companion had disappeared into the late spring afternoon, replaced by a new wave of pedestrians going about their business.

Kristina headed into the restaurant to pick up her order. She wanted to stretch her legs, get out of the office, and figured the less than ten-minute walk from her office on Dalton Street to the restaurant would do her good. It had rained earlier in the day, and the mottled gray sky had turned clear and sunny.

She approached the hostess at the reception podium of the restaurant and provided her name.

"Your order will be right out," the woman said with a friendly smile. Her round cheeks and high ponytail reminded Kristina of Holly Wilson, the teenage babysitter her parents sometimes hired to watch Kristina and her brother Cameron when they were growing up in the Chicago suburb of Hickory Hills.

Holly had a soft spot for Cam and let him stay up way past his bedtime. Kristina never squealed on them, not once.

An idea occurred to her as she waited her order, watching people filing in and out of the restaurant. The hostess's name was Emily, Kristina learned from her nametag.

"Say, Emily, tell me if I'm being too nosy, but there was a couple in here earlier getting their takeout. The guy was hot."

Kristina leaned in conspiratorially and gave a description

of Abbie and the man with her. "I know the woman; her name is Abbie. We're old acquaintances, but I don't know the guy.

"Do you remember his name from his lunch order? I want to ask Abbie about him next time we run into each other. It would be nice to have a name instead of saying that guy you were with the day you went for takeout."

Emily's eyes lit up as though she and Kristina were high school friends dishing about the boy all the girls had a crush on.

Emily said, "All the women in here were checking him out. He was so cool about it though, you know, humble."

His name, please. I don't have all day, Emily.

"So you remember his name?"

"Yeah, it's Christian."

"Are you sure?"

"Yeah."

"Did you hear what he and Abbie were discussing while they waited?"

Emily frowned.

"Oh, sorry. I'm not a stalker or anything like that. I just want to make sure that he and Abbie aren't involved. It would be awkward if they're dating and I expressed an interest in him, you know what I mean?"

"Abbie wore a wedding ring. How come you don't know she's married if she's an acquaintance, as you claim?" Emily picked up a few menus and handed them to a passing server. "I have to go. Your food should be out any minute."

Damn it, Kristina had pushed too hard. Asking for the last name on the credit card Christian used to pay for his order was out of the question. Emily would probably call the cops on Kristina, accuse her of trying to steal Christian's credit card details.

After she received her lunch order, Kristina headed back

to the office, using the ten-minute walk to let her mind wander freely. It flashed back to the lobby of the Savoy when Abbie introduced her kids, before she found out Ty was their father. Kristina remembered thinking one of the kids stood out, but she hadn't given it much thought at the time—still reeling from the shock of seeing Abbie after so many years.

What was the boy's name? Oh, yes, Lucas. Lucas's ice-blue gaze had sliced right through Kristina. He had assessed her with suspicion and the I-don't-like-you vibe thrown in just in case Kristina didn't get the hint. What a weird kid. Though Lucas said hello after Abbie gave him the side eye, Kristina couldn't figure out what his problem was.

A teenager with attitude was not headline news, but what struck her as odd was Lucas's resemblance to Christian and someone with the same ice-blue gaze who had treated her with cool indifference. The man who assaulted Abbie.

CHAPTER 11

ABBIE

FTER A LONG, hot shower, I towel off and massage the creamy, luxurious lotion into my damp skin, the fresh vanilla-and-orange scent wafting throughout the bathroom. Standing in front of the mirror, I draw a smiley face into the steam on the mirror with my index finger. Because I'm happy. We're happy. Our family is perfect.

At thirty-three, I've had my share of nightmares but always came out on top, scars and all. The notion that Kristina poses a threat to my family is more than I can bear. The past few years have been peaceful. No drama, no nightmares, no psychopaths plotting to take me down. Tears prickle at the corners of my eyes as I stare at my anxious reflection.

I've been stalked, blackmailed, kidnapped, and sexually assaulted. Then the unthinkable happened. Every parent's worst nightmare. Lucas went missing. Is it too much to ask for a reprieve? Better yet, how about a normal life? I like normal. I need normal. I crave normal.

Picking up my hairbrush off the sink, I brush my thick, glossy, shoulder-length tresses in smooth, even strokes, trying and failing to squash the bad feeling that's been shadowing me since this afternoon.

Some call it gut instinct, intuition, or a sixth sense. I couldn't shake the feeling of being watched when I stepped out for lunch with Christian. To make matters worse, my mother's warning kept circulating in my head, an endless loop on autopilot. *Have you forgotten, Abbie? This won't be our family's first brush with an unhinged woman fueled by jealousy and obsession.*

Kristina couldn't be the reason for the bad feeling, could she? Has she resurrected her obsession with Ty? But she's thousands of miles away in London. There's no reason to be paranoid. I set down the brush with a clang and sigh. I'm overworked and overstressed. That's it. The fatigue is clouding my judgment, making me see things that aren't there, feel things that aren't real.

"Cooper, are you going to stay in the bathroom all night?" Ty's voice breaks through my anxious thoughts. "I have a surprise for you."

"Coming."

I grab the blush-pink terry bathrobe off the hook on the back of the door and hurriedly slip into its soft cotton comfort. When I step into the master suite, Ty waves his phone excitedly, a big grin plastered on his face.

"What is it?" I ask.

"Come and see." He pats a spot on the bed next to him. I do as he says. He drapes an arm around my shoulders and holds the phone at our line of vision with his free hand.

A video fills the screen. Lush, tall palm trees sway in the breeze. Next, images of turquoise-blue waters and white, sandy beaches appear. I open my mouth to say something. Ty places an index finger over my lips to silence me.

My eyes remain glued to the screen, absorbing the slew of images that could only be described as paradise on Earth. Massive luxury suites with verandas and ocean views, delectable dishes made from fresh local ingredients, outdoor pools flanked by palm trees with yellow and white cabanas facing the ocean.

The gorgeous skies and clusters of hibiscus and lobster claws among the bold, tropical flowers complete the picture. The video ends with the tide, white and frothy rolling inland.

"Wow! Does this mean what I think it does?" I ask, wide-eyed and excited. "You've booked this place for us?"

"You guessed correctly."

His eyes sparkle under the dimmed lights of our bedroom, a large suite I've gone through great pains to turn into an oasis of calm and relaxation. The walls are painted a soft, pale blue. A vanity stool, nightstands, and an accent chair are cream colored with gold accents. A gorgeous handmade rug rests on the hardwood floors at the foot of the bed, and an aroma machine diffuses the scent of fragrant oils at pre-programmed intervals.

"When? There's so much to do. Requesting time off from work, asking our parents to watch the kids, and..."

Ty silences me by brushing his index finger across my lips once more. But it's not an admonishment to keep quiet. It's playful, sensual. "Already handled," he says.

"What do you mean?"

"In a couple of weeks, you and I will be frolicking in this tropical paradise for a second honeymoon. Your only concern should be all the naughty things I have planned for you."

"Oh my, do spill the tea," I say, my hand flying to my chest. "What are these naughty things you speak of?"

My sass only encourages him. Ty inches closer and whispers something so thoroughly scandalous in my ears that I can't help but giggle, and then I burst out laughing at his outrageous suggestions.

"You know that's physically impossible, right?"

"Says who?"

"The laws of gravity."

I adjust myself on the bed, sitting upright, my back against the headboard with my legs pulled up and arms resting on my knees. I've missed this playful, flirtatious side of Ty. We're both so caught up in the daily grind and our numerous responsibilities that we never allow ourselves time to slow down and just be us.

When he lifts my hand and draws it to his lips for a kiss, my heart flutters. I'm reminded of the handsome teenage boy I fell in love with freshman year of high school, after I caught him studying me from across the room at a welcome reception.

He had broken away from his group and strolled toward me, holding a plastic cup in one hand. When he got close enough, he said, "Why are you standing in the corner all by yourself? Are you anti-social or what? It's a mixer, but I don't see you mixing or mingling."

Then he smiled at me. A dazzling, hypnotic smile. Fourteen-year-old me almost melted in a puddle right then and there. He wore a light-blue button-down shirt and jeans. And he smelled incredible. Fresh and clean with a hint of citrus thrown in.

"I'm Ty Rambally," he had said, extending a hand. It took me a moment to get words to leave my mouth. I took his outstretched hand and introduced myself in a voice that sounded like a frog got caught in my throat.

"Abigail Cooper," he repeated, trying on my name for size.

"Everyone calls me Abbie," I interjected.

"I think I'll call you Cooper instead." He nodded as though it was the most brilliant idea he'd had in a while. "Yeah, sounds cool."

"Um, okay," I said, not sure how else to respond. No one had ever volunteered to address me by my last name before.

"What about you?" I asked. "Your last name is unusual, isn't it?"

"Yeah. I get that a lot. My dad is Indian, from Guyana."

Because I didn't want to appear like a total idiot in front of this guy whose presence hit me like a lightning bolt, I scanned my brain, willing it to recall relevant geography lessons.

"South America," Ty said, as if he could read my thoughts and knew I had no clue where Guyana was. "Guyana is in South America, the only English-speaking country there. The culture is similar to the Caribbean islands."

"Oh, right," I said, embarrassed.

We found a seat and ignored everyone else for the remainder of the event. Ty was beginning his junior year and was a member of the committee that set up the welcome reception for freshmen. Ty and his family lived in Scarsdale, a wealthy suburb in upstate New York. Both his parents were doctors, his dad a plastic surgeon and his mom, originally from the Bahamas, was a reproductive endocrinologist.

I nodded like I knew exactly what a reproductive endocrinologist did and made a mental note to research it the minute I got home. By the end of my freshman year, Ty and I had become inseparable.

We've been best friends ever since.

"Where were you just now?" he asks, bringing me back to our complicated present.

"Freshman year at St. Matthews. When you used that weak pick-up line on me about being anti-social." He draws closer to me.

"It worked, didn't it? Could have predicted that eighteen years later we'd be here?"

"No, I couldn't."

Ty leans in and kisses my forehead. Then he says, "Promise me nothing will ever come between us. We belong together, Cooper."

Where did that come from? I squint at him. "Are you okay?"

"Fine," he assures me. "You're not keeping anything from me, are you?"

Guilt stalks my conscience like a lion on the prowl for its next meal. I didn't tell him I met up with Christian for lunch this afternoon. Ty already expressed concern about Christian sharing his problems with me. It was just an innocent lunch. No reason to get Ty upset over lunch. He has enough on his plate already.

"No, Ty. I'm not keeping anything from you."

Forcing my brain to dissolve the guilty thoughts, I switch gears. I cross over to where he sits and straddle him. He opens his mouth to speak, but I silence him. "Shhhhh, Dr. Rambally. Enough talking." I unbutton his shirt and peel it off his body. After I remove his belt, I say, "There are so many interesting things we could do besides talking."

He beams at me, stroking my arm. "What are these interesting things you speak of?"

"It's best if I show you."

CHAPTER 12

TY

HAVING CAUGHT UP on paperwork, Ty hurried down the corridor to catch the elevator that would take him to the ground floor. The summer schedule at Harvard Medical School started up in August. As an assistant professor of surgery, he couldn't miss the meeting.

The parking situation at the Longwood Campus where he taught already annoyed him and he hadn't even left MGH yet. Parking in Boston was notoriously challenging, and the Longwood area was no exception.

With his phone in hand, he fired off a quick text to Cooper, smiling as he did so. Several colleagues and staff offered greetings as they passed him by. He acknowledged the greetings without looking up from his phone.

> Heading to Longwood. See you tonight.
> Might I interest you in a repeat of last night?

Followed by a series of fire emojis.

Her response came in swiftly.

Cooper

What do you have in mind?

Cooper

Tell me in one word.

Ty barely heard the elevator ding. He was floating on air, grinning like a fool. The perfect response he formulated in his brain—*one word isn't enough to describe what I have in mind*—never made it into the flirty text exchange.

"Hello, Ty."

His blood chilled. *It couldn't be.* Ty looked up from his phone, and like an apparition, a figment of his imagination, a smiling Kristina stepped out of the elevator and stood less than a foot away from him.

Ty said nothing at first, just studied her as his body pulsated with dread. Then he summoned his inner calm, much like he did when performing complicated surgeries that looked like the patient would take a turn for the worse. He faced life-and-death situations almost on a daily basis. Surely, he could handle seeing the ex he thought he left behind in London.

"Kristina. What brings you to Boston?" he asked, his tone pleasant and relaxed.

"Would you believe me if I told you the hospital begged me to be the new assistant director of development for the MGH Annual Fund? They made me a great offer, and I thought it would be nice to come home to America."

Ty didn't know what to say. He fumbled for the right words, but his brain wouldn't cooperate. Finally, he said, "Well, Boston is a great city. Congratulations on the new role. I wish you the best."

Taking that elevator was out of the question, so he started walking away. He would catch another bank of elevators on the same floor. Or perhaps he might take the back stairwell and walk to the next floor and catch the elevator there.

Ty wasn't a coward. He just needed a minute to calm down. How was he going to break this news to Cooper? What was Kristina doing here? Of all the hospitals in all the world, she ended up at MGH? Did such coincidences exist?

Kristina called after him as he walked away. "Ty, I'm hoping you can spare me a few minutes of your time to discuss a possible co-chair run for next year's campaign?"

Glancing at his watch, Ty turned to face Kristina and frowned, anxious he would be late for his meeting at the medical school if he didn't keep it moving.

"I was co-chair this year, before you came on board. I'm skipping next year to give another physician an opportunity to serve. Now I really must run, Kristina. Good luck."

She persisted. "Perhaps Abbie might be interested in volunteering in some capacity and convince her friend to make a generous donation. He looked like someone with deep pockets."

"What friend?" Ty suspected Kristina might be playing some angle, but curiosity overrode his common sense.

"Well, I don't know his name. I just moved here. He and Abbie were at lunch yesterday—tall, blond guy, really good looking, gorgeous actually." She paused, waiting for Ty's response. He said nothing.

She continued, "Anyway, I assumed you were all friends. Abbie seemed comfortable with him. They were playful, laughing and carrying on."

Ty almost blurted out Christian's name. Cooper never mentioned Christian came to town, let alone that they had lunch together. And why does Kristina know this? Was she spying on them?

Why didn't Cooper say anything?

But a voice deep in the far corners of his mind advised him to recognize Kristina's tactics. Not only was she fishing for information, wanting to know who the man was, but also to gage Ty's reaction.

"You'll have to talk to Cooper about volunteering; it's her call. And, yes, she was out with a friend. I couldn't join them as we had planned. Now I really must run."

Ty didn't wait for a response. He couldn't get away from Kristina fast enough, a series of careening thoughts bombarding his mind.

CHAPTER 13

ABBIE

DEEP, IMMOBILIZING PANIC followed me most of the day. I couldn't believe the words staring back at me from my screen when Ty texted after several failed attempts to get me on the phone.

Ty

Kristina is here. She got a job at MGH.

For several minutes, I couldn't respond. I sat in my office staring at the text, willing the words to dissolve as though they never appeared in the first place. When my vision got spotty from gazing so long and hard, I put the phone away to collect my bearings and calm my galloping thoughts.

It's dinnertime. We sit around the island in the middle of the kitchen. Chinese takeout containers and plates are strewn all over the quartz countertop. I'm too tired to cook. It's as though the news about Kristina drained all my energy the moment I read Ty's text. Lucas and Blake are arguing over who gets the last Peking ravioli, while Alexis prattles on about Camp Greenaway, a brother-sister summer camp in New Hampshire she will attend with her siblings.

Alexis ticks off all the activities she's looking forward to: sailing, photography, and tennis. But I'm only half listening. Ty has been uncharacteristically quiet. He's barely touched his food. Something else is on his mind besides the shock of discovering Kristina is in Boston and works at MGH.

"So, when did Kristina start at MGH?" I ask.

He shrugs. "I don't know. She must be a brand-new hire. I just ran into her at the elevator this morning. She pitched me on the idea of co-chairing the MGH Employee Fund campaign. I shut her down, but she might reach out to you."

"Why?" I say, a bit too loudly, drawing the kids' attention. They look up from their dinner, surprised by my outburst. "Sorry," I say.

"Kristina said she wanted to find out if you'd be interested in volunteering. I told her it was your decision."

"Are you talking about Mrs. Saxena?" Alexis interrupts. "Now that she's in Boston, we can invite her to dinner like you promised while we were in London, Mom."

I give my daughter, almost thirteen, an admonishing glare. "Alexis, how many times have I asked you to stay out of adult conversations? This doesn't concern you. If I want your opinion, I'll ask for it."

"Calm down, Cooper," Ty hisses. Blake and Lucas, eyes wide, shrink back in their seats.

Before I can respond, Alexis says, "It was your idea in the first place, Mom. You don't have to get all salty out about it. If you want me to stay out of adult conversations, then don't have adult conversations around me."

That does it. My patience has officially run out. Anger oozes through my veins, making their way up to my tongue. Of all my kids, Alexis likes to test me, see how far she can push me. Ty opens his mouth to say something, but I hold up a palm, signaling that I will handle Alexis.

After a sharp intake of breath, I say, "Go to your room. Now! I don't want to hear a peep out of you the rest of the night."

Alexis pushes back from her chair, making loud scraping sounds against the tiled kitchen floor, and storms out. She trudges up the stairs like an angry herd of hippos, each step loud enough to be heard down the street. The mood has soured at the table. Ty nods in the direction of his home office.

"Finish your dinner and then load the dishwasher afterward," I say to Blake and Lucas as I trail Ty out of the kitchen.

I close the door behind me and lean up against the back, arms folded.

"Don't you think you were a bit hard on Alexis?" Ty asks, his tone measured, the way he does when trying to disguise how annoyed he is with me.

"No, I don't. Kristina being here and landing a job at the same hospital we work in is not a coincidence. That coffee meet-up in London was not the end. It was the beginning of whatever scheme brought her here.

"The last thing I need is our daughter sticking her nose into a situation that doesn't concern her, asking to have Kristina over for dinner. She's just a kid and needs to stay out of this."

Ty shoves his hands into his pockets and stares aimlessly at the wall, his gaze eventually landing on a photo of the two of us taken aboard the Wheeler family yacht in the Caribbean. Katherine invited us to an intimate birthday bash she threw in Alan's honor. Ty and I had a blast at that party.

Why is he staring at the photo?

"You didn't pull me aside just to discuss Alexis," I say, prompting him to reveal the reason we're in his office.

"Kristina asked whether you could convince your friend to donate to the MGH Fund because he looked like he had deep pockets. What friend is she talking about, Cooper?"

I say nothing at first, trying to make sense of the question. I can't. According to Ty, he ran into Kristina today, and I haven't laid eyes on the woman since that awkward encounter at the Savoy a few weeks ago.

"What friend? I have no idea what Kristina is talking about. I haven't seen her since London."

"Perhaps she saw you with another man. Don't get me wrong, I know she mentioned it on purpose to gage my reaction, but you never said anything about this male friend."

I take a steadying breath, trying to decipher what it means. There's a strong undercurrent of accusation in Ty's voice and posture, though he's trying to downplay the situation. He knows full well I don't have any male friends except Christian. Where would Kristina have seen me with Christian? The development office is on a different street from where I work.

Was Kristina stalking Ty? Does she have spies around the hospital already? *Question everything when it comes to Kristina.* My mother is inside my head again. She's right, though.

Then it all snaps into focus for me, like a puzzle piece that finally fits. "Kristina must have spotted us grabbing lunch at the Bristol Gardens Restaurant.

"It's a ten-minute walk from her building on Dalton. Christian was in town for the day on some business. Sorry, I just forgot to mention it. No big deal."

"You and Christian don't see each other often. Strange you wouldn't mention the visit. Unless he comes to Boston regularly and his visits are now the norm, not worth mentioning."

Ty has ice in his eyes. Leaning up against the neatly organized oak desk, he grabs the three stainless-steel bearing balls on the desk and rotates them in his right hand repeatedly, the balls making a loud, clacking sound as they collide against one another.

"I spent all of twenty minutes with Christian. We went to pick up takeout and continued on with our day separately. This wasn't some clandestine meeting, Ty. It slipped my mind, that's all. Do I need to report to you every time I go to lunch with someone?"

"Christian came to Boston on business and went out of his way to visit you at work for twenty minutes and then you grabbed take-out lunch. So the entire visit lasted roughly forty-five minutes to an hour. He couldn't resist, even if it was just for an hour."

"Are you accusing me of something? Because if you are, just come out and say it." The interrogation is irritating me, exacerbating my exhaustion and shattered nerves. "You never had a problem with Christian in the past. What's changed, Ty? Why is he a pariah suddenly?"

Instead of answering the question, Ty lobs one of his own. "Why is it so hard for you to say no to him?"

"What?"

"You take his calls, no matter where we are or what's going on. You drop everything to go to lunch with him. You always say yes when he's in the picture. Are you still carrying a torch for him, despite your denials?"

I glare at Ty. Raw, unfiltered anger engulfs me. It's mostly directed at Kristina, who turned an innocent lunch into something ugly, and here I am, defending myself to my suspicious, doubting husband.

"I'm surprised you can't see this for what it is, Ty. A simple slip of the mind has now turned into a full-on inquisition about me and Christian because Kristina made you suspicious? A woman you know despises me and made that clear as recently as a few weeks ago?"

His shoulders relax, and he breaks away from my stare, embarrassed.

When he refocuses his attention on me, he says, "We confide in each other; nothing's too big or small. That's the way it's always been with us. It's not like you to hold back."

He adds, "All it takes is just once, one time you don't tell me something, no matter how trivial it may seem. Then it happens again, and again. Next thing you know, we're keeping secrets from each other."

"Let's focus on the threat under our noses. Kristina. The woman is a menace. Why is she here, mere weeks after seeing you in London? She's been living overseas for fifteen long years, almost two decades. One day, she lays eyes on you for a few minutes, and suddenly, she's back in the States. Don't you find that suspicious?"

"I plan to stay far away from Kristina and whatever scheme she's cooking up. I don't see what she could possibly do that's a danger to us. If she's entertaining ideas about me, well, that's just her fantasy and has nothing to do with reality."

"It's a mistake to underestimate her," I warn. As I dole out the warning, I feel it deep in my bones. An arctic blast of foreboding about the damage Kristina could cause.

I say, "It was an honest omission, not telling you about lunch with Christian. Let's stop fighting each other and recognize the real threat, Ty. Now that Kristina is here, it'll be easier for her to gather information on us.

I don't add that I have a sickening feeling that Kristina *is* already digging into our lives.

CHAPTER 14

June 17

I couldn't believe my eyes. But there she was. The love of your life flirting and carrying on with another man, not a care in the world. How it sickened me. You know me, I don't hold back, and although you told me to back off your wife in London, I can't, not after what I saw.

Is this the woman you defended with such passion, a woman who is so reckless with your heart? How can you stand it? She doesn't deserve you. I will never stop believing that.

You made the wrong choice of a bride, Ty, a terrible mistake. I would NEVER do that to you, take you for granted. You deserve so much better, someone who only has eyes for you, someone who would be proud to stand by your side, someone who understands you and would do anything for you. Not a woman who sneaks off to lunch with another man.

I can be that someone if you would let me. You would never need to question my fidelity or commitment.

I'm confident that in time you'll see your wife for who she really is—a manipulative, conniving woman who's never satisfied. You are enough, Ty. Enough for me.

CHAPTER 15

───◆───

TY

THE PLANE TOUCHED down and accelerated before beginning its unhurried approach to the gate. *Cooper got it all wrong*, Ty thought. The real threat wasn't Kristina; it was Christian Wheeler. For three years, everything was fine. They had a deal. The dark secret between them would remain a secret forever. Cooper would never find out. For three years, Christian had kept his promise.

He knew Christian still carried a torch for Cooper. But there was an unspoken rule that served as a buffer, the line they both knew could never be crossed.

Unfortunately, Christian's actions in recent months revealed a man who had no qualms about pursuing another man's wife. If he thought Ty would sit back and let that happen for fear the secret would come out, he was mistaken.

At a few minutes after one in the afternoon, Ty meandered through the streams of people deplaning the American Airlines flight at JFK International airport. He hurried to ground transportation where he grabbed one of the dozens of yellow taxi cabs lined up.

If things went as planned, he would be back in the air in two hours, three tops, and make it home in time for dinner.

Cooper would be none the wiser.

It didn't matter that he gave no advanced warning. The cab arrived outside the fifty-three-story glass tower in mid-town Manhattan. Ty paid the driver and sprinted to the main entrance and then took the elevator to the fifty-second floor.

"Hello, Courtney," Ty said pleasantly with a hint of a smile. He jammed his hands into his pockets and strolled toward the massive, polished mahogany desk flanked by two large potted plants.

She stood. "Dr. Rambally. It's good to see you again. We weren't expecting you. Can I get you anything, coffee, tea?" Courtney was wringing her hands, a telltale sign that his unscheduled arrival had upended her boss's calendar.

"No, I'm fine. Thanks." Ty winked at her reassuringly. "Don't worry. This shouldn't take long at all."

Courtney epitomized the perfect executive assistant—beautiful, poised, stylish, and efficient, running her boss's affairs with military precision. She smiled weakly and then went around her desk and picked up the phone.

"Dr. Rambally is here to see you." She all but whispered the phrase.

Ty's back was to her as he took in the sweeping views of the city through the massive windows that let in sunlight.

"You can go in," Courtney said.

Ty ambled into Christian's office as though on a leisurely afternoon stroll.

"This is an unexpected visit," Christian said, leaning back in his executive leather chair and gesturing for Ty to have a seat.

"Is it, though?" Ty asked, taking the seat offered.

"Yes. You didn't call first, and it's dumb luck that you caught me. I was about to head out."

"You had to know I would call you out."

"What are you talking about?" Christian asks, a frown creasing his brow.

"When another man makes a play for my wife, I'm not going to be polite about the situation."

"Whoa! Hold on a minute." Christian popped into a sitting position and assumed a rigid body posture. The relaxed, in-charge executive from moments ago evaporated into the afternoon air.

"Where is this baseless accusation coming from, Ty? Are you and Abbie having problems and you're looking for someone to blame? If that's the case, man up. I don't much appreciate you coming at me like that."

Ty leaned forward, his hands steepled together. In a measured tone, he said, "I'm not stupid, Christian, don't insult my intelligence. Your tactics may be more subtle and sophisticated than most—you haven't done or said anything blatant—but it still boils down to one simple fact: you want her."

Christian glared at him, a withering gaze that suggested he was quickly losing patience.

Ty added, "If you think you can leverage our secret, that I'm going to sit back and let you interfere in my marriage, you're mistaken."

Christian's eyes darkened. The temperature in the room dropped several degrees, indicating a seismic shift in their relationship just occurred. Ty had made unwelcome ripples in an otherwise calm and unlikely alliance.

Christian said, "I don't know what your problem is, but it's just that, *your* problem. Nothing in my relationship with Abbie has changed. I've never done anything to compromise or disrespect her, and you know that. So what's this visit really about, Ty?"

Christian sounded so convincing Ty almost believed him. Ty was right to come, force a face-to-face meeting to let

Christian know that Cooper was off limits. Ty also needed to know whether Christian would reveal their pact, given the right motivation.

Ty swatted away the dark thought. Christian had as much to lose as he did, mutually assured destruction if the truth of what they did came to light.

"Cooper has a lot on her plate. Just give her some space to breathe. You don't need to see her every time you fly up to Boston or call her every time you and Alan get into a sparring match. She's not your shrink, Christian."

"What's really going on, Ty? I thought we were good. Now you barge in on me all confrontational and accusatory. I'm not the enemy here."

Christian leaned in closer, his expression like thunder. In a venomous voice, he said, "But I can be."

Was that a threat? Christian's blue eyes bored into Ty who had never seen Christian this angry, not that they'd spent a lot of time together. Ty held his gaze, refusing to back down.

"Find someone else to share your burdens with," he said, ignoring the threat hanging in the air. "What you're doing isn't good for her."

"Did Abbie tell you that?" Christian asked.

"She didn't have to. I'm her husband. It's my job to pay attention to her well-being."

Christian's gaze was suffused with suspicion, as though Ty was hiding his real motive for this ambush behind a veil of concern for his wife's well-being.

He said, "It's admirable that you take your role as her husband seriously. Abbie deserves that and more. But why the need to confront me about something that doesn't exist?"

"So you're denying you still harbor feelings for Cooper, is that it?"

Silence pulsated through the room. Christian's jaw ticked, ever so slightly. Then he broke out in a boisterous laugh meant to display confidence, but Ty detected a slight wobble in his voice.

"Your suggestion that I'm making a play for your wife is preposterous. The fact that you mention this scenario tells me you don't trust Abbie. Do you actually think she would betray you like that?"

Ty observed that a lot of words were coming out of Christian's mouth, but none of them the truth. That in itself was a revelation, confirming what he had long suspected.

"I'm asking you man to man to stop it," Ty said. "That's all I came here to say. Cooper is not for you, never was and never will be. If you're holding out hope that someday things will change, they won't."

"When I saw Abbie in Boston, it was obvious to me something was bothering her," Christian said, ignoring Ty's request to leave his wife alone. "She was tense, nervous. Perhaps you should focus on what's causing her anxiety and stop wasting time accusing me of something I would never do."

Christian stood, removed his cell phone from his pocket and strolled over to the window nearest his desk. He took a cursory glance at the screen and then shoved the phone back into his pocket.

Facing Ty, he continued, "I only got a snippet of the story that Abbe tried to brush off as nothing because she was protecting you. But she believes your ex could be trouble. She didn't say the words. I could read it on her face, in her body language."

I could read it in her face, her body language. The nerve of this guy, the hubris it took to pretend he knew Cooper better than Ty, her own husband. But did Kristina's arrival spook his wife so badly that she confided in Christian?

Ty couldn't deny that he felt betrayed, but he also had to consider the possibility Christian could be exaggerating to get a rise out of him. Ty quickly composed himself.

"Cooper and I are fine. She doesn't need you to protect her."

"Because you're doing a bang-up job? Hasn't she been through enough?"

Christian's words landed like an ice cube rolling down Ty's back in the middle of winter: jarring and unpleasant.

Keeping his temper in check, Ty said, "I don't want any animosity between us, Christian. But I couldn't stand by and pretend I don't know how you feel about *my* Cooper. See that you don't cross the line."

"Or else what?" Christian challenged.

Ty stood. Then with bored detachment in his voice, he said, "Grow up, Christian. We're too old to be playing these games. See you at Lucas's graduation."

Ty saw himself out without another word or backward glance.

CHAPTER 16

CHRISTIAN

CHRISTIAN SAT AT his desk for a full ten minutes after Ty left, silent, not moving a muscle. Guilt engulfed him. Shame and embarrassment made his blood run cold. How could he let it come to this, chasing after her so brazenly, like some lovesick, infatuated teenage boy?

For goodness sakes, he was a grown man—a man about to take over the leadership of a global multi-billion-dollar media empire in a few short years—the livelihood of thousands of employees around the globe resting on his shoulders.

Yet, he had allowed himself to appear weak. Ty was upset with him, but it would blow over. Both men had a lot to lose. Christian had no intention of being a loser when he'd been a winner all his life. He was a Wheeler, and Wheelers weren't allowed to lose.

Except he hadn't won the Abbie lottery, a ghost that still haunted him seventeen years after they first got together. Christian didn't make a habit of bragging, but he could have any woman he wanted: princesses, heiresses, celebrities, corporate executives, and entrepreneurs. Still, he couldn't help how he felt about Abbie.

He hadn't yet figured out how to exorcise that particular

ghost. Did he want to, though, especially since he knew Abbie was keeping a secret from Ty? He swore to her he would never tell. And he would keep his word. If Christian broke her trust, he would never get it back.

Though emotions had flared during the conversation with Ty, Christian couldn't back down. Especially since he had received information about the state of Ty and Abbie's marriage from an insider. Someone he would never betray under any circumstances. Lucas. Christian had grown close to his nephew, and they had built up a strong bond.

Lucas had called, unbeknownst to his parents, scared and anxious. According to Lucas, his mother went off on Alexis. Lucas had never seen his mother so upset. Then a short time later, his parents disappeared into his father's office.

Lucas and Blake followed and listened outside the door to find out what was going on, even though they were supposed to be loading the dishwasher.

"Mom and Dad had a huge fight about this woman named Kristina," Lucas said. "We met her in London. I didn't like her, to be honest. Do you think my parents are splitting up? The fight was pretty intense."

Christian had rushed to offer reassurances that married people sometimes fought; it didn't mean they were getting a divorce.

"Your parents aren't splitting up, Lucas. Couples sometimes get really mad at each other. But then once they cool down, everything returns to normal. You don't need to be afraid."

"Mom said Kristina is a menace," Lucas had informed him. "I think it's because Kristina ratted her out to Dad. Kristina told Dad that she saw you and Mom together, and Dad got upset because Mom never mentioned it. Anyway, my parents never fight. This is serious. You have to do something."

"I'm sure your parents will cool off, Lucas," Christian had said. "It's nothing for you to worry about, your parents aren't going anywhere. They just need to fix this little problem they're having and everything will be fine. Do you remember Kristina's last name?"

"Mom introduced her as Mrs. Saxena. Said they knew each other a long time ago. She went to Yale with Mom and Dad. But I could tell Mom didn't like her. Alexis said Kristina likes Dad. A lot."

Christian tried to hide his surprise and took a minute to project a calm, reassuring tone for his nephew's sake. "Is that why you're afraid your parents are splitting up? Because Alexis said Kristina likes your dad?"

"Yeah. She has a crush on Dad, and Mom doesn't like it. Anyway, Alexis and Blake don't like Kristina either. She's trying to break up our family. If she didn't show up, Mom and Dad wouldn't be fighting."

Christian saw the problem clearly. Kristina came to Boston for the sole purpose of breaking up Ty and Abbie. She was the ex-girlfriend Abbie mentioned when he visited her.

This was huge. Christian wasn't *that* guy, the outsider who would come between a man and his wife, but if Abbie needed a shoulder to cry on, he would happily offer up his. She had done the same for him many times, and he wouldn't let her down.

Abbie had put everything on the line when he was in a very dark place last year. He owed her and would always protect their secret no matter what.

CHAPTER 17

KRISTINA

THEY AGREED TO meet at a bar inside the Lenox hotel. After a quick glance at the drink menu, she ordered a Vegas Poolside—a drink made up of Bacardi rum, coconut puree, pineapple juice, lime, and mint. Kristina wasn't much of a drinker, but this concoction sounded yummy. She figured she could nurse it for the entirety of her meeting.

The thirty-something bartender with long hair and a goatee took her order and tried to strike up a conversation. "First time here? I haven't seen you around before."

"I'm meeting someone," Kristina said, hoping Mr. Goatee would take the hint and leave her alone. He did. Luckily, it didn't take long for the man of the hour to arrive.

In his mid-fifties, she estimated, fit with a light tan and graying hair, he sidled up next to Kristina. He was dressed in jeans and a polo shirt, with a large envelope tucked under his arm.

"Vodka Martini," he told the bartender, a woman this time, not the guy who tried to engage Kristina in conversation earlier.

"Found anything interesting?" Kristina asked.

"It depends on what you mean by interesting. I got the information you requested, but..." He trailed off.

"But what?"

"The guy and his wife came back cleaner than a load of laundry fresh from the dryer. Not even so much as a speeding ticket."

Kristina turned the information over in her head. She was certain an investigator of Henry Dalton's background could ferret out whatever secrets Ty and Abbie were hiding. Everyone had secrets. Were Ty's and Abbie's secrets buried so deep that they were nearly impossible to dig up?

Henry came highly recommended to Kristina before she even left London. He worked for a top law firm in Boston and branched out on his own after a ten-year stint. Prior to that, Henry put in sixteen years with the Boston PD.

Keeping in touch with a handful of friends and acquaintances in the States paid huge dividends for Kristina. Danielle Oppergard had been Kristina's roommate at Yale, now a junior partner at the law firm for which Henry worked as an investigator. Danielle also used her contacts at MGH to ensure Kristina snagged the assistant director of development role.

Over the past week, Kristina and Danielle met for lunch and dinner in the South End. Kristina told Danielle she was looking for an investigator to do some background work on a potential suitor. Kristin neglected to mention that she was still very much married to Callum Saxena. She settled on a lie instead. She had been divorced for a few months and was dipping her toes into the dating pool.

"Are you sure there weren't any flags?" Kristina asked Henry.

"I looked at it from every angle," Henry said. "I also dug into whether the Ramballys had any disciplinary action brought against them by their employer. Dr. Tyler Rambally is a well-respected surgeon and doesn't have a single blemish on his record. At least none I could find."

"What about his wife?"

"Dr. Abbie Cooper Rambally received both her undergraduate and graduate degree from BU. She also works for MGH as a neuropsychologist. From what I can tell, like her husband, she's well respected and really good at her job. In fact, she also works with researchers at the NeuroRecovery and NeuroTech research centers."

Henry paused, as though recalling the rest of his summary. The details would be included in the report he compiled. Most of the information in the summary, Kristina already knew, but she waited patiently for him to finish.

He added, "She's the mother of three. The Ramballys have lived in Lexington for almost fourteen years. Believe me, I turned over every stone. These two are a golden couple."

"What about any business dealings, financial issues?" she asked, not willing to concede that Ty and Abbie were the golden couple as Henry proclaimed.

Dr. Rambally is heavily involved with a biotech start-up. He's on the board and serves as a scientific advisor. They're in the process of securing Series A funding."

"Who are the investors? Which venture capital firm is backing them?"

"Not sure yet. I'm still waiting on that detail."

Henry handed Kristina the envelope. "Everything I know so far is in here, including their home address."

This news was the highlight of her day. She kept her expression neutral, not wanting Henry to detect how much the news thrilled her. Kristina wanted to head to her suite right away. She didn't bother ordering dinner to go. Room service at the Mandarin Hotel would suffice.

"Thanks, Henry, this is just brilliant," she said, waving the envelope. "I'll be in touch soon."

"Any time," he said, giving her a mock salute. Kristina got

off the bar stool and started to walk away when Henry said, "Oh wait. There's something about one of the kids that might be of interest to you."

Kristina walked over to him and said, "Go on."

"Their son Lucas was kidnapped three years ago."

"Kidnapped by whom?"

"Some crazy woman named Brynn Harper."

"Why did she kidnap Lucas?" This newsflash stunned Kristina. As much as she was intrigued by the tidbit, however, the news wasn't part of Henry's report. How come? He told Kristina he found nothing suspicious, yet he neglected to mention a kidnapping?

Henry shrugged. "I don't know. The motive is a bit murky. Brynn Harper is doing life in prison."

Kristina's eyes widened. "For kidnapping?"

"There was more to the story. Brynn also stood trial for a double murder. Something having to do with the Ramballys' nannies."

Had she just walked into a hornets' nest? Kristina had been so focused on Ty and Abbie's marriage it never occurred to her that other aspects of their lives might serve up a treasure trove of information. But what a tragedy. Kristina needed the backstory. What a doozy it must be. Double murder?

"Glad you mentioned it, Henry." She thanked him again and took off so fast she might have left skid marks in her wake.

KRISTINA SAT ON the massive king-sized bed in her suite, legs tucked under her as she poured over the documents Henry had provided. Room service had delivered dinner; penne pasta with Bolognese sauce and grilled chicken breast. She took two bites and shifted her focus to Henry's report.

She Googled the town of Lexington, Massachusetts, to

get a feel for the kind of place Ty and Abbie called home, the place they decided to raise their children.

Lexington was a wealthy suburb ten miles northwest of downtown Boston. It was steeped in history, most famously known as the place the first shot of the American Revolutionary War was fired. But the town was also known for its family-friendly communities, excellent schools, beautiful parks, and historical architecture.

Next, Kristina pulled up their home on Zillow. According to the real estate website, they made the purchase three years ago. A five-bedroom, three-and-a-half baths, four-thousand-square-foot colonial on a cul-de-sac. The house stood on just under an acre of land on Hummingbird Drive. With its beautifully manicured lawn, front garden, and tall mature trees flanking the property, the home looked like something out of a storybook.

But according to Henry, Ty and Abbie were long-time Lexington residents, almost fourteen years. They changed homes. Why? Did it have anything to do with Lucas's kidnapping? Did their previous home hold bad memories?

Kristina's mother, Aasvi, was expecting a call, but the newsflash about Lucas's kidnapping added an extra shot of adrenaline to Kristina's plan. She didn't want to lose that momentum. So Mom would have to wait a bit longer.

Kristina felt guilty about putting her mother on the back burner like that. Kristina had been back in the States for weeks and had not made a single move to book a flight out to Chicago for a visit.

With fingers feverishly working the keyboard of her laptop, Kristina was surprised to discover there wasn't a ton of information on the motive in Lucas Rambally's kidnapping. Henry was right.

She clicked on the first link and read an article from one of the local news stations about the kidnapping. Lucas was snatched in the dead of night without waking the household. He was then taken to Canada by Brynn Harper. Local law enforcement worked with the Montreal police to find him.

There was only a vague reference to motive. Brynn Harper claimed Lucas was her only living relative and she just wanted to spend some time with him. There wasn't much information regarding Brynn's involvement in the nannies' murders either.

Kristina frowned. Wait a minute. Trial transcripts. Henry didn't mention those. Why not?

Henry picked up on the second ring. "Transcripts," Kristina said without preamble. "How long would it take to access the transcripts from the kidnapping trial? And what about the nanny killings? Brynn would have stood trial for the kidnapping and murders separately."

"That's right," Henry said. "The murders and the kidnapping were closely related, but yes, she stood trial separately. I didn't mention transcripts because the judges assigned to both cases issued gag orders. Most of the court documents are sealed."

"What? Why? I thought the Freedom of Information Act gave the public access to court transcripts."

"There are exceptions to every rule. The court can seal records involving personal and delicate or sensitive matters. Courts protect the rights of individuals in certain cases for specific reasons."

"So you're saying we can't get those records at all?"

"You can try, but I doubt you'll succeed."

After she ended the call, Kristina hopped off the bed and went to stand at the window, drawing back the thick drapes for a nighttime view of the city. How strange. What was so sensitive that those documents were sealed and information about the case limited?

What were Ty and Abbie hiding?

CHAPTER 18

ABBIE

I BOOT UP my laptop for a video chat with one of my dearest friends, Frances Lin Everly, an award-winning journalist turned producer for one of the BBC's top-rated newsmagazines.

Once we're live, she says, "Your first trip to London in years, and you didn't visit us. Hugh is taking it harder than me. He looked forward to introducing Ty to his friends on his cricket team."

Glamorous as always, even at the late hour London time, Frances's long dark hair cascades past her shoulders. Her makeup is flawless, and she sports a blazer over a light-pink corset blouse.

Frances, Callie, and I met freshman year of high school and dubbed ourselves the Rainbow Posse because of our diverse ethnic backgrounds—Chinese, Italian, and African American, respectively. Our Latina sidekick from Columbia, Anastasia Cruz, left St. Matthews at the end of sophomore year.

After graduating from Northwestern University in Chicago with a journalism degree, Frances chased a story all the way to London and fell in love with the city. She met her husband Hugh, a lawyer, during an interview and, like Kristina, made London home.

"There wasn't time, Frances. We only had a few days, plus

the kids in tow. No real time to catch up."

Twirling her hair, a habit since our school days, she says, "It's okay. I'll forgive you eventually." Frances says it with her trademark attitude. But she doesn't mean anything by it. It's her way of expressing her affection for our friendship.

After a brief catch-up on what's going on with each of us, she moves on to the reason we agreed to this video chat. It pays to have an award-winning journalist as a close friend, I'll soon discover.

Frances says, "This Kristina chick is some piece of work. I don't know why she decided to come for you, but you're right to worry."

I inhale deeply and slowly let out the air. I had done a basic Google search on Kristina, including her married name in the search. A few interesting hits came back. But I figure Frances can fill me in on the non-public version of Kristina's life in London.

"Okay, tell me what you know."

"Kristina's husband, Callum Saxena, is a big deal on the London business scene. And quite the playboy. It's no secret he has a roving eye, despite his wedding to Kristina making the papers when they first got married eight years ago. They're well known as a power couple in certain circles."

"Yeah, yeah, that's all well and good, but tell me something Kristina wouldn't want me to know."

"I'm getting to that. Just know that my sources tell me the marriage has been in trouble for some time."

"Are you suggesting our trip to London, seeing Ty, triggered Kristina and planted the idea that getting Ty back would be a way to move on from Callum?"

"Could be. Anyway, be on guard. She's bringing the crazy."

"What does that mean?" I lean closer to the screen.

"There was an incident a couple of years ago."

"What incident?"

"No one had solid proof of anything, but rumors started circulating that Kristina ordered a vicious attack against a woman Callum was involved with."

I slowly ease away from the screen. Tendrils of distress invade every cell of my body. I didn't know what to expect, what Frances would find, but certainly not this. Kristina had a possessive, controlling streak when she dated Ty back in the day, but what Frances is describing is some next-level psycho.

"I'm guessing there's more?" I ask, after taking a moment to catch my breath.

"There is," Frances says.

She goes on to explain that Kristina's husband was involved with a beautiful Bollywood actress, Sita Kapoor, who was on the cusp of a major breakthrough role on American television.

Just before she flew to Los Angeles to begin filming, two thugs followed Sita home from the gym where she worked out and attacked her in the parking garage of her apartment building.

The attackers, who looked like Ninjas dressed in black from head to toe, also threw acid in Sita's face. The woman survived the attack, but her life and career were destroyed.

"Again, no proof of Kristina's involvement," Frances reiterates. "The Kapoor family didn't want to open a case, especially since Sita couldn't identify her attackers." Frances looked down as if reading notes.

"But Sita and Kristina were seen arguing at a party two weeks earlier. Kristina threw a glass of champagne in Sita's face and was heard making threats. *One way or another, you'll stop seeing Callum. I promise you that.* Then Kristina left the party in a rage."

I blink several times and then stare at my friend openmouthed. But as shocked as I am to hear this incredulous story, it's not completely surprising. In addition to pursuing Ty, I wonder whether Kristina's move to Boston was also an opportunity to put some distance between herself and the attack she allegedly orchestrated. But Frances said the attack happened two years ago.

"Frances, you said your sources told you Kristina and Callum's marriage was in trouble. Have you heard any rumblings about them being separated or talking divorce?"

"No, I haven't. Why?"

"Because if they're still together, that tells me Kristina gave Callum the slip and moved to Boston without telling him the truth of where she was headed or for how long."

Frances cocks her head to one side, giving the statement some thought. Then she said, "That makes sense. If she told him she was going away on an extended business trip, then he wouldn't question her absence."

Frances adds, "How long ago did she pop up in Boston?"

"Three, maybe four weeks."

"That's a long time to be away. Callum is bound to start asking questions soon if he hasn't already."

I ask, "But if the marriage is in bad shape and her husband cheats on her, why does Kristina tolerate that kind of treatment? It doesn't sound like the Kristina I know."

"It's possible she asked for a divorce and Callum refused. I heard he's controlling, a real prick. One moment he can charm a snake, and the next, he's screaming at an assistant because the temperature of his coffee was one degree off."

"So they're both volatile, it sounds like." I allow my thoughts to drift but can't ignore the clanging alarm bells going off in my head. "Frances, just how dangerous is Kristina?" The answer should be obvious, but I have my reasons for asking.

Frances rubs her chin, pondering the question. An intense

look of concentration blossoms across her face. After a few beats, she says, "Do I think Kristina is a total psycho and capable of anything? The answer is yes."

I swallow hard. "Could you use your contacts to find out whether Kristina has ever been admitted to a psychiatric hospital or saw a therapist?"

"It wouldn't be a shocker if she was seeing a psychiatrist. I'll see what I can find out."

"Thanks, Frances. I owe you."

"Don't think I won't collect, Abbie." She grins.

"I promise to come see you and Hugh, kid-free. When are you coming back Stateside anyway?"

"Can't say for sure. I'll let you know."

I thank her again and promise to check out the links and other materials she's sending my way; then we log off.

A crazy idea works its way into my brain. It's risky and could possibly backfire, but I feel compelled to give it a try.

CHAPTER 19

ABBIE

"O H MY GOODNESS, with a body like that, it would look spectacular on you," Shay, the sales associate, gushes.

I stand in the dressing room of Brandi's Diva Boutique, an upscale establishment on a side street in Burlington, fifteen minutes from home. An orange bikini with teardrop cut-outs and cross back straps caught my attention. Shay insists that I try it on.

Despite the recent tension between Ty and me, I'm excited about our upcoming second honeymoon trip to Montego Bay and have spent the past couple of days shopping for clothes.

One-piece bathing suits are more my style, but Ty insists that I model for him, his own private fashion show once we arrive in Jamaica. And that includes the lingerie he's already picked out and won't let me have a peek. He's such a tease.

The dressing room mirrors in stores are meant to flatter, or so I've heard, but stepping back and taking in my reflection, Shay is right. This bathing suit is a great choice. But I'm afraid I'll need to up my exercise game if I'm going to keep this slim figure. I loathe working out or going to the gym, so I walk, take the stairs at work, and attend Pilates class when I can.

"How's it going in there?" Shay asks. "I brought you a few more to try."

I open the dressing room door halfway and take the bathing suits from her. "How is the orange one?"

"It's perfect; you were right.

"See, I knew it would look great on you. You have the body for it. Not everyone can pull that off. You're so lucky. Let me know if you need any more help."

I thank her, shut the door, and get to work trying on the new batch of bathing suits and matching wraps. Shay is speaking to another customer. I strain to hear what they're saying.

My body stills instantly. I recognize the voice.

Taking several deep breaths, I separate the bathing suits into two piles. The ones I will purchase and those I'll leave behind. I scoop up my purse and sling it over my shoulder while clutching the bathing suits in both hands. I slowly exit the dressing room.

"How did you make out?" Shay asks, turning to me, her face bright and beaming.

I don't answer right away. My eyes are fixated on the other customer: Kristina. *What the heck is she doing here in Burlington?*

We stare at each other for a beat, each not knowing what to say. An uncomfortable silence hangs in the air like a bad odor you're desperate to escape before it makes you gag.

"Hello, Kristina." I greet her, my voice even. I almost sound pleasant.

"Abbie. Nice to see you. What a coincidence, running into you here."

Her expression says she's anything but happy to see me. In fact, I don't think her presence at this store is accidental.

Shay's eyes dart from Kristina to me and back again, although Shay's doing a terrible job of pretending she's not paying attention. I hand her the pile of bathing suits I decided against.

"I'll purchase these," I say, handing her the second pile to ring up at the register.

Turning my attention back to Kristina, I say, "Yes, quite a coincidence running into each other here." She's decked out in jeans, stilettos, and a pretty bell-sleeve blouse in fuchsia.

"But you know us girls; we love to shop. No distance is too great to travel when we're on the hunt for the perfect outfit." Kristina must live in or near Boston. What is she doing here in Burlington, forty-five minutes away?

"You're right," she says. "Luckily, I didn't need to travel too far to discover this little gem of a boutique."

With an overabundance of confidence brimming from her and spilling out all around us, Kristina lets the comment hang in the air, daring me to dig for details. She didn't have to travel too far. What does that mean? *You know what it means.* I am curious but don't want to give her an inch, thinking that whatever game she's playing has any effect on me whatsoever.

Then she takes advantage of my indecision by dropping a grotesque bombshell on me.

"Living in Bedford, so close to this boutique might be bad news for my credit cards. I could shop here non-stop."

She smiles big and wide, her frost-white teeth in perfect alignment. But the diabolical glint in her deep-brown eyes is unmistakable.

I swallow the rage rising up from the pit of my stomach. Bedford is ten minutes or less from Lexington where we live. Bedford is literally the next town over. Why would Kristina choose to leave the excitement, history, and culture of Boston to schlep all the way to a suburb forty-five minutes away from the city where she works?

She's lived in London, for goodness sakes. A suburban lifestyle for someone who's lived in one of the world's oldest and most sophisticated cities seems odd.

With forced enthusiasm, I say, "Bedford is a great town.

You must be experiencing culture shock though. Settling in a little suburban town of less than twenty thousand after living in London."

Without waiting for a response, I turn to Shay who had been organizing clothes on a rack after she rang up my order. "All of your choices were spot on, Shay. Thank you."

Shay's face lights up. "That's great, Abbie. You will be the envy of every woman on the beach. Enjoy." She hands me my purchases in the boutique's signature shopping bag.

As I head out with my purchases, I say, "Happy shopping, Kristina."

In a tight parking spot behind the boutique, with the car engine running, I take a moment to calm my frayed nerves and steady my breathing before driving home. It's hard to remain composed when someone gets under your skin the way Kristina does mine. The news that she now lives a few minutes away from us is distressing.

While I was preoccupied, convincing myself I was being paranoid, Kristina had made moves to solidify her plan. Her plan to steal my husband.

CHAPTER 20

---❖---

KRISTINA

TOSSING THE SHOPPING bags on the carpeted bedroom floor, Kristina flopped down on the bed, screaming her frustration into the down feather pillow. During the fifteen-minute ride from the boutique to her luxury garden apartment in Bedford, her fury steadily progressed. And now she was officially ticked off.

The tidbit she casually dropped in Ty's lap days ago, about Abbie and the blond, good-looking man, Christian, had no effect. *They're taking a second honeymoon.* The thought sickened Kristina. She couldn't tell whether it was from jealousy or anger or both.

Abbie didn't deserve a second honeymoon. Not after what Kristina witnessed. Abbie was practically flirting with Christian. She didn't believe Ty's story that he was supposed to join them for lunch. Kristina could tell the news angered him.

After Abbie left the boutique, Kristina pumped Shay, the salesgirl, for information, making the comments sound casual and non-invasive.

"You did such a great job recommending the right style and color for Abbie. I'm hoping you could make some recommendations for me as well?"

Kristina had flashed her practiced, I'm-clueless-and-desperately-need-help smile. The one she spent years cultivating when she wanted others to do her bidding.

Shay responded the way Kristina hoped, with unbridled enthusiasm. "I'm sure we can find something to your liking. What kind of outfit do you need? What's the occasion?"

"A party. I'm new in town, just started a job at MGH. I will be attending a fundraising gala hosted by a wealthy donor. Looking for something sexy but tasteful." She feigned embarrassment. "There's someone I'm hoping will notice me at the gala. He's a surgeon and single."

"Oh, well, in that case I have an outfit that just might work. Don't worry, I'll find you something amazing."

Minutes later, Shay returned with several dresses and made Kristina try on every single one of them. The girl was eager to please, and that made her chatty and easier to extract information from.

"After this fundraiser, I could use a vacation," Kristina said, as she stepped into yet another outfit and assessed her appearance in the dressing room mirror. "A tropical resort where I can lounge by the beach all day and have someone deliver fruity cocktails with umbrellas. Seems like Abbie has the right idea." Kristina stepped out of a gown made for someone with a more statuesque figure.

Kristina appreciated that the boutique wasn't teeming with customers, making it easier to monopolize Shay's time and attention as Shay busied herself outside the dressing room.

"Abbie and her husband are heading to Jamaica for a second honeymoon next week," Shay said. "That's why she was shopping for bathing suits."

"How exciting," Kristina gushed, infusing her tone with

just the right amount of casual enthusiasm. She didn't want to come off too animated. It might make Shay suspicious and cause her to clam up.

Shay said, "I would be happy with just one honeymoon if I ever land a husband. It's so hard, and I'm tired of kissing frogs. I just want Prince Charming to show up already."

"Tell me about it. Abbie and I go way back. We weren't friends or anything, just acquaintances. I hear she's married to a surgeon. Perhaps some of her luck will rub off on me at the gala."

"I'm sure you will do fine," Shay said. "That doctor is an idiot if he doesn't sweep you off your feet."

"Well, I'm going to put out good vibes and hope he takes me on a honeymoon in Jamaica. I've always wanted to go there. To see the house where Ian Fleming wrote the first James Bond novel, *Casino Royal*."

Kristina made up the story on the fly. She needed to know exactly where in Jamaica Ty and Abbie were headed. She couldn't come right out and ask Shay for fear the girl would go tight-lipped like Emily had at the restaurant when Kristina inquired about Christian.

"I'm a big fan of the franchise because of my mum," Kristina continued. "I bet Abbie is visiting while she's there. She seems like the kind of girl who would do something like that."

"Well, I don't know where the Ian Fleming house is, but Abbie said they're going to Montego Bay," Shay revealed. "I've never visited the island either. My friend Michelle was a bridesmaid at a wedding there. You know, one of those fancy resorts. She said it was absolutely fabulous. Showed me pictures. I was so jealous."

Kristina couldn't fly out of the store fast enough. She bought a dress and a red blouse and black pencil skirt to go with it.

She slipped off the bed and put away her purchases—the slinky, black, clingy number with a slit up the side she would wear to the gala as well as the skirt and blouse.

Bedford would not have been her first choice after living in London for so long. Abbie was right about that. But it turned out there was more to this little suburban town than met the eye. First off, her apartment had everything she could possibly need.

Her place boasted every modern amenity she could think of. Granite countertops and stainless-steel appliances, a washer and dryer in the dwelling, a twenty-four-hour fitness club and yoga studio, a screening room, and a game room with Wi-Fi.

The outdoors were surrounded by lush trees and landscaping and a wooded nature trail. The best part was easy access to major highways, dining, and entertainment.

Walking around the bedroom, picking up dirty clothes strewn all over the floor, Kristina recalled the horrified look on Abbie's face when she saw Kristina at the boutique earlier. The element of surprise worked in her favor. Abbie would be playing defense for a long time, and that made Kristina pump her fist in the air.

As she poured laundry detergent into the appropriate compartment in the washing machine, she silently congratulated herself. Was it risky moving to Bedford, the next town over from Abbie and Ty? Yes. But Kristina had never been shy about taking risks. What was the old Latin proverb? *Fortune favors the bold.*

Everything was going according to plan. Bit by bit, Kristina would chip away at Ty's resistance. Over time, sooner rather than later, he would see her as a friend, not a threat. With a combination of endless patience, understanding, and kindness, she would encourage him to confide in her, further deepening the relationship.

Once that happened, Kristina would be at the finish

line. Convince Ty to leave Abbie. But he would do so willingly because it would be *his* idea.

When a couple had been married as long as Ty and Abbie, there were bound to be issues, no matter what it looked like to the outside world. No matter if they were headed on a second honeymoon.

There was always something lurking in the background, waiting for the right moment to rupture.

CHAPTER 21

——◆◇◆——

TY

H E TAPPED OUT a quick text on his way to the cafeteria and waited for a response.

> Kristina, this is Ty.
> I hope this isn't too awkward.
> Can you meet me in the hospital cafeteria on Fruit Street?
> I'll be there for the next half hour.

He had purposely timed the communication during lunch. The development office where Kristina worked was only a couple of miles away from Fruit Street. He needed to infuse the right balance of urgency and nonchalance in his text and hoped he had succeeded.

Kristina

> Not awkward at all. See you then.

"Thanks for coming," Ty said fifteen minutes later. The lunch rush was underway. Hospital staff of every level and function, mixed in with visitors, rushed in and out with Styrofoam containers, while others snagged seats or spots in the long lines for the food stations.

Ty cradled his coffee container. He hadn't touched the chicken sandwich on the paper plate.

Kristina said, "I was surprised, well shocked actually, to hear from you. But curiosity got the better of me."

"I'm afraid what I have to say isn't that interesting or dramatic. The simple fact is, Cooper and I have been less than gracious to you since you came to town. She said she ran into you at a boutique in Burlington a couple of days ago. Cooper said the encounter was tense. She regrets that."

"Does she now?" Kristina's skepticism couldn't have been more obvious if she wrote it using block letters and a red sharpie across her forehead.

"She does. That's why I've been instructed to invite you to a dinner party at our home this weekend. Just a small get-together with a few friends. I apologize for the short notice. And it's perfectly fine if you have other plans and need to decline."

Ty wanted Kristina to know it made no difference to him whether she accepted or not. At least, that was the impression he wanted to project.

Kristina's expression fishtailed, going from shock to a glimmer of excitement, then stoic cynicism, and back to cautious excitement, all in the span of a heartbeat.

Then she said, "Why the sudden one-eighty? Abbie can't stand the sight of me, and you've been cold and indifferent toward me. At least that's the way I read it when we met up in London and when I ran into you at the elevator. So what's changed, Ty?"

He needed to play his cards right. If he messed up, Cooper would never forgive him. "You're right, Kristina. But you took me by surprise in London. I felt ambushed if you want to know the truth. And I wasn't about to sit back and allow you to bash my wife."

"But you and Abbie have warmed to the idea of me, is that it?"

"Don't be churlish, Kristina," he admonished. "We're all adults. You and Cooper will never be best friends, but she's extending an olive branch because that's who she is. If you don't want it, that's fine. Just say so, no hard feelings."

Indecision floated across Kristina's face. Ty didn't want to give her time to overthink the invitation. He stood, even though he hadn't touched his chicken sandwich. "I'll take that as a no. I'll tell Cooper I tried my best."

Kristina grabbed his arm. "No, I mean, yes. I'd love to come to the dinner party. Tell Abbie I'll be there and thank you."

"Great. I'll text you the details. See you then."

CHAPTER 22

June 20

You made my day. No, you made my year. I couldn't stop smiling after you extended the dinner invitation. It's as though the world went from drab gray to glorious color. That's how you make me feel, Ty. After London, I thought you would never speak to me again. You were so angry with me for saying those awful things about Abbie. I was jealous. It ripped my heart out when I saw that you and Abbie were married and had a family.

Sometimes I wonder what if you had made a different choice. That you had picked me instead of her. Why wasn't I good enough? I could have made you happy, but you never gave me the chance to prove it.

Anyway, this gesture, inviting me to your home for dinner, your desire to hit the reset button, is an unexpected gift, one I shall cherish always.

You haven't changed, Ty. You're still the kindest, most considerate, and most generous man I've ever met. And that's why I never stopped loving you and never will. Does that sound sappy, ridiculous? Maybe. But it's the truth.

CHAPTER 23

ABBIE

"YOU LOOK SENSATIONAL," Ty says, appraising me with an admiring gaze.

I return the compliment. He sports a navy-blue, striped herringbone dinner jacket and matching dress shirt.

"Kristina might have to pick her jaw up from the floor," I tease. "She could barely control herself when she saw you in London. The woman almost fainted."

We're in the master bedroom, getting ready for the dinner party. I settled on a navy-blue, V-neck dress with a coup skirt that flounces just above the knee. With my hair in an elegant updo and wearing an heirloom gold necklace with matching dangling earrings, I'm satisfied with my appearance.

"You exaggerate, Cooper. No one reacts to me that way. Besides, it doesn't matter what Kristina does. I only have eyes for you." He draws me close, snaking his arms around my waist, devouring me with his sensual gaze. He adds, "Relax. Everything's going to be fine."

"You promise?"

"I get why you're nervous, but don't be. I will be right there at your side. We're a team."

"Okay. I trust you. I just hope nothing goes wrong."

"WELCOME," I SAY, a saccharin smile pasted on my lips.

"Thank you for inviting me," Kristina says, with an equally sweet smile.

She looks stunning, her choice elegant but bold. Sporting a red fit-and-flair cocktail dress with a deep V neckline, accessorized by metallic gold stiletto sandals and matching purse, Kristina is dressed to impress.

I take the bottle of wine she offers and ask her to follow me through the foyer, past the living room and kitchen, and out to the patio. We moved to this gorgeous Colonial on a quiet street after Lucas's kidnapping. It felt wrong to remain in our old home, the place he was taken, the place with so many painful memories.

Police cruisers in the driveway and officers all over the house and yard, looking for clues. The press conference on the front lawn, pleading for Lucas's return. Telling the kids that their nanny had died. Our collective fears that another tragedy would occur. I'm not saying the old house was cursed. Just that the energy had been tainted somehow. It made sense to move.

The new house is larger and set back from the street, providing an extra layer of privacy. Decorating was a familial affair. The kids were so thrilled to share their ideas for the new digs. They're especially fond of the family room, decorated with bright rugs and sofas and a fireplace flanked by built-in bookshelves. But their absolute favorite is the upstairs lounge, their own teenage sanctuary to hang out with friends and each other.

"Everyone is out on the patio," I say to Kristina. "It's such a lovely evening. We want to enjoy the outdoors before we sit down to dinner."

Scattered across the patio, cocktails in hand and socializing, are my in-laws, Bobby and Jenny; my parents; and my younger brother Miles and his fiancée, Layla.

"Hey, everyone, this is Kristina. She's new to Boston and just started at MGH in the development office."

Everyone at various volumes says hello. Ty's father, who is closest to us, extends a hand in greeting and welcomes Kristina.

Layla, my sweet but fiercely protective and soon-to-be sister-in-law, says from her seat on the sofa, "Welcome to Boston, Kristina. You must spill the tea. What were Ty and Abbie really like back in the day before they became respectable parents and citizens?"

Everyone voices their enthusiastic agreement with Layla. I say, "Don't listen to them, Kristina. They're a bunch of troublemakers."

Kristina visibly relaxes, pleased that she's been accepted. "I don't mind a few troublemakers, Abbie. They keep things interesting."

"That's right," Layla agrees. "Troublemakers get things done."

"Abbie was a couple of years behind Ty and me, so I didn't get to know her that well," Kristina says. "Ty was always a go-getter, knew what he wanted. And he still found time to be the perfect boyfriend."

An awkward silence descends over the patio. Layla shoots me an accusing glance as though admonishing me for inviting Kristina, a woman who clearly has no filter. Knowing Layla, she's probably offended on my behalf by Kristina's reference to Ty being the perfect boyfriend.

Kristina's obsession with Ty is making her stupid, causing her to lose her sense of decorum and appear desperate and immature. Miles takes up a spot next to Layla on the sofa, his way of making sure she doesn't say anything embarrassing because Layla never holds back, sweet as she is.

Layla says, "Yes, I'm sure Ty was the perfect boyfriend,

Kristina. But that was so long ago. Now he's Abbie's husband." She turns to me. "How long has it been, Abbie? Fifteen years? I hardly think a brief college fling can stack up against fifteen years of marriage." The scorn in Layla's voice could cut through steel.

I don't answer Layla's rhetorical question. Miles clears his throat and says to an embarrassed Kristina, who has a death grip on her purse, "Please forgive my fiancée. She's overprotective when it comes to my sister. She didn't mean any harm, did you, babe?"

Layla ignores Miles and sips her drink. Kristina must be over her embarrassment because she now looks like she wants to pour scalding hot water all over Layla's flawless face, which resembles a filtered Instagram photo.

I don't want Layla disfigured before she officially becomes my sister-in-law, so I quickly ask Kristina, "What are you drinking? We have both red and white wine. Unless you want something stronger?"

"A glass of white wine, if it's not too much trouble."

"No trouble at all. I'll ask one of the waitstaff to bring it out. I should check on Ty, see what's keeping him."

At the mention of my husband's name, Kristina's face brightens, ever so slightly.

"You made it." Kristina whips her head around to face Ty who just joined us. "Cooper and I thought you might cancel at the last minute."

"That would be rude of me, after you went through so much trouble to invite me, wouldn't it?" A flash of triumph spreads across her face but then disappears just as quickly.

Ty says, "Well, we're glad you're here."

"My pleasure." Then she says, "Your parents, they no longer live in Scarsdale?"

Kristina acts as though I don't exist, and I'm happy to remain quiet for now. Her attention is squarely focused on Ty, her eyes shining, head tilted back, and lips slightly parted. The reference to his parents' residence is meant to imply intimacy; that once upon a time, she knew everything about Ty and his family.

"They moved to Massachusetts to be closer to the grandkids."

"Oh. Are they retired then?"

"Not quite. My father still operates, but he only takes on special cases. He's also part of a lucrative private practice."

"He's a plastic surgeon, right?"

"Yes, and my mother is still a practicing reproductive endocrinologist."

Then I almost choke on my own saliva when Kristina says, "Is your Mom taking on new patients? Callum and I, well, we've been struggling to conceive for a while. We've seen some of the top fertility specialists in London, but I'm not ready to give up just yet. Perhaps Dr. Whistler might succeed where others have failed."

Kristina patiently waits for a response with the most casual of demeanors like she just ordered breakfast instead of revealing a deeply personal issue between her and her husband.

I break the silence. "It's a good thing you came tonight then. You'll be seated across from my mother-in-law at dinner."

"Oh, brilliant," she says. "I look forward to it."

A five-course dinner stretches before us in the dining room. Kristina is seated next to my father on her left and my mother to her right. Across from her, as promised, are my mother-in-law Jenny and father-in-law Bobby.

Ty and I sit across from each other with Miles to my right. The seat across from Miles is empty. It's reserved for a special guest who should be joining us soon. And Layla sits across from my dad at the far end of the table.

Classical music plays in the background. A series of floating candles in champagne-gold candle holders are strategically placed on the table, complementing the red silk tablecloth. Everyone digs into the first appetizer—shrimp supreme with a French baguette dipped in olive oil.

I say, "Kristina, you don't have any food allergies, do you? I apologize. I forgot to ask. The shrimp…"

Ty jumps in. "Our niece, Gabrielle, Lee's daughter, is deathly allergic to tree nuts so we're sensitive to allergies. I can't believe you forgot to ask before tonight, Cooper." The accusation in his tone and look of condemnation floats in the air, heavy and uncomfortable.

"I'm really sorry," I say quietly. "It was an honest oversight."

A look of delight embeds itself in Kristina's face. She says, "Thanks for looking out for me, Ty. No food allergies, no need to worry. Unless the shrimp has penicillin hidden in it. Does it?" Then she laughs, breaking the tension.

After the awkward allergy question, dinner runs smoothly. The third course—mini crab cakes with orange sauce and a rich, buttery lobster bisque—is a hit. Snatches of conversation take over the room, but nervous tension roils in my stomach. The time is approaching when our surprise guest should arrive.

Kristina says to my brother, "So, Miles, when is the big day? You're a bit young to be getting married, aren't you? You don't look a day over twenty-one."

Layla shoots daggers at Kristina but is smart enough to know Kristina is baiting her. Miles does look young for his age; Kristina is right about that. Though Miles is over six feet tall, he has that perpetually youthful appearance enhanced by two dimples and a playful, mischievous personality that my adore. Uncle Miles lets them get away with everything.

Miles says, "I'm twenty-nine. I had to snap up this incredible woman before someone else did." He looks in Layla's direction, and she blows him a kiss.

"And what do you do for work?" Kristina asks.

Kristina is clearly trying to pay back Layla for embarrassing her earlier on the patio by engaging Miles and ignoring Layla. The verbal volleyball match helps keep my mind occupied, preventing me from getting sick with anxiety over what will happen once our guest arrives.

"I'm an analyst for a tech research and advisory firm. Perhaps you've heard of them." Miles tells her the name of his employer.

"Of course. What space do you cover?"

"Worldwide telecom."

"That's brilliant. And what do you do for fun?"

Okay, you're getting weird, Kristina. You should stop now. Thankfully, Dad speaks up.

"How are things going at the hospital, Kristina? Do you like the new job?"

"I've never felt more at home in any job," Kristina says. "There are so many talented people at MGH. It's like I've finally found my tribe."

She's finally found her tribe? Seriously? Could she suck up any louder? It takes enormous willpower not to roll my eyes. Besides, I promised myself I would stop doing that. Alexis has picked up the bad habit, which she's embraced with reckless abandon.

Just then, the doorbell rings. I send up a silent prayer that this works out the way I planned.

CHAPTER 24

ABBIE

H E'S BETTER LOOKING in person. The tailored designer suit, a light-blue silk-and-wool blend fits him like a glove. With a thick head of coal-black hair, just a hint of gray at the temples, and mocha-brown eyes that look like they're always scheming, I ought to tread carefully.

I extend my hand in greeting and he takes it, lightly brushing the back with his lips. "Madame. It's a pleasure," he says, in a posh British accent.

"The pleasure is all mine. Do come on in"

I enter the dining room and announce, "Everyone, I'd like you to meet Callum Saxena. Kristina's husband."

Kristina gasps. I mean the kind of gasp that draws attention, as though she just woke up from a nap and discovered a dead body next to her. A panicked expression flitters across her face. Her eyes seem to sag out of their sockets.

Ty pushes back from the table and strides over to greet our guest. "Welcome, Callum," he says, extending his hand.

Callum makes the rounds, greeting each person at the dinner table. He walks over to Kristina and says, "It's wonderful to see you, darling. You look ravishing. I've been so worried and missed you terribly." Then he plants a lingering kiss on her check.

I retake my seat next to Ty. Curious stares are leveled at Kristina's reaction to Callum. After Callum is seated, Kristina shoots daggers at him. From the expression on her face, she's wishing he would drop dead from her glares.

Continuing her death-stare offensive, Kristina says, "You've never had business in Boston before. What brings you here?"

Callum responds, "You were very naughty, not calling to let me know where you were. I got worried, naturally. Any loving husband would want to make certain his beloved wife was safe. Isn't that so, Ty? If Abbie disappeared, you would do everything in your power to find her, wouldn't you?"

"Of course I would," Ty responds, enthusiastically. "Good on you for tracking down Kristina, Callum. She's lucky to have a husband who looks out for her and would travel across an ocean to make certain she's okay."

Everyone at the table says, "Here, here." Then my dad proposes a toast. "To Callum and Kristina," he says and everyone clinks their glasses in a toast. Callum toasts. Kristina doesn't. *What an odd pair.*

The waitstaff enters the dining room in a flurry of activity to serve the main course of grilled rack of lamb paired with a pinot noir. After the staff exits, the conversation picks up again with the clanking of silverware adding to the background ambience.

Addressing Callum, I say, "It's a good thing you caught up with Kristina. It's difficult to conceive if you're a continent away from each other, isn't it?"

Eyes pop, jaws drop, and Kristina has officially turned purple with rage. Callum says, "I beg your pardon?"

"Well, Kristina mentioned in passing that you were having difficulty conceiving, and she wondered whether my mother-in-law might be of some assistance. Sort of a last, desperate hope, if you will."

Callum tries and fails to mask his shock with a strained smile. "Is that what she told you?" Then he flashes Kristina a look of frustration and disdain. He doesn't want to outright call Kristina a liar in front of an audience, but that's the takeaway from his body language and expression.

Kristina stabs vigorously at a piece of lamb on her plate, not meeting Callum's gaze. Then she looks directly at me. She says, "Abbie, I mentioned that to you and Ty in confidence. I didn't expect the subject to become dinner-table fodder."

Jenny shoots me a quizzical look. "Sorry, Jenny. I jumped the gun a bit. Kristina wanted to discuss her case with you, asked if you were taking on new patients. I told her she could ask you directly."

Turning to Kristina, I say, "I owe you an apology as well. When you mentioned to Ty and me that you and Callum were having fertility issues, I assumed you were comfortable discussing the matter openly." I take a sip of wine and carefully place the glass down on the table to gather my thoughts.

I add, "Otherwise, why bring up the subject to people you haven't seen and have had no contact with for fifteen years? Anyway, sorry I embarrassed you."

The room goes quieter than an Anechoic chamber. Kristina says nothing, her head bowed as she moves a piece of food around her plate.

Ty breaks the silence. "Callum, seems that you and Kristina should get on the same page. If this is a private matter you wish to keep private, then you should both keep it that way."

Ty dabs the corners of his mouth with a linen napkin. He adds, "I'm sure Cooper was only trying to help, but to her point, Kristina brought up the infertility issue. We're sorry if it made you uncomfortable. Let's put it behind us and move on with our dinner, shall we?"

A big sigh of relief echoes throughout the room. Kristina stands and says, her voice shaky, "Excuse me." Then she bolts from the dining room, headed for the bathroom I assume.

I say to Callum, "Perhaps you should check on Kristina, make sure she's all right?"

"No, Abbie. I think I'll sit here and enjoy this delicious meal. Kristina is more than capable of taking care of herself." With that, he digs into a slice of glazed carrot and starts chewing.

I gape at Callum. Despite the tension we all witnessed between him and Kristina, his nonchalance surprises me. But then again, Kristina's reaction to his presence didn't exactly scream, *I'm thrilled to be reunited with my husband.* I don't want to get in the middle of their mess, so I don't push Callum.

Dinner is over. The last of our guests spill out into the hallway in a flurry of air kisses, hugs, and promises to do this again soon. Only Kristina and Callum remain.

Ty shakes Callum's hand and thanks him for coming. Callum says, "It's been a rather enlightening evening, hasn't it?" He tosses a glance in Kristina's direction, and she looks away.

"All couples face challenges, Callum," I say. "You and Kristina will be fine."

He nods and starts heading toward the door. Kristina lingers. Callum says, "Are you coming, darling?" Kristina doesn't respond.

Callum heads out the front door. Ty suddenly remembers something that needs his urgent attention, leaving Kristina and me alone in the hallway. She says, "Well played, Abbie. Your actions tonight were needlessly vindictive. You're still that same conniving, manipulative girl I knew from college. Nothing has changed."

"That's where you're wrong, Kristina. Everything has changed. Ty is my husband and father to my children. He's not a toy to be borrowed or shared with you.

115

"What you don't understand is we've faced insurmountable odds that would have pulverized other couples. And you think you can just swoop in and shatter our family?"

"You don't deserve Ty," she sneers. "You never did. One way or another, you'll lose him."

One way or another, you'll stop seeing Callum. The conversation with Frances floats into my head, like a chilling reminder echoing throughout the foyer. Those were Kristina's words to Sita Kapoor, the woman Callum was seeing before the acid attack two weeks later.

"You should have stayed in London, Kristina. I strongly suggest you return with your husband and resume the life you've built. Or you'll learn the hard way just how conniving and manipulative I can be."

CHAPTER 25

---◦---

ABBIE

FROM WHAT I observed tonight, the Saxena marriage is in shambles. A few thoughts strike me as I sit in my home office, dissecting the evening and everything I've learned since Kristina arrived in Boston. I grab a notebook from my desk and begin scribbling notes.

> One: Kristina has no more use for Callum. Why would she when she's set her sights on my husband?
>
> Two: Kristina is a pathological liar.
>
> Three: Kristina is mentally unstable, which makes her dangerous.
>
> Four: Callum Saxena has no more use for Kristina, but he's a prideful man. His wife flew halfway across the Atlantic to chase after another man, and Callum's ego won't stand for it.
>
> Five: Kristina is hiding dark secrets.

Getting inside her head is the easy part. But what will I do once I uncover all her secrets? How far am I willing to go to stop her from wrecking my life? Every human being has a dark side. Most of us keep it in check, that line we won't cross. Call it a conscience or moral compass. What happens when we're pushed beyond our limits? What does it take to obliterate that line?

I close the notebook and stick it in the desk drawer. I shut off the lights and head upstairs to our bedroom. Ty is sitting up in bed, waiting for me.

"Some dinner, huh?" I say.

"Yes, there were definitely fireworks. Kristina was fuming, had that determined glint in her eyes, like no matter what happened, nobody was going to get in her way."

I flop down next to him, and he goes to work, unclasping my necklace. "Kristina doesn't scare me. She's a bitter woman who still lives in the past. It's sad when you think about it."

Removing the hairpins from my updo, Ty says, "It is sad. Looks like Kristina ran away from Callum; there was so much tension between them at dinner. All I'm saying is… I want you to be cautious where she's concerned."

You don't deserve Ty. One way or another, you'll lose him.

I shift my body and turn around to face him. "I don't want to talk about Kristina anymore. The only thing I want to think about is… in seventy-two hours, I'm going to be sitting on a beach in Montego Bay."

His eyes glint with mischief. "And what else?" he asks, his voice low.

"And my gorgeous, babe magnet of a husband is going to be right next to me, slathering sunscreen all over me with his strong, capable, surgeon hands."

CHAPTER 26

KRISTINA

HOW COULD SHE have allowed that spoiled, conniving witch to ambush her like that? Kristina's hatred of Abbie moved like a force, every cell in her body consumed by it, pounding with rage and venom.

Abbie had the audacity, the gall, to corner Kristina and tell her to go back to London. Who did Abbie think she was? The nerve of that woman. She needed to be blasted from her perch, Kristina decided.

"What? What are you smiling about?" she shouted at Callum.

Callum had insisted he come to Kristina's apartment following the dinner party. When she refused, he informed her he would get an Uber and knew exactly where she lived. Callum then rattled off her address to prove he wasn't kidding around. So, reluctantly, Kristina acquiesced.

"Oh, darling," Callum said from the living room sofa, "do calm down. So Abbie got one over on you, good for her. You should have known who you were dealing with. Did you think she would just step aside and let you have her husband?"

"How could you allow them to use you to humiliate me like this?"

119

"What? I did nothing of the sort," he protested. But she knew he was lying. He reveled in humiliating Kristina.

"Did Abbie contact you to betray my whereabouts?"

"Does it really matter how I found out you were in Boston, chasing after a married man?"

"You will do anything to hurt me," she spat. "That's the reason you cooperated with their scheme. I bet it was Abbie's idea and she contacted you, not Ty."

"Right you are. Mrs. Rambally was concerned that you left London without telling me the truth about where you were headed. She didn't think it was fair to me. I agreed."

"What is that supposed to mean?" Kristina asked, now standing directly in front of Callum.

"If word got out that you left me, it would hurt my reputation. So when Abbie called, I saw the perfect opportunity to spin the story in my favor." Callum sat up straight, adjusting his body as though his next statement was of the utmost importance.

He continued, "You went away on a long business trip to Boston. I missed you so much, I decided to join you, and together we returned to London, ever the happy couple."

"I'm never going back to London with you, Callum. All you're concerned about is gaining the upper hand."

"Well, yes. It's one of my more attractive qualities, I'm told. It's the reason I'm a highly successful businessman."

"You won't get the best of me, and neither will Abbie Cooper."

"It's Rambally, dear," Callum said, mocking her. "She carries her husband's surname professionally. Unlike her mother-in-law. I looked it up."

Callum leveled a devious grin at her. She couldn't stand it. Kristina leaned over, picked up one of the throw pillows from the sofa, and pushed it down over Callum's face. She couldn't suffocate a man who was bigger and stronger than she was, but she didn't care. Despair had taken hold.

Callum shoved the pillow off his face with force. Kristina stumbled backward. She had gone too far. He stood, his entire body a live wire ready to burn anyone who came near him. Kristina slowly backed away.

"Stop behaving like a dog in heat," he hissed. "It's embarrassing. Have you no shame? Are there any lengths you won't go to for this man? What in the bloody hell is wrong with you?"

Kristina stood frozen under his scrutiny. Heat warmed her cheeks. When she put her mind to something, she didn't stop until she had accomplished her goal. This was no different. No matter what Callum or anyone else thought.

Abbie had taken what didn't belong to her and caused Kristina's miscarriage. The emotional rollercoaster of losing Ty, the stress, anxiety, and heartbreak had been too much for her little one to take, and he or she decided it was best to leave. Kristina had suffered alone while Abbie went on to bang out kids like someone passing out candy on Halloween.

Abbie needed to pay for causing the miscarriage. Abbie didn't deserve Ty, a prestigious career, or three gorgeous children who looked like they stepped out of a television ad for a luxury brand, while Kristina didn't have a single child of her own.

Abbie didn't deserve that palatial home with the elegant staircase, vaulted ceilings, and large private backyard with a patio and lush gardens. A home fit for a queen. *Well, Abbie, your reign will soon come to an end.*

Kristina gave Callum a withering look and said, "This doesn't concern you. I could do without your commentary or insults."

Callum stood, grabbed her by the arm, and said, "Stop it! I will not allow you to continue to embarrass and humiliate me. Have some self-respect. Don't you think Abbie told everyone at the dinner party that you're after her husband? Do you think it was a coincidence her parents and in-laws were there?"

"You're hurting me," Kristina said and pulled her arm away from his grip.

"Abbie Rambally isn't stupid, and you would do well not to underestimate her. Stop this ridiculous campaign and leave that woman and her family alone. It's for your own good."

"Since when have you been concerned about what's good for me? You don't care, Callum. I was nothing more than an acquisition.

"An acquisition who was supposed to give you children, stand by your side, and smile in public. Then shut up the rest of the time while you ran around doing whatever you wanted with whomever."

"That's not true. I loved you. It was good in the beginning. Wasn't it?" His tone was softer, his face laced with regret.

Loved. I loved you. Kristina didn't know why, but that statement hurt more than the insults. And suddenly, she felt so alone, tossed aside like an old toy that had outlived its usefulness, never to be looked at again.

Kristina walked away from Callum, went to her bedroom, shut the door behind her, and collapsed on the bed. Big, body-wracking sobs overtook her, as though she were pouring out her heart and soul onto that pillow. She was being rejected. Rejected by Ty. Now rejected by Callum. And it was all Abbie's fault.

Ty left Kristina because of Abbie, dumped her like an underperforming investment fund. Now Callum was here because of Abbie, telling Kristina that his feelings for her were in the past.

So what are you going to do about it? Are you going to let Abbie get away with what she's done?

Kristina catapulted out of bed, trotted to the bathroom, and splashed water on her face. Once she returned to her bedroom, she slipped into a silk nightgown and sat on the bed with her legs tucked beneath her. She didn't care whether Callum had left. He was old news. Kristina picked up her phone and punched in a number.

A groggy voice answered, "Yeah."

"I can't go on like this. I'm ready to jump off the bloody John Hancock Tower."

Kristina explained her predicament and then asked for a favor that would rid her of Abbie Cooper permanently.

PART III
DEADLY HONEYMOON

CHAPTER 27

ABBIE

WE ARRIVED IN Montego Bay two hours ago. Our eyes widened when we stepped into the elegantly appointed one-bedroom suite with its rich cream-colored décor and walls adorned with bold, tropical paintings, which created a sense of luxurious relaxation.

The breathtaking ocean views bowled us over. I can't wait to fall asleep to the soothing sounds of the waves crashing inland, although Ty says we won't be doing much sleeping.

Ty is on a call with a potential investor in the biotech start-up he's trying to get off the ground. I leave him to it and head out to the balcony again, to breathe in the tropical air and luxuriate in the stunning ocean views. The Caribbean Sea sparkles like crystals under the bright tropical sunshine.

I tear my gaze away from the ocean and turn to my right. I squint for a second. Goosebumps cover my arms. There, two balconies over, stands a woman taking in the view. I can't help but stare at her. Or rather, her profile.

As though she senses my gaze upon her, the woman turns quickly and scrambles back to her room. How strange. And her face. I only caught a glimpse, a split second, but I could swear she looked like me. I think.

Ty makes it out to the balcony and says, "Cooper, what are staring at?"

"Nothing." Ty is now next to me.

"Are you sure? You look dazed."

"I thought I saw someone who looked like me."

"What? Cooper, is the tropical heat getting to you already? Maybe you should come inside."

Maybe Ty is right. I'm not used to the intense tropical heat and it's making me hallucinate. I hope I'm not coming down with something. It would be awful to be sick on a second honeymoon. Or perhaps I'm just exhausted and conjured up a lookalike. The last several months have been both physically and emotionally draining. If I'm being honest, I'm nowhere near my best self, my peak.

We curl up on the sofa. I shiver, trying to banish thoughts of what I thought I saw on the balcony. Then I change the subject.

"How did the call go?" I ask Ty.

"They're interested. But until we agree on an investment amount and their stake in the company, all of this is just talk. Anyway, now that the call is over, we can concentrate on our second honeymoon. No more work or business-related interruptions."

"Good. Let's make this trip unforgettable."

CHAPTER 28

THE SNIPER

THE SNIPER STUDIES the map of the resort with intense concentration, his third go-round. Having caught a glimpse of his subject once today, he has a good idea where to take the shot. But he always had a backup plan, and his backup plan also had a backup plan.

Placing the map into his pocket, the sniper focuses on his surroundings. He's at the Blue Calypso, a beachfront grill house serving fresh seafood. The place isn't quite yet busy, just a smattering of people, so he orders a pineapple mojito and enjoys the ocean view. He is a patient man. Waiting comes second nature to him.

Thirty minutes later, at six, as the place starts hopping with guests, she appears with her husband at her side. They stand for a minute or two, and then the husband pulls out a chair for her and they sit.

The target wears a long, floral sundress with a tropical flower tucked above her ear. With his baseball cap pulled low and sunglasses, the sniper gets a good look at her. An unobstructed view of her face. *She really is beautiful*, he thinks.

The sniper sighs with regret. It's too bad Abbie Cooper Rambally won't get to enjoy her second honeymoon.

Because before the week is out, she'll be dead.

CHAPTER 29

ABBIE

THE SALTY OCEAN air and sound of the waves crashing inland and out to sea again shower me with calm. We sit in an oceanfront cabana on a private section of the beach. The Caribbean Sea stretches out to the farthest point of the horizon where the sky kisses the water's surface. A few sailboats appear as dots on the horizon with their sails barely visible.

"This is the life," I say, turning to Ty and sliding the sunglasses halfway down my nose.

"We could come back every year, make it a tradition," he says.

"I could get used to that tradition. No kids, no work. Just beauty, pampering, and relaxation."

"I don't know, Cooper. All this doing nothing may take some getting used to. I'm having work-withdrawal symptoms. Last night I dreamt I missed a page and a patient died."

"Relax. It's only day two. There's still a lot to do. By the time we leave here, you'll be clamoring for a repeat."

Ty reaches over and moves his fingertips across my shoulder and down my back like a spider, except it tickles and I giggle. He says, "Anything that gets us alone has my vote. I miss you, Cooper."

"What do you mean? I'm right here."

"I miss our closeness. Our long talks, confiding in each other, teasing each other. We're so busy that sometimes it feels like we're two ships passing in the night. That's on me."

"How do you figure?"

"The past year has been tough on you. I'm sorry I took you for granted. We both have demanding jobs, but you still run our household and take care of our family. Because you do it so well and never complain, I let things slide when I should have stepped up to take some of the burden off your shoulders."

Ty's usually vibrant hazel eyes now brim with regret and hurt, as though he's done something truly unforgiveable. He adds, "I apologize for my selfishness. But I'll make it up to you, Cooper. I don't know how yet, but I will. You're the most incredible wife and mother, and you deserve to be supported. I let you down."

A tsunami of guilt and shame explodes in my chest, rendering me speechless. I didn't think he'd noticed. Why didn't he say something before, before…before I made a terrible mistake?

After swallowing several times, I stroke his arm and say, "Ty, I don't want you feeling guilty. I should have said something but remained quiet instead."

"That's no excuse, Cooper. We're a team, and I let you do all the heavy lifting. Again. After you sacrificed so much, raised our kids while supporting me through medical school and residency, you deserved better."

I lower my gaze, unable to look him in the eyes. The thickness in my throat returns, and suddenly, I can barely breathe let alone get words out. A year ago, I was at my lowest point in many years—stressed, overwhelmed, and drowning in a sea of constant exhaustion.

Just two years out from post-doctoral work, I had a lot to

learn and even more to prove as a neuropsychologist at one of the country's top hospitals. The pressure to succeed was crushing at times. So was battling self-doubt.

With an additional role as a psychology instructor at Harvard, and the demands of being a mother of three, I couldn't catch my breath. Worse, I was ashamed to raise my hand, admit I was drowning. Turns out women all over the country were facing similar struggles balancing their families and careers.

Ty was hardly around. Not only was he a busy surgeon and a member of the faculty of Harvard Medical School, getting the biotech company up and running took up whatever time he had left, despite having two other partners working with him. The cooking, cleaning, and child-rearing weren't about to slow down so I could catch a break.

Nothing justifies my actions that fateful day, however. I convince myself it was a mistake never to be repeated. A moment of weakness, that's all it was. Ty didn't need to know because it would rip our family apart. What would be the point of causing long-term damage over something that was only a blip, a tiny speck in the fabric of our lives? There was no reason to add unnecessary stress on our marriage, I rationalized.

Now my kind, wonderful husband is blaming himself for what he considers a major failure on his part. I was a weak, duplicitous wreck of a woman when it happened. But I can't take back what I did, no matter how much I try to pretend it never happened.

"Cooper, say something." Ty gently lifts my chin so I can look him in the eye, which takes a major effort.

"Thank you for understanding. I didn't think I had the right to complain. We have a great life because of all your hard work, and you're still working hard for our family."

"My number-one job is to protect and support you. It took

me too long to recognize you were struggling. What hurts even worse is that I made you feel as though you couldn't come to me."

"It's not your fault, Ty. Yes, I should have come to you, but I didn't. We can't change that."

We both go silent for a beat. The breeze gently rocks the palm trees that arch over the cabanas, as the sun's bright rays cast shimmering reflections on the turquoise-blue water.

Breaking the silence, Ty says, "I have another surprise for you."

"Oh? Are you going to tell me what the surprise is?" I'm grateful for the reprieve from my guilt. I remind myself to stay grounded in the present. Enjoy every moment of this glorious trip my husband went through so much trouble to arrange. *Live in the moment, Abbie.*

"No, I'm not telling you what the surprise is. At least not yet."

"Come on, give a me a hint. Please."

"Okay. You'll be wearing a very beautiful dress and the ocean will be the backdrop for what I have in mind."

"Wait, are you saying what I think you're saying?" Excitement bubbles up inside me. "Are we renewing our wedding vows? Is that it?"

"Now you've spoiled the surprise," he says, a big grin on his face.

I lean over and plant a slow, tantalizing kiss on his lips. After we catch our collective breaths, I say, "You've made this the most memorable trip."

"We'll be married fifteen years this December. That day we ran into City Hall in New Haven without telling anyone and walked out husband and wife."

"Gosh, we were so young. I was nineteen and you twenty-one. What were we thinking?"

"We were thinking about our future. Our family."

"Lucas was on the way. I sometimes wonder what life would have been like had I stuck to my original plan to terminate."

"I couldn't go through life without you by my side, Cooper," Ty says. "If it meant having a family sooner than we intended, that was an easy decision."

I stare blindly at the ocean. My mind rewinds to fifteen years ago when I tried to terminate my pregnancy, multiple times. The days when I was filled with despair that an unwanted child was growing inside me.

This many years later, guilt still creeps up on me. Every so often, I take Lucas's side in a dispute with his siblings. I spoil him to death and convince myself he needs all the love and spoiling his heart can hold. Blake and Alexis were conceived in love. Lucas, not so much. I'm still working to ease my guilt for trying to get rid of him.

"Look where we are now because a couple of crazy college kids decided they would become a family before they even graduated. Before they had a chance to really experience life," I say.

"Those crazy college kids made it because they held on tight to each other and never let go. Don't ever let go, Cooper."

"I won't. Can you promise me the same, that no matter what, you'll always fight for us?"

"I always have and always will."

"I'll hold you to that promise for eternity, Ty."

The promise is music to my ears. I allow the pledge to embrace me like a warm blanket. Ty is a man of his word, and I trust him with my life. But would my husband be so quick to fight for our marriage if he uncovered my duplicity?

Would he let go if he discovered I betrayed him with another man?

CHAPTER 30

⸺◆⸺

ABBIE

New York, One Year Earlier

WHAT A SPECTACULAR view," I said. "Thanks for bringing me up here."

"You can have that view any time you come to New York. I mean it. You're always welcome."

I stopped by to visit Christian at his Lennox Hill Penthouse, twenty minutes from Levitron-Blair headquarters in Midtown Manhattan. We trotted into the massive living space after spending an hour admiring views of the city from the rooftop Solarium.

I came to New York to attend the International Cognitive Neuroscience Conference. It was the last day, and Christian invited me to dinner at his place.

In his gourmet kitchen, outfitted with Italian Calacatta marble, was a sumptuous meal prepared by Aaron, Christian's personal chef. Dessert was a rich, decadent Brioche and Amber Rum Custard. After dinner, he took me to his art studio to show me his latest paintings.

I'd never seen his art so dark, full of despair. Each painting depicted someone being consumed by tragedy: a man trying to escape a raging fire, the flames lapping at the edges of the canvas. The rest of the pieces—including a young man drowning and a barren landscape void of a single living creature—looked as though the color had been sucked out of the paintings, leaving the canvases void of hue and life.

Christian's art had always been his refuge, a place of joy and peace. His previous works were laced with optimism, the brush strokes a medley of dancing, shimmering color on canvas. What happened?

We returned to the living room and sat next to each other on a luxurious, royal-blue sofa with blue and white throw pillows. The stone fireplace crackled, smoldering embers adding a cozy feel to the room despite its massive size.

"I had no clue you were in such a dark place. What I observed doesn't look like your work at all. It's as if someone else painted those images. How did you get here, Christian?"

He shrugged. "There's no recording I can go back and watch, pinpoint the exact moment in time when I started feeling as though my life was in free fall."

"Is this about taking over as CEO of Levitron-Blair?"

"Maybe. Dad's cronies would like nothing more than to shout from the top of the Empire State Building that I'm not fit to lead the company."

"Is that what you believe?" I ask.

"I don't know what to believe, Abbie. What if they're right?"

"What makes you say that?"

"I'm not sure who I am besides Alan Wheeler's son and heir to LB. Don't get me wrong, I'm not complaining. I've had it easy compared to most."

He took a steadying breath and then added, "Now a multi-billion-dollar global corporation is being handed to me on a silver platter because my last name is Wheeler. And let me tell you something, Abbie. Wheelers are not allowed to fail. Ever."

Christian gazed at me with a panicked intensity, his expression haunted. In that moment, I understood, more than I ever did before, the crushing burden he was about to inherit. The constant struggle and fear of wondering whether he was cut out for the task at hand.

With the additional pressure and scrutiny of his detractors, those who doubted his ability, the situation was a recipe for disaster.

I squeezed his shoulder, trying to reassure him that everything would work out. Then I said, "No wonder your art is so dark and chaotic. I'm glad you have that as an outlet when you're feeling overwhelmed. Have you spoken to either one of your parents about how you're feeling?"

"And appear weak? No way, Abbie. My father only understands strength and decisiveness. There's no room for error."

"I understand that more than you know," I said. The words escaped my brain before I could stop them from spilling out.

He blinked at me and then said, "What's going on?"

"Nothing. I'm fine."

"You're not fine. The minute I saw you, I knew, but I didn't want to pressure you into telling me if you weren't comfortable."

I hesitated. I'm supposed to be helping my friend, not unloading my problems on him. "I'm okay." I touch his arm in a reassuring gesture.

Christian stared at me, his face twisted into a solid mask of skepticism and doubt, as if he didn't believe me. "Don't give me that look."

He stubbornly held on to his position, not blinking and not saying a word.

"Stop that. You're creeping me out." Then I said, "How old are you, three?"

Christian refused to relax his expression. "Gosh, you're annoying. Are you going to stay silent the rest of the evening because I said I'm fine and you don't believe me?"

I picked up a throw pillow from the sofa and gently tossed it at him. He didn't move out of the way, and the pillow fell to the floor.

I broke away from his gaze. I wasn't playing fair. The man bared his soul to me, revealed his deepest vulnerabilities and doubts without hesitation because he trusted me implicitly. I didn't take that lightly.

But there was a difference between Christian and me. I was married and he wasn't. Ty should be the only man I turned to for safety and comfort when life got difficult and tumultuous. He was ninety-nine percent of the time. The remaining one percent had been causing turmoil, making me feel unbalanced, anxious, and fearful.

Was it fair to unload this on Christian, no matter how much he pressed me to reveal what was bothering me? Should I take him up on his offer to be a listening ear?

"Okay. I've been feeling lost lately. It's no big deal. Life happens and we have to roll with it."

"Lost how, Abbie?" The intensity returned to his face.

I gave his question careful consideration. It had been a challenge articulating what the issue was. "I'm losing my footing, losing my way, but I can't express that."

"What are you talking about?"

"My kids told me I look exhausted. I believe the word they used was *whipped*. They're right." Tears stung my eyes. But I didn't want to have a meltdown in front of Christian. I came to be a support system for him, not fall apart.

He said, "Tell me what's going on, Abbie. Don't hold back. I'll listen with no judgment. The way it's always been with us."

His kindness made me want to break wide open and drown in a pool of my own sorrow. I tried to hold it in, the emotions that had been threatening to bury me alive. The feeling that my insides had been stripped raw from pretending everything was fine. Fearing that if I complained, I would come across as weak and ungrateful.

Through multiple pauses and apologies, the story came pouring out of me as if someone unscrewed a pressure valve.

"Some days, I'm physically unable to function. I'm working four jobs: mother to three kids, a twenty four-seven role; my career, which is two separate jobs; and wife of a busy surgeon. There's no time to breathe or slow down."

I paused and took a minute to compose myself. All the feelings came roaring back. Feelings of worthlessness. Feeling that I wasn't successful at any of the roles I signed up for. It seemed as though everyone else had their act together and had purposely kept the recipe for success from me.

"I'm struggling to balance it all. Like you, I can't afford to fail, but I am. Sometimes I can't even focus, and all I want to do is get away from my life for a while. And worst of all…worst of all, I'm starting to resent my husband."

Christian said nothing for a few beats. I observed his restless fingers and the tick in his jaw. Then he said, "Abbie, that's a lot for one person to handle. How could you even think you're a failure? And what is Ty doing to help you?"

"Ty doesn't know."

"Why not?"

"Because I don't want to appear ungrateful. Ty works hard for our family, and the truth is, we don't need my salary. Our lifestyle wouldn't change if I quit my job. But I wanted a career of my own, and we made sacrifices to make it happen. How would it look if I started complaining?"

Christian nodded. "I get it, but tell me why you're starting to resent Ty."

I swiped my fingers under my eyes, both slick with tears. "I assumed once I finished up my Ph.D. and Ty wrapped up his residency, that somehow, magically, I would get more help with raising our family and running the household."

"But instead, you got your Ph.D., took on two additional jobs outside the home, and the child-rearing, cooking, cleaning, and running of the household still all fell on your shoulders."

"Exactly. I was a stay-at-home mom for ten years, and the kids don't know any other way of existing. They still expect me to do it all. And Ty keeps getting busier."

I further explained the main reason I haven't discussed the issue with Ty, the crushing guilt and fear of judgment. From the outside, it looked like I had it made: three healthy, wonderful children; a thriving career; a great husband; and a beautiful home in an affluent suburb. What did I have to complain about, right?

What people didn't see were the days I came home from work exhausted and had to muster the energy to cook for a family of five. Check homework. Do the laundry. Create a meal menu. Manage the family calendar, including the kids' activities. Or the days I needed to leave work early to take the kids to some appointment or the other.

Heading to the supermarket late at night to do grocery shopping because the weekends were crazy and went by too fast. Or the meltdown I had in a Target parking lot because the kids were too demanding that day and I wanted to get away from them. Dealing with the self-loathing that followed because I shouldn't have such thoughts.

A deep, pained stare bloomed over Christian's face. "I'm glad you told me, Abbie. But you can't go on like this. It's not fair."

"I know I can't go on this way, but I don't know what the

solution is. Besides, I'm a coward."

"Is that so?" Christian asked, a sarcastic edge to his voice. "You're the most fearless person I know. I've had a front-row seat to every grenade life has thrown at you. Did you allow any of those grenades to take you out? Absolutely not. This situation is no different."

"Then why am I afraid to tell Ty how I'm feeling? We've been through a lot."

"Maybe you're afraid he won't understand. If he's hardly home, that means the two of you don't spend much time together. Telling him how you feel could be a shock to his system, and you want to avoid what you would consider as blindsiding him."

Christian was right. He understood, just like I knew he would. I turned over the conundrum in my head dozens of times and still couldn't figure out the solution. Sure, I could ask for time off from work, but that would take massive coordination and effort for what would amount to one week, two weeks at the most. Then I would return to the same issues, ten-fold.

Christian must have sensed my distress. He reached out and cradled my face in his hands. He asked, "Abbie, are you depressed? You can tell me."

It took me a moment to register the question. Then the gravity of what he asked dawned on me. "What? No. I'm not depressed."

"It's nothing to be ashamed of, if that's the case," he said, gently.

"I'm not depressed, Christian. I'm temporarily overwhelmed. Everything will work out," I said. My voice wobbled, sounding small and pathetic. "It's just a temporary situation. I can handle it." Tears pooled in my eyes and then trailed down my face, spilling unto Christian's hands.

"I'm sorry…I'm falling apart. I don't know what's wrong

with me." Then big, uncontrollable hiccups took over, and it seemed as though I couldn't catch my breath. Christian's voice was calm and soothing as he pulled me into his arms and held me.

"It's okay, Abbie. You're going to be fine. We'll figure it out. I'm right here. I'm not going anywhere."

His gentle words of encouragement made me wail even harder, and the next thing I knew, he was kissing my wet cheeks and stroking my hair.

But I couldn't explain what happened next, why it happened. Christian kissed me on the mouth, his lips soft and inviting. And though I knew I was supposed to break away, pull myself together, leave—no, run!—out of his penthouse, I didn't. Instead, I kissed him back.

The part of my brain that should have been screaming *stop* checked out. Christian continued raining fiery kisses all over my face, neck, chest, and shoulder. Before long, clothes were coming off fast and furious, tossed in all directions in a frenzied symphony of want and need.

Afterward, we lay motionless for a long while. Then Christian asked, "Are you okay?"

"Yes."

"You don't have to pretend with me."

"I know."

We both fell silent again. Then I said, "I need you to swear."

He looked me square in the eyes. "What do you mean?"

"Swear that no one will ever know what we just did. It has to stay a secret between us."

Christian hesitated, as though confused by my request. He asked, "Are you saying you regret it?"

I sighed wearily. "Christian, I don't have the mental faculty to analyze what just happened. The only thing I know for sure is that it can never happen again under any circumstances, and we need to keep it a secret."

"A secret from your husband, you mean."

"Yes. And every other human being on the planet." It was unfair to place that burden on Christian, but my brain was slowly beginning to function again and reality began to set in. There was no other way but absolute secrecy. No other way to protect my marriage and keep my family intact.

"I understand." Christian's voice sagged with something I couldn't identify. Disappointment? Sadness? Resentment that I had put him in the position of co-conspirator? I couldn't tell.

"Look, on some level I understand why it happened," I offer. "We were both hurting and turned to each other for comfort. That doesn't make it right, but that's my fault."

"How do you figure? I'm equally to blame."

"No blame game here, Christian. Just promise me this will remain our little secret."

"I would never betray your trust or cause problems for you, Abbie. You know that. I understand the implications if our secret gets out."

"Thank you," I said, a wave of gratitude flooding my body. "But I have to go now."

"Why? It's late. You can sleep in one of the guest bedrooms. My driver will take you to the airport in the morning."

"Thanks for the offer, but I must get back to my hotel. Ty and the kids plan to video chat. If I'm not in my room, I'll have some serious explaining to do. Besides, your girlfriend may drop by unexpectedly. That would be awkward to say the least."

"As always, you make perfect sense. But you shouldn't worry so much."

"I do worry. I could lose everything, including my children if anyone finds out."

Well you should have thought of that before you got naked with him. I swatted away the convicting thought.

Christian said, "That won't happen."

I said nothing but suddenly felt shy and exposed. "Um, do you think you could find my clothes?" I asked. I had no idea where they landed and no desire to strut around naked trying to find them.

Christian gave me a mischievous grin and then cocked an eyebrow as if to say, *you weren't so shy a few moments ago.*

"Yes, I'm a hypocrite," I said. "Sue me."

He broke out laughing but did as I asked. He handed me the clothes. I dressed hurriedly, pulled up the Uber app on my phone, and booked a ride to my hotel.

"May I see you out?" he asked.

Without hesitation, I said, "We might run into someone you know. Better I do this alone."

I gave him a quick peck on the cheek and left.

CHAPTER 31

THE SNIPER

FROM HIS VANTAGE point on the roof of the building, he has a perfect view of the space. The sun is beginning its descent over the horizon. A pillar of pink and white flowers and the majestic Caribbean Sea serve as a backdrop for the vow renewal. He gazes through the telescopic lens of his rifle with the patience and expertise of the well-trained professional he is.

The target comes into view.

She's dressed in a pale-pink strapless tulle gown with embroidered flowers. A pink tropical flower is tucked into her hair on the left side. Her husband stands next to her in a blue suit, white dress shirt, and a pink tie that compliments her dress.

A thorough but careful search of their room yesterday produced the itinerary for this vow renewal ceremony. The sniper's discovery of the itinerary was a stroke of luck he hadn't anticipated.

It's showtime. The sky is clear. There's no wind that could affect the bullet trajectory. It's all systems go. Adrenaline pumps through his veins. He puts the plugs into his ears. The minister officiating the ceremony stands in front of the couple. The sniper has a clear shot.

As he places his finger on the trigger of the rifle, a woman

145

appears and whispers into the target's ear. The target turns to engage the woman in conversation.

No go. Disappointment courses through him. He sweats profusely. A rooftop stakeout in the sweltering Caribbean heat could do that. The woman who interrupted now steps aside. The sniper could see the target once again, but she was not optimally positioned. He couldn't get a clean shot.

CHAPTER 32

ABBIE

MY HANDS SHAKE as I hold on to my gorgeous bouquet of tropical flowers. I could blame my trembling hands on the heat, but that would be ridiculous. The sky is streaked purple, orange, and pink as the sun begins its descent over the horizon.

Three other people are present for this momentous occasion. The ceremony officiant, one witness, and the photographer to take a few shots. We plan to surprise the family. They have no idea we're renewing our vows.

The officiant Reverend Horton says, "Tyler and Abigail have written their own vows. Tyler, would you like to begin?"

I hand over my bouquet to the witness, and Ty takes both of my hands in his. I gaze into his eyes, now wide and glowing with adoration. My breath quickens.

Ty says, "On the night I proposed to you, I said I couldn't imagine life without you. I've said that many times over the years, but Cooper, it's so much more than that.

"You bring me peace and joy and happiness so I can be the best version of myself. You've always been a safe place for me when life gets hard, my port in the storm."

My heart swells with happiness and pride. How lucky am

I to hear this wonderful man recite these words to me, share his heart with unabashed honesty?

Ty continues, "If I live a thousand lifetimes, I want to be your husband in every single one of them. I don't know what I did to deserve you, but I thank God for bringing you into my life.

"So today, I just want to say, from this day forward and into eternity, I'm yours. Will you have me?"

My heart races, and my palms get sweaty. Why am I nervous? I should be giddy, am giddy with happiness. I'm renewing my commitment to the man who has always protected me, loved me, made me laugh. The one who makes me feel like the most cherished woman on Earth. A model father, husband, best friend, and lover.

And how did you repay him? By sleeping with another man and keeping it a secret. You're a faithless, deceitful woman. But you don't have to be. You can tell him the truth. But you won't, will you, Abigail?

An electric charge zings through me, and for a moment, guilt-ridden, accusing thoughts bombard my mind. *Liar, cheater, ungrateful wife.*

Faster and faster the thoughts spiral through all the way down to my chest and land like a boxer throwing punches at his opponent repeatedly with no way to deflect the blows: *adulteress, deceiver, schemer. Kristina would never cheat on Ty. Maybe he married the wrong woman. One way or another, you will lose Ty.*

I can't catch my breath. I struggle to push through, get my breathing under control, and proceed with the ceremony. I close my eyes tight.

Ty says, "Cooper, what's wrong?" His tone is concerned and anxious. "Cooper, open your eyes, is everything okay? You're trembling."

I suck in air and then slowly open my eyes. Reverend Horton says, "Are you okay, dear? Do you need a minute?"

I swipe my hand across my eyes. "No, I'm fine. I don't need a minute. I'm sorry, Ty. I just got a bit emotional, that's all. You've turned me into a blubbering mess. Now I've ruined my makeup."

The photographer reaches into her pocket and hands me some tissue, which I use to dab my eyes and nose. Ty beams at me with that wide, confident smile of his that tells me everything will be okay. It will be. It has to be.

The reverend gestures for me to proceed with my vows as the photographer, who had stopped clicking away during my meltdown, takes her position again.

"Ty," I say, grabbing both his hands. "I hit the jackpot with you, and sometimes I'm afraid someone will come along and say oops, we made a mistake, he was meant for somebody else.

"I'm the luckiest girl because I get to do life with my biggest cheerleader, a man for whom I have tremendous respect and admiration, a man I adore more and more with each passing year."

I add, "Plus, you're gorgeous and a talented surgeon. A nice bonus. So yes, I'll be your forever girl. I'll be yours for eternity, Tyler."

Ty pulls me into his arms. Not caring that three people are present, he lays a deep, penetrating, passionate, can't-breathe kiss on me. I match his passion and intensity, and only come to my senses when we're pronounced husband and wife. Again.

CHAPTER 33

ABBIE

WE'RE BACK IN our suite after a private, candlelit dinner on the beach. Ty has made this second honeymoon spectacular, but with every thoughtful gesture, loving glance, and cherished moment, I'm one step closer to a meltdown.

Over the past year, I kept the guilt and shame under wraps from the one mistake that could demolish the life we've built. Was I deluding myself to think I could put it out of my mind and that would be the end of it? Why is my guilt flaring up again, on a second honeymoon of all places?

I force the careening thoughts to come to a screeching halt so I can focus on the night ahead of me. The fluttering island breeze drifts into the room from the open balcony door. A compilation of sexy R&B hits from the nineties and romantic ballads spring from the floor speakers. The mood is further enhanced by dozens of small candles giving off the aroma of guava with notes of soft caramel and brown sugar.

The aroma is already working its magic. I'm beginning to relax as I take in the hundreds of rose petals strewn all over the floor, leading to the bedroom from the living room area.

"I have something for you," I say to Ty, who comes out of the bedroom sporting a blue silk robe with an elegant jacquard pattern.

"What is it?"

I whip my hand from behind my back and hand him a small gift box. "I hope you like it."

He takes the box from me, his face beaming, and lifts the lid open. "Wow, Cooper."

I take the box from him, and he tries on the Bulgari WorldTimer watch with a blue sunburst dial accented with small diamonds.

"It has automatic winding and twenty-four different time zones, including New York, London, and Dubai."

"I can see that," he says, examining the watch. "I love it, Cooper. Thank you."

"I thought it was time to replace the one I got you for Match Day. That seems forever ago."

"I cherished that watch. It's how I carried you with me every day of my lengthy and sometimes painful residency."

After he plants a lingering kiss on me, he tugs at the belt of my white silk Kimono robe and says, "Are you going to show me what you're wearing underneath that robe? The suspense is killing me."

"Patience, my love," I tease. "There'll be plenty of time for you to have a peek."

"Just a peek? His face contorts in feigned disappointment. "That's not fair."

"My poor baby." I stroke his face. "I'll make it up to you. But in the meantime, how about a spin around the dance floor?"

CHAPTER 34

---◆---

THE SNIPER

*I*T HAS TO *be tonight*, the sniper reminded himself. The kill
shot. A reggae concert started an hour ago, which is why
he chose this night. With the music amplified and pulsating
throughout the property, no one would hear the shot.

He is exhausted, however, having traveled over twenty
hours from Nairobi, Kenya, to Montego Bay. He had been a
big-game hunting guide for some billionaire and his pals who
wanted to hunt buffalo. The sniper couldn't turn down the
lucrative pay and convinced himself at least they weren't illegally
hunting elephants.

When he received her desperate call, he was fearful she
would do what she threatened to do—jump off Boston's John
Hancock Tower. The sniper did some research and learned it
was the tallest building in the New England region of the U.S.,
clocking in at one hundred stories.

He couldn't let her jump.

Wiping his tired eyes, and shaking the fog from his
exhausted brain, the sniper does what he was trained to do. Wait.
And wait some more. Three hours into his stakeout, the target
comes into view, sporting a white robe. Her hair is loose now,
not pulled back in an elegant chignon as it had been during the

ceremony. The tropical flower is still tucked in her hair though.

It's time. He didn't want her scooting back to her room before he finished the job. With his rifle in place, he adjusts his night vision goggles and double checks that the ear plugs are firmly in his ears.

The sniper curls his finger around the weapon and squeezes off one shot. Her body goes toppling over the balcony. From his earlier reconnaissance, there was a plunge pool beneath her balcony on the ground level, so she must likely fell into the water.

He quickly disassembles his rifle and leaves the roof. The sniper must leave Montego Bay first thing in the morning. Before the police launch an investigation.

CHAPTER 35

―◦―

KRISTINA

I S IT DONE?" she asked. "Is she dead?"

"I never miss."

"And you're sure none of this can be traced back to us?"

"What do you take me for, an amateur?"

"Do you have pics of the body?"

"No, Kristina," he snapped. "I figured it was more important to get out of there. Are you out of your mind? Do you want me to get caught?

"This is a civilian you asked me to take out. A mother, for goodness sakes. These kids will grow up without their mom. It's a terrible way to grow up. Trust me."

"Don't you think I took that into consideration? They will grieve for a bit, but I will soon be their mom, new and improved."

"And Dr. Rambally? The man you claim to love so much. What about his pain and suffering?"

"I'll be there to soothe his wounded soul. Don't you worry about that. I know what I'm doing."

Seamus said, "I'm hanging up. About to run out of minutes on this burner phone. Heading back to London before the local police start asking questions. It would be a disaster if they start restricting guests' movements."

After she disconnected the call, Kristina plopped down on her bed and took a long, deep breath. An eye for an eye. A life for a life. Abbie caused the death of Kristina's unborn child when she convinced Ty to break up with Kristina. The stress had been too much for her body to handle. With Abbie gone, justice had been served. Finally.

Kristina could focus on the future. Ty would warm to the idea that she had been the woman for him all along. She would be his shoulder to cry on, his support system to help him through his grief. Kristina would help him with the children of course. They might be resistant at first, but with a little patience and understanding, Lucas, Blake, and Alexis would eventually embrace her.

Kristina rolled onto her back and stared up at the ceiling. Finally, she would become Mrs. Rambally, the way it should have been from the beginning. She pondered how to make the transition smoother, especially for the children.

I could never replace your mom, but I hope to be a mother figure. Your mom loved you very much, and you will carry her in your heart always. Your mom is in Heaven now. I'm here to help you and your dad. We're a new family, but your mom will never be forgotten.

Ty would see how hard Kristina tried to make everything okay for the children. He would have no choice but to fall madly in love with her.

A memory crawled its way into Kristina's brain. The day she found out Ty had proposed. Abbie sporting that massive diamond, with the scornful, superior air Kristina so despised. Abbie had said, *I'm sorry your heart is broken. I really am. But Ty is no longer your concern. It's time to move on.*

"Well, he's my concern now, isn't he, Abbie?" Kristina said aloud to the room. "And don't you worry. I'll take good care of Lucas, Blake, and Alexis. Ty and I will have a couple of little ones of our own obviously. We'll be one big happy, blended family."

Seamus was angry with Kristina. His fault really. Seamus shouldn't have gotten drunk and spilled his guts. That's one of the reasons Kristina drank alcohol only occasionally. When people drank too much, it ruined lives. Take Seamus, for example. He was drunk out of his mind when he confided his deep dark secret to Kristina, what he and his mates did in Afghanistan. She leveraged the secret to gain his reluctant cooperation.

Kristina had only one major obstacle left. Divorcing Callum. Once she became Ty's wife, she would take care of her irksome little infertility problem, the reason she and Callum couldn't conceive. The problem wasn't that Kristina couldn't get pregnant. It was that she didn't want to, not with Callum as the father.

After she had Ty's ring on her finger, Kristina would have her tubes untied.

CHAPTER 36

TY

A N ODD SENSATION prickled at the back of his neck. A sensation of foreboding that something dark had happened or was about to happen.

Ty headed to the concierge off the main lobby to confirm the private pool cabanas he rented were ready to go. Ty and Cooper planned to spend the day reading, relaxing, and enjoying cocktails delivered by the beach butlers.

Several guests were scattered around the lobby area, and they all seem to be doing the same thing: whispering. The hotel staff was stone-faced and urgent in their movements.

Ty approached the clerk manning the front desk, a pleasant-looking woman with a round face and bright smile. "What's going on? Why is everybody whispering and pointing?"

The woman hesitated. Ty said, "Can I be of help? I'm a medical doctor. My wife and I came to the resort for a second honeymoon."

Playing the doctor card always worked. The clerk said, "You're too late, doctor. She's gone."

"Who's gone?"

The clerk, Lydia, looked to her left and then right, scanning the area for anyone who might overhear what she was about to say.

Leaning in, she said, "A guest was found in the plunge pool under one of the west-facing balconies this morning. She drowned."

Ty stepped back from the desk as though some invisible force wanted to protect him from the tragedy.

"That's awful. When did they find her?"

"Late last night. Another guest was on his way back from the concert. He saw a body in a white robe floating in the pool. That poor woman. Savannah. Just got married right here at the resort and was enjoying her honeymoon."

Chills ran up and down Ty's spine. He couldn't say a word. Lydia continued. "I checked them in myself, lovely young couple. She had the most beautiful smile and always had a kind word."

Lydia shook her head as though grappling with the senseless tragedy.

"I'm guessing they closed the pool until further notice?" Ty asked, finally finding his voice.

"Just the area where she was found. Such a sad, sad situation. Her poor husband is beside himself. Losing his wife and unborn child like that."

Ty's head snapped to attention. "She was pregnant?"

"That's what her husband said."

"Lydia, you're needed in the back." A sharp, commanding island-accented voice sliced through the conversation. A tall, distinguished man with graying hair and thick eyebrows—the manager who had checked in Ty and Cooper upon arrival—appeared seemingly out of thin air. He did not look happy.

The manager made no effort to hide his annoyance with a staff member caught gossiping with a guest. Ty figured a dead body in one of the pools on the property was not the kind of information the hotel wanted the public, or other guests for that matter, to get a wind of.

Lydia scuttled away from the desk and disappeared into another room off the reception area.

The manager, Conrad, turned on a cordial smile and said, "Dr. Rambally, how may I be of service?"

Ty didn't know what to say for a moment. Fear unfurled inside him like thickening storm clouds. Cooper told him on their first day in Jamaica she saw a woman who looked like her out on the balcony, although she wasn't a hundred percent sure.

In an artificially light voice, Ty said, "I just want to know one thing. The woman found in the pool, was she black, tall and slender, really attractive?"

"Dr. Rambally, I'm not at liberty to discuss what happened—"

"Please," Ty said, interrupting him. "It's important. Urgent even."

The man hesitated and then said, "From what I've heard, that sounds about right. Now is there anything else I can do for you, sir?"

An eerie calm flooded Ty's body. He said, "I'm all set, thanks."

Then Ty slowly backed away from Conrad without saying another word, turned on his heels, and lumbered toward the bank of elevators.

CHAPTER 37

TY

W E'RE LEAVING. TODAY," he said.

Cooper gaped at him, wide-eyed and confused. She had slipped into a sexy, orange bikini with a matching semi-sheer sarong. Her sun hat rested on the sofa, alongside her beach bag and sunglasses.

"What are you talking about? We're spending the day at a private, poolside cabana catching up on our reading and sipping tropical drinks with umbrellas."

He took her by the hand and led her to the sofa. After they were both seated, he said, "I wouldn't make it if I ever lost you, Cooper."

"Ty, you're shaking." She took his hands in his hers and placed them on her knee. "What the heck happened downstairs?"

Where to begin? The news was still raw, but even worse, it took tremendous restraint to keep at bay the horrifying thought that… that…it could easily have been Cooper they found in that pool. Ty supposed local investigators would swarm the hotel wanting to speak to guests. He didn't want to be around when that happened.

There was a ton of work waiting for him when he returned home, and he didn't want either of them caught up in some death-in-paradise investigation.

Besides, there were the kids to consider. Lucas's graduation coming up in a week, and then all three kids would be off to summer camp in New Hampshire for a few weeks. Ty and Cooper couldn't afford to be detained. They didn't know anything anyway, so it would be a waste of everyone's time—theirs and the police's.

"Something happened at the hotel last night, Cooper."

"What something?" She regarded him with a blend of anxiety and curiosity, those big, expressive doe eyes of hers pleading and vulnerable. Ty just wanted to get her home safe and sound. Lydia said the woman fell off the balcony, but what if someone pushed her?

What were the chances that two women who looked alike ended up at the same resort at the same time wearing the same robe on the same night, and one of them wound up dead? Ty shivered.

"Ty, you're scaring me. What's going on?"

"Cooper, I think that lady you told me about, your doppelganger, is dead."

She flinched. "What? Where did you hear that?"

"I went downstairs to confirm our cabana for the day, and people were in the lobby whispering."

He explained what Lydia at the front desk told him and how he had provided the manager with a description of Cooper. Conrad confirmed the dead woman, Savannah, fit the description.

Cooper's face crumpled like wet tissue. "That's awful, really awful. I don't understand how something so horrific could happen to her, here. It doesn't make sense. How does someone go on vacation and fall off a balcony to their death?"

"According to the front desk clerk, she came to the resort

for her wedding and honeymoon. Her husband confirmed she was pregnant. So far they think she just fell over the balcony. Maybe she leaned over too far and couldn't right herself in time. An accident. No sign of foul play." Ty shivered again.

"What?" Cooper asked.

"You've seen the pools, right? The ones that run beneath the balconies on this side of the resort?"

"Yes, the plunge pools. What about them?"

"They're not too deep. Say Savannah fell off the balcony, as they suspect, isn't it possible she could have survived the fall?"

"Anything is possible," Cooper said.

"Maybe Newton's second law came into play. Mass times acceleration meant that she hit the water with such force that she drowned before she had time to straighten out and come up for air. I don't know. Something about this isn't right."

"I think I understand what you're trying to say." Cooper shivered too. "Savannah was dead before she hit the water."

They both fell silent. Despite the splendid tropical sun filtering into the room, caressing the walls, a dark cloud hung in the air between them. How could it not? Ty surmised his wife was thinking the same thing he was. The strange coincidence of seeing someone who resembled her two balconies over, only for the woman to wind up dead days after their initial sighting.

Breaking the silence, Cooper said, "You're right. We should leave today. I don't feel safe."

PART IV
THE UNRAVELING

CHAPTER 38

KRSITINA

PANIC SPREAD THROUGHOUT her body like wildfire. Kristina literally clutched her expensive pearl necklace. How on earth could she salvage this dreadful debacle? Her breaths came out in short, erratic bursts. She moved away from the counter, away from the article. Seamus had made a colossal mistake. A spectacular failure that put them both at risk of getting caught.

Kristina took a deep breath and slowly expelled it to calm her thundering heart. She repeated the exercise several times until she calmed down long enough to give her brain a chance to start thinking rationally.

Standing at the center of the small kitchen—dressed in a pink silk blouse, black pencil skirt, and heels—she fidgeted with the necklace again. She needed to leave for the office soon but had pulled out her laptop to do some quick online research, see if the story had made the papers in Jamaica at the very least.

He took out the wrong woman. How was that possible with his training? *Okay, calm down. Think!*

Seamus was halfway around the world when she called him and asked for this favor, and he hadn't sounded well. Did exhaustion cause him to make a mistake? Flying from Nairobi to Montego Bay on short notice was enough to test the patience and stamina of even the most seasoned of world travelers, Kristina reasoned.

The woman he took out, Savannah Davis Patterson, looked just like Abbie. *Mistaken identity.* The statistical possibility that both Abbie and her doppelganger would show up at the same resort, at the same time, in a foreign country was next to zero. Kristina would bet money on it. Yet, it had happened.

On the positive end of the spectrum, Abbie had no way of knowing that bullet was meant for her or who took the shot. Nobody could trace the murder back to Kristina or Seamus. The odds were still in Kristina's favor, despite the debacle.

As long as she remained calm, everything would work out. No more losing her temper; it clouded her judgment. She had been angry with Abbie the night after the dinner at her house for the Callum ambush. Fortunately, Kristina managed to convince Callum to return to London.

Kristina's rage had caused her to act irrationally. She could see that now. But she was good at planning. She was patient and always several steps ahead of Abbie, which gave Kristina an advantage.

Pacing the kitchen floor, Kristina decided to tackle the problem from another angle. She needed a weakness she could exploit, a crack she could widen. Then she snapped her fingers as a possibility came into focus. It had been lying beneath the surface, waiting for her to dredge it up like lost treasure.

With excitement buzzing through her, Kristina picked up her cell phone from the counter where it lay next to her laptop and pulled up the photo app. She scrolled until she came to the right images. Photos of Abbie with Christian Wheeler on the street near the Bristol Gardens restaurant.

She recalled how uncomfortable it made Ty when she

166

casually mentioned Christian and Abbie had gone to lunch. Ty's contention that he was supposed to join Abbie and Christian but canceled at the last minute had rung hollow to Kristina and still did.

Ty was upset about Christian spending time with his wife. But why, if they were so-called friends?

A new plan to get rid of her nemesis wormed its way into Kristina's head. Christian Wheeler was going to help her take down Abbie. He just didn't know it yet.

CHAPTER 39

ABBIE

W E ARRIVED HOME from Jamaica yesterday without giving the family advance notice our trip was cut short. Ty and I need the time to come to grips with the tragedy.

I walk over to the stainless-steel coffee machine in the kitchen to brew myself a fresh cup. Drumming my fingers on the counter while the machine hisses to life, a toxic tornado of chilling thoughts bombard my brain.

It could have been me. I was on the balcony of our suite the night Savannah died. I couldn't sleep. The semi-darkness, tranquility, and sound of the waves crashing inland helped to calm me.

I took the time to examine why I almost fell apart during the vow renewal. Why the guilt over what Christian and I did resurrected suddenly, like a long dormant disease.

If Ty discovers I was unfaithful, it could be the end of us. But what sends shooting pains through my chest is the possibility the killer was after me and got Savannah instead. I could chalk up such dark thoughts to paranoia, shock, or my history of people committing vicious crimes against me. But the feeling in the pit of my belly, the sixth sense that grows more intense by the minute, won't let me brush aside those thoughts.

One way or another, you'll lose Ty. Kristina's words echo through my brain. I pick up my coffee with trembling hands and head for the kitchen table. I place the mug down, spilling a few drops, not bothering to clean the mess. *There's more than one way to lose someone*, I think.

Did Kristina mean I would no longer be with Ty if I was dead? Or did she mean she would do whatever it takes to wrestle him away from me, from our family?

Kristina threatened Sita Kapoor, the Bollywood actress about to make her debut on American televisional at a cocktail reception, and look what happened. When Kristina ordered the two thugs to attack Sita, did Kristina just want to scare her, or was the attack a murder attempt gone awry?

I sit at the table, pondering my next move. My original plan was to check for news about Savannah's death in the local papers of Montego Bay. Then I would move on to stalking Kristina on social media to gather information.

I decide spying on Kristina is more urgent. I can't do anything to bring back Savannah. I change the browsing mode on my own LinkedIn profile so I can browse Kristina's profile privately. Within minutes, I have the name and location of her three previous employers, organizations she belongs to, and a plethora of other information. Next, I pull up Facebook.

Kristina's Facebook page is loaded with glamor shot after glamor shot of her at elegant gatherings dressed in designer duds and expensive jewelry: galas, cocktail parties, ribbon-cutting ceremonies, weddings, club openings.

My eyes glaze over from trying to keep up with the captions on the dozens upon dozens of photos with accompanying likes, comments, and emojis. From the photos, it's obvious Kristina had also traveled extensively: Abu Dhabi, Jakarta, Johannesburg, Marrakesh, Istanbul, and a bunch of other places, including tropical vacation destinations.

I don't see anything useful but force myself to scroll farther down. Now we're getting somewhere. Family photos, her mother and brother. Friends. In one photo, Kristina is surrounded by two women and a man. The caption suggests it's a night out celebrating a birthday with friends at an upscale restaurant.

All three friends are tagged in the photo, including Poppy Taylor and Sienna Evans. The man, Seamus Jones, intrigues me. He sports a black baseball cap with a logo that looks like a giant X with a crest at its center.

I click on the photo to enlarge it. The X is comprised of two intersecting swords and a lion with a crown on its head. But the word beneath the logo makes my heart drop to my stomach.

Army.

Sweat prickles at the back of my neck and forehead. I open a new browser window on the laptop and Google British Army logo. It's the same logo on the cap that Seamus Jones is wearing in the restaurant photo.

Breathe. Don't jump to conclusions. But my fingers aren't listening. They fly over the keyboard, typing in the name of the resort in combination with Montego Bay and accidental death. Several hits come back. I click on the link from the *Jamaica Observer.*

WOMAN TUMBLES OFF RESORT BALCONY, DROWNS IN POOL

I almost jump out of my seat. I'm staring back at my own face. I didn't get a good look at Savannah the day I first spotted her on the balcony, when Ty and I first arrived in Jamaica. The photo sends chills up and down my spine. I had no idea how much she looked like me. We could be identical twins. Only in this photo, the name is Savannah Davis Patterson. Knowing her full name makes the tragedy all too real.

I scroll and take in more of the story, searching for details. Savannah was thirty-two years old, a year younger than me. Savannah and her fiancé Don Patterson came to the resort for their destination wedding and honeymoon. They were both from Torrance, California.

Savannah was a software developer and Don a project manager. They worked for the same tech company.

I start to choke up, tears circling. I don't know if the tears are for Savannah and her unborn child or because I could have ended up the way she did. I read the story to the end.

Investigators discovered a bullet hole in Savannah's neck. I was right. She was dead before she hit the pool.

CHAPTER 40

CHRISTIAN

T HE WAY HER mouth twitched indicated she was angry about something. Sam had passive-aggressive down to a science and Christian had learned to read the signs. What had he done now?

She suggested coming over to his place for a quiet evening, having canceled the Broadway show they planned to attend. After a rough day at work for them both, staying in made sense.

"What movie do you want to watch?" he asked. "Lady's choice."

"I'm fine with anything. I might fall asleep halfway through, anyway."

As if to drive home the point, Sam yawned and then stretched. She was dressed in slim-fitting jeans and a sleeveless top, her blond hair pulled back in a high ponytail. Even in a casual getup, she exuded confidence and glamor.

"Is everything okay?" he asked.

"Why wouldn't it be?"

"I don't know. You seem preoccupied, like something is on your mind."

"No, I'm great. Couldn't be better." She sighed loudly and angled her body away from him on the sofa. Usually when they watched a movie together, Sam curled up next to him and placed her head on his chest.

The words spilled out of Christian's mouth before he could think of a gentler approach. "If you have something to say, just say it and quit pouting."

Sam glared at him without blinking. Her mouth twisted into an expression resembling a sneer. Sometimes it was hard to tell with Sam, even after three years.

"Do you talk to her that way, get brusque with her? I bet you don't."

"Who? What are you talking about?"

"*Her*, Christian. I'm talking about Abbie." Sam inspected her fingernails, waiting for him to react.

"What does Abbie have to do with us?"

"Everything. She's the reason you won't propose, isn't she? What, you think she'll leave her husband for you and the two of you will ride off into the sunset together?"

Heat flushed through his body as a cold silence descended over the room. The cold silence then morphed into a crackling hostility, unspoken but palpable.

Sam knew Christian and Abbie were close friends, he made no secret of it. What sparked her aggression? The two women met on a couple of occasions. Once at Callie's fashion show and at a charity event. They were cordial, no tension whatsoever. What changed?

"My relationship with Abbie is not for you or anyone to dissect or pass judgment on. We've been friends for the better part of seventeen years. She's an integral part of my life, and that will never change. What's really going on, Sam?"

"You can hide behind your so-called friendship all you want, but I know the truth."

"What truth would that be?"

"You won't propose to me because you want her. And I'll tell you something else, Christian. I'm nobody's second choice. There are plenty of men out there who would be delighted to have me."

Sam fumbled in her purse and pulled out a cigarette. She smoked whenever she got anxious. But she didn't light the cigarette, just held it between her fingers as though she needed a prop.

She continued, "I know my worth and refuse to sit around waiting for you to recognize it." She gave him a disdainful stare, her eyes two gray pods of burning resentment.

"Is that a threat?" he asked. "Because I don't respond well to threats. What's really eating you up inside?"

"Oh, you want the truth, do you? I'll tell you the truth. Your obsession with Abbie is making you stupid and reckless."

Christian folded his arms and said, "Well, don't hold back, you're on a roll."

"She chose someone else. It's time you got over it and focus on what's in front of you. I won't live in limbo anymore, waiting for you to stop behaving like a lovesick puppy every time you see her."

Sam got up from the sofa and stood off to the side. She added, "You think I don't notice how you always find excuses to talk to her over the phone? During Fashion Week last year, you couldn't tear your eyes away from her once she hit the runway for the showstopper of Callie's collection. I deserve better, Christian."

She began pacing. "Damn you, Christian. Damn you!" She placed her hand on her forehead shaking it, the unlit cigarette poking through her fingers.

He stood also. "You too, Sam? Like I don't have enough pressure on me without you acting like a drama queen because I won't do what you want on your timeline? I'm not your father. You can't twist me around your little finger."

She whipped around to face him and let out a thin laugh. "Of course not. Because there's only one woman who has you wrapped around her little finger. Abbie. And you know full well this has nothing to do with pressuring you. I won't be one of those women who turns a blind eye to her man's cheating ways."

"Excuse me? What is that supposed to mean?"

Sam laughed once more, but there was no humor in it. "This thing with Abbie isn't some platonic affair of the heart. Or the so-called friendship mantra you keep tossing around like a badge of honor."

Sam inched closer to him so they stood face-to face. He felt her anger pulsating throughout her body, as though it were a force about to spill out through her clothes and into the room.

She continued, "Let's call it what it is, once and for all."

Christian didn't flinch when he asked, "And what would that be, Sam?"

"It's an intense sexual attraction wrapped inside a deep, emotionally complex bond that has consumed you most of your adult life. That's the truth. We both know it."

He blanched at her analysis, which was spot on, not that he would ever admit it. She caught him off guard. Sam wasn't dumb, but her powers of observation and deduction were limited. So where were her sudden insights into his relationship with Abbie coming from?

Christian attempted to coax Sam back to the sofa. She withdrew from his touch and remained standing. He let his hands drop to his sides and took a seat.

He said, "That's an interesting assessment, Sam. Why are you throwing unfounded accusations at me?"

"It's not just me, Christian. Your father also has concerns."

And there it was. The source. What had his father said to Sam?

"My dad doesn't know what he's talking about. And you just accepted information he spoon-fed you?"

"No, Christian." Sam dug into the pocket of her jeans. "I didn't just accept what Alan said. I have proof." She held out her palm.

A gold earring shaped like a Faberge egg sparkled under the living room lights. *Abbie's earring.*

Under the brutal spotlight of Sam's hurt and anger, there was no way to explain it away.

"What, nothing to say?" she asked.

If he pretended it didn't belong to Abbie, then he would have to explain what another woman's earring was doing in his apartment. If he admitted the truth, that the piece indeed belonged to Abbie, many lives would be impacted.

"I entertain here frequently on behalf of LB. You know that, Sam. Anyone could have dropped that earring. Why do you assume it belongs to Abbie?"

"Do you take me for an idiot?" she shouted. "Her initials, ACR, are carved into the earring. Here." She shoved the offending jewelry into his hand. "See for yourself."

He took it from her, gave it a cursory glance and asked, "Where did you find the earring?"

"Under a sofa cushion."

The next question died on his tongue. Asking Sam what she was looking for under a sofa cushion would only make matters worse, so he suppressed the urge to ask.

Sam said, "Did Abbie leave the earring behind to mark her territory after you two slept together?"

"Don't be crude." Christian's heart thudded in his chest. "Abbie is not that kind of woman."

"So you didn't have sex with her, in this apartment?"

Christian promised Abbie he would protect their secret.

He wouldn't go back on his word. There was too much at stake for them both. If he admitted the truth, Sam would make sure everyone in their circle knew it. Then the news would spread like wildfire. Abbie would believe Christian betrayed her, and he couldn't—wouldn't—do that to her.

"As I said, Abbie has been here before, and obviously the earing fell without her noticing. I don't know why you're jealous about her all of a sudden."

In a steady, low-pitched voice, Sam said, "You still haven't answered my question. Look me in the eye and tell me you didn't sleep with Abbie, a married woman, mother of your nephew no less, in this apartment."

Sam stood directly in front of Christian. Her eyes shot daggers at him, daring him to fess up.

Christian held her gaze and didn't move a muscle, forcing himself into a state of calm and focus. He said, "I didn't sleep with Abbie in this apartment. Or in any other apartment at any time. Got it? Stop allowing my dad to fill your head with lies."

Sam backed away, ever so slightly. Her lips pressed together in a grimace as tears pooled in her eyes. "I won't let you do this to me. I deserve a man whose heart belongs to me, and only me."

She slid her feet into the flats on the floor near the sofa, picked up her purse, and walked out of his apartment. Christian didn't stop her. What would be the point? She was upset and wouldn't listen to anything he said.

Flopping down on the sofa once more, Christian pondered how far he was he willing to go to protect the secret he shared with Abbie. Would he consider giving Sam what she wanted to keep it from spilling out further? It wasn't just Sam and Abbie he needed to worry about. He had to consider Lucas as well.

If Ty Rambally found out Christian slept with his wife, there was a high probability he would divorce her. Ty was a prideful man who adored Abbie, a woman Christian heard Ty refer to as his queen more than once. To discover his queen had betrayed him would send Ty over the edge.

If that scenario played out, the consequences would bleed far and wide. It would upend Lucas's life, destroy the security and stability he'd always had. His nephew did not handle change well. If his parents split, Christian didn't know what it would do to Lucas.

He needed to figure out a better way to deal with the situation. The lid on the secret had cracked open, thanks to Sam. Would it stay that way, or would the crack get bigger and bigger until the secret was exposed for all to see?

Christian had a sickening feeling that no matter what he did, it was already too late. The die had been cast.

CHAPTER 41

ABBIE

KRISTINA'S FACE REGISTERS shock and then morphs into a cloak of utter misery like a tragic heroine in a Puccini opera. She stands there, doorknob in hand, raw and awkward. She's decked out in black high-heeled pumps and a belted linen dress in navy blue with gold buttons. A leather bag is slung over her shoulder.

I don't take my eyes off her as I casually sip my coffee. Then I give her a big, bright smile that says, *I know you tried to have me killed in Jamaica, you scheming, vindictive, viper.*

"Abbie, what are you doing here?" she asks, stepping into the room finally.

"I thought I'd stop by. See if we could bury the hatchet."

She narrows her eyes at me, as though she doesn't believe me. I don't care. She places her bag at the far corner of the desk and stands behind the chair, leaning over it.

I remain seated. Kristina doesn't intimidate me. Her tactics may be scary and desperate, but she's on my territory, attempting to mess with my family, trying to steal my husband, and for that, I will make her eternally sorry.

"What?" I ask. "I'm just saying we should call a truce before something truly horrible happens."

I let the statement hang in the air and watch her closely. Fear stretches across her face. She rubs her arms as though warding off a chill, but it's the last week of June.

"Look, Abbie, you resent me for no logical reason I can fathom. All I did was take advantage of a great career opportunity, and it's obviously upset you. I thought we buried the hatchet when you invited me to the dinner party at your home."

Kristina taps nervously on the armrest. She adds, "The dinner turned out to be an ambush, a brutal attempt to humiliate me in front of your family. I'm sorry but you have zero credibility with me, and you are deluded if you think I'll ever trust you again."

Oh, she's good. An Oscar worthy performance, right down to the eyes narrowed in confusion and her pursed lips.

"Fair enough," I say. "That's why I'm here. Ty said I was too hard on you and asked me to apologize. I didn't reveal my plans for Callum's appearance at the dinner until it was too late for him to do anything about it. Sorry."

"I figured the dinner was your idea. Ty is kind and considerate. He would never do anything so blatantly devious. When we were together, he was protective, always made sure I was okay. And he was so gentle…"

She trails off, but I catch her hidden meaning. I won't take the bait she's so desperately dangling before me.

"You're right. Ty is all of those things. It's what makes him a great husband and father." I lean in closer, as if we're friends revealing our deepest, darkest secrets.

In a breezy, friendly tone, I say, "You have every right to be skeptical. To prove my sincerity, I'll talk to my mother-in-law on your behalf."

Kristina finally takes the seat behind her desk, her attention anchored on me. "What do you mean?"

"Well, you never got the chance to talk to her about the

fertility issue. Remember? Jenny isn't taking on new patients at all. Her schedule is booked a year out. People come from all over the world, desperate to see her. But I could convince her to squeeze you in."

I suspect the so-called fertility issue is another one of Kristina's lies, a lie to gain sympathy and deflect attention from the real reason she's in Boston. Callum confirmed this whopper of a lie during the dinner, non-verbally of course. The man was too shell-shocked to speak.

Kristina frowns at my suggestion. "Don't worry," I say, holding up a hand. "I have no desire to be in your private business; that's between you and your husband. All I'm volunteering to do is to talk to Jenny."

"Why would you do this for me?"

"Because Ty said I had to make it up to you, that what I did, the whole Callum thing, was mean." Ty said no such thing, but Kristina doesn't know that.

Kristina visibly relaxes, her body sinking back into the chair, her facial muscles at rest. She says, "Yes, it was very mean-girl of you. I'm glad Ty called you out. I'm surprised he didn't cancel the trip to Jamaica after what you pulled."

Interesting that she's bringing up Jamaica. I want to see where this goes.

"Why would he?"

"You said yourself. He was upset at what you did."

"Well, first off, the trip was already planned, and second, I'm not a child who needs punishment for bad behavior. Both Ty and I needed to get away, so we did."

I add, "Aren't you going to ask me how Montego Bay was? It's the polite thing to do when someone returns from vacation."

Kristina crosses her arms in front of her chest and presses her lips flat. "Well, we're not friends, are we?"

"No," I say slowly. "But we are trying to build a bridge of some sort, so it couldn't hurt to start with common decency, politeness."

In a reluctant tone, she says, "I assume Montego Bay was fabulous. Who wouldn't have a good time in a tropical paradise surrounded by great weather, turquoise-blue water, white sandy beaches, and great food and service? All these places are the same after a while. If you've been to one, you've been to them all."

"I disagree, Kristina. The place definitely helps, but I think it comes down to the people. A couple can get away to a tropical paradise and have an absolutely miserable time."

My gaze never leaves her face. I catch a hint of something. She runs her hand through her hair. Silence hangs between us. Then Kristina reaches for her bag at the far end of the desk, unzips it, and roots inside as though looking for something important. In the end, she pulls out her laptop and boots up.

Then she says, "So you and Ty had a great time. Good for you."

"Thanks for asking. Yes we did, but it was more than a good time. It was a time for reflection and to reinforce our commitment to one another, to our family.

"The vow renewal ceremony was a wonderful surprise. It meant so much to me that Ty went through the trouble of planning the event. But as you've pointed out, he's kind and considerate."

If Kristina's jealousy could spring to life, it would grow legs, walk across the desk, and punch me in the face. That's the vibe I'm getting from her sullen expression and clenched teeth.

She says, "Look, Abbie, I have a busy day ahead. I don't mean to be rude—"

"Say no more." I cut her off. "I have a pile of work waiting for me as well."

But I don't get up from my chair. My eyes scan the office. With the exception of a couple of plants and generic prints on the wall, there are no personal touches. No wedding photos or shots of family and friends. Not even a diploma on the wall.

Kristina follows my gaze. "Your diploma is missing from the wall. I would have thought you would proudly display it."

"What are you talking about?"

"You went to Oxford, right?"

"Right."

"So where is your diploma? People who attend prestigious universities like to display their diplomas in their workspace. You should have both your Yale and Oxford diplomas on the wall. You've earned it."

A half smile tugs at her mouth. "Showing off really isn't my thing."

"You're no fun," I say, pretending to tease her. "I'm sure MGH asked for proof that you graduated from both Yale and Oxford. They can be such sticklers. So why not show off your accomplishments? Put it right where everyone can see."

I'm met with stone-faced silence. I stand. "Well, I'm glad we chatted. Let me know about asking Jenny."

"I'll think about it."

"Good."

I leave Kristina's office without a backward glance. Murder for hire may be the most heinous of her crimes—okay, *alleged* crimes since I can't yet prove she hired Seamus Jones, ex- British military, to fire the bullet that ended Savannah Davis Patterson's life. But she's not above committing other ugly crimes. Like fraud.

CHAPTER 42

KRISTINA

ABBIE KNEW SOMETHING. Kristina leaned forward, clutching the edge of her desk. She tried to concentrate on work yet couldn't.

Panic swirled around her, a relentless grip that made her ill. Abbie's entire visit was suffused with suspicion and disdain, her attempt at civility obviously designed to mess with Kristina.

But it didn't mean Abbie had proof of anything, right? She was just fishing. *Calm down. Breathe. You know what happens when you panic.*

Why did Abbie mention Oxford, though? She couldn't possibly have uncovered Kristina's secret shame? *Stay calm. Abbie was testing you, bluffing.*

Letting go of the desk, Kristina stood and ambled toward the window. Splashes of sunshine seeped through. She needed a minute to calm her riotous insides that had ignored all the alerts her brain doled out about remaining calm. She could do that. She had to before her first meeting of the day.

Do not underestimate Abbie, her brain screamed. Callum told Kristina the same thing at her apartment, after that awful dinner at Abbie and Ty's house.

Could Abbie have discovered that Kristina only attended

Oxford for one year? She was not proud of the fact that she quit her master's program because boredom set in. She wanted to be out in the world, making things happen, meeting people, traveling.

Perhaps she opted for Oxford too soon after she graduated from Yale. A few years off before diving into another rigorous academic program made sense in hindsight. But at the time, Kristina had been trying to forget: the miscarriage, Ty, his betrayal, her broken heart. Taking on a master's program seemed like the perfect anecdote to her troubles.

Kristina wouldn't give Abbie another chance to ambush her or suspect Kristina of malfeasance or make thinly veiled accusations or whatever. Abbie might have escaped death in Jamaica, but Kristina wasn't done with the woman yet. Not by a longshot.

CHAPTER 43

ABBIE

B Y LATE MORNING, I start feeling normal again after the meeting in Kristina's office. Building a psychological profile on someone is one thing, but seeing those characteristics play out in front of you is another. I shiver and reach for the coffee on my desk.

Look, Abbie, you resent me for no logical reason I can fathom. All I did was take advantage of a great career opportunity, and it's obviously upset you. I'm the problem. An innocent career move by Kristina turned me into an evil witch. She's blameless, innocent. As harmless as a newborn baby. I almost laugh out loud at the absurdity.

I take a sip of my coffee. Someone knocks on the door, and I invite them in.

She plops down in the chair across from my desk. I ask, "Do you have it?"

"Yes." She reaches into her bag, pulls out a package, and plunks it down on my desk.

"You avoided cameras, kept your head down, and paid cash like we discussed?"

"Yes, Abbie. I'm not stupid."

"I'm just nervous. I don't want this coming back to haunt us."

"It won't," Layla says. "People buy burner phones all the time. You don't need to be paranoid."

Layla is a successful realtor and had a showing in Concord, the other town that borders Lexington where we live. After showing her client the house, Layla hopped on Route 3 North and drove forty minutes to Nashua, New Hampshire, and found a convenience store to purchase the two burner phones. Purchasing the phones from a known retailer like Wal-Mart or Target is a recipe for trouble. Some random convenience store out of state makes me feel less anxious.

"Now is the time to back out if you're having second thoughts. Once we set this in motion, there's no going back. Are you sure you want to be part of this?"

Layla glares at me.

"What? I'm giving you an out, last chance," I say. "This isn't my first tango with a raving sociopath who decided to come for me. Things could get messy and complicated."

Plus, there is a possibility the police could come knocking on our door, but you don't need to know that because it's just my paranoia talking.

Layla says, "I told you I would help you with this problem. I won't go back on my word. I'm all in."

I relax into the chair. I had reservations about roping Layla into this plan, but after the dinner at our house, Layla wanted the lowdown on Kristina and what the tension she observed at the dinner was all about. So I told her the truth: Kristina wants my husband.

After that conversation, Layla's dislike for Kristina turned into a bright, hot, intense hatred. As an only child, Layla wholeheartedly embraced the Cooper clan after she and my brother Miles got engaged. Layla's father, an immigrant from Ethiopia, died when she was six, so it's been Layla and her mom Zoya for most of her life. Now she's about to inherit a big, crazy, family.

"I know you won't. The plan is risky. I don't want you to get burned.

"I got your back, Abbie," she says with confidence. "Trust me, Kristina is going down."

"She is," I concur. I open the package, remove the red burner phone, insert the SIM card, and compose a text message to Cheryl Barnes, Kristina's boss.

CHAPTER 44

ABBIE

LAYLA IS BARELY out the door when my cell phone vibrates with an incoming call. I scoop up the phone off my desk. It's Christian.

"We need to talk. It's urgent," he says when I answer.

I press the phone to my ear. "What's going on?"

"Trouble might be heading your way."

My blood curdles. The last thing I need is trouble. What could Christian possibly have to warn me about?

"What kind of trouble?"

"I'm heading up to Boston in a couple of days for a meeting with a guy who wants to pitch his new gaming platform to LB. We should meet, but not in your office."

That sounds ominous. Christian is nervous and scared. "Okay. The weather is nice, let's meet at Boston Common."

"Sounds great. Let's do it."

"Aren't you going to give me a hint?"

"Not over the phone. I'll text you my availability, see if any of the time slots work for you."

After I hang up from Christian, I glance at the framed family photos on my desk. Fear sparks in my chest. Will my actions a year ago shatter my perfect family before Kristina has

189

the opportunity to do just that? Is that what Christian is about to tell me?

Christian would not go back on his word to keep our indiscretion a secret, but something has changed, something big enough to make him nervous, to call me and request a face-to-face meeting.

I pick up the first photo and trace my fingers around the image. We sit on the front steps of the house. Ty and I are next to each other, Alexis sits in front of Ty, his hands on her shoulders. Blake and Lucas sit next to me. We're all grinning. Two large flower pots bursting with daisies create the perfect backdrop. Our own version of a Norman Rockwell painting.

I want my kids to have the same upbringing that I did, with a mom and a dad, stability, security, love, and laughter. Ty and I have provided that for them, our greatest accomplishment. But is the clock ticking? Is my betrayal about to ruin my family?

I place the family photo back on the desk and turn my gaze to a wedding photo. Because we first got married at city hall without telling anyone, the family threw us a lavish wedding a few months after Lucas was born. In this photo, Ty is leaning toward me, his hand extended, his face radiating pure joy. I'm sitting with my wedding gown spread out all over the ivory and gold Louis XIV style antique sofa.

My cell buzzes, bringing me back to the present. It's a text message.

Lucas

Is Uncle Christian coming to my graduation?

I think so. Why do you ask?

I shouldn't make promises to my son, not knowing what kind of trouble Christian is about to reveal. What if his news impacts the graduation plans? If Christian doesn't attend, Lucas will be devastated. I can't have my little boy heartbroken on one of the biggest days of his young life.

Whatever Christian has to say, we'll keep it under wraps until after the graduation celebration. I won't allow anything to ruin this day for Lucas.

CHAPTER 45

June 28

Imagine my surprise when she showed up uninvited to my office. But then she shared the most wonderful story. That you asked her to apologize for ambushing me the night of the dinner. My heart leapt for joy. Abbie treats me with contempt, but you see me, Ty. Not as some object of loathing but a real living, breathing human being with feelings, someone worthy of respect and consideration.

Remember when you admonished Abbie for not knowing whether I had any food allergies ahead of the dinner? You stood up for me in front of your family. I can't remember the last time anyone came to my defense. It just made me love you more, miss you more. Want you more.

I know I shouldn't say such things but I can't help how I feel. Besides, I've suffered enough with Callum. I'm almost ashamed to admit that my husband, hopefully soon-to-be ex-husband, has never been faithful to me in the entire eight years we've been married. I couldn't in good conscience bring children into the world, his children, knowing how he treated their mother. Divorce would be inevitable, and I couldn't do that to them. I hope you understand.

I worry about you in that marriage of yours, though. I worry that Abbie will destroy you. Please consider me a friend. If Abbie can have a friend, Christian Wheeler, why can't you? Why can't you have someone you've known for years as a friend to share your burdens? It's only fair.

Will you let me be there for you?

CHAPTER 46

ABBIE

TWO DAYS AFTER the ominous call from Christian, we meet up at Boston Common. It's a beautiful summer day in late June. Sunlight glints off the gold dome of the Massachusetts State House across from the park.

We sit on a bench close to the pond, with low-hanging tree branches that provide shade from the sun. Joggers pass by with ear buds firmly in their ears, while streams of people, both locals and tourists, take in the beauty of the park.

"You got my attention," I say. "It's all I've been thinking about since I received your call. What's going on?"

Christian bites his lips. "It's about what happened last year, between us."

"What about it? We promised to keep it a secret."

"The secret is out, Abbie. I'm really sorry. That's what I wanted to tell you in person so you can prepare."

His words land like a gut punch. All hope that we could keep a lid on our infidelity drains from me. Christian promised. Who did he confide in? I thought I could trust him.

With a false sense of calm, I say, "Please explain what happened."

"One of your earrings fell in between the sofa cushions.

Sam found it, and she confronted me. My denials didn't make a difference. She told my father."

This is bad! Really bad. I had noticed the earring went missing, but I didn't think I lost it at Christian's place. It's one of my favorite pairs, and I wear them often. There were any number of places I could have dropped the missing one. The car, my office, at home. Eventually, searching for it fell way down my long list of priorities.

"I need details. Tell me exactly what happened." I'm surprisingly calm for a woman whose life is about to implode.

"Like I said, Sam found the earring, but I don't know when. The confrontation happened a week ago. She pulled the earring from her pocket and showed me. The one that looks like a Faberge egg, in gold."

"How did she know it belonged to me?" I sound whiny and desperate. "No offense, but you have a playboy reputation. That earring could have belonged to any woman, again, no offense."

"None taken. And just so you know, I never fooled around on Sam. Well, except for our dalliance last year. Anyway, your initials, ACR, were carved into the earring." Christian bounces his right knee and then rubs his neck again. His nervousness is contagious.

I place my hand on his knee. "Stop doing that. Tell me why you're afraid. Don't hold back. I'm not that fragile."

Christian explains Sam's reaction and her accusation that he still carried a torch for me, ending with her refusal to be with a man whose loyalty is divided.

I turn away from Christian, shame and guilt assaulting me. I blink back tears. Not only was I reckless with my marriage, but I also didn't stop to think how our tryst would affect his relationship with Sam. Since promised to keep it a secret, there was no reason to worry. Until my missing earring turned up and exposed us both.

Returning my gaze to him, I say, "I'm sorry. If there is anything I can do to help, I will. But I doubt Sam wants to hear from me, pleading your case."

"I'm not sure if anything can be done."

"Just because my marriage may fall apart doesn't mean your relationship with Sam has to end. Convince her she's the one for you. Ask her to marry you.

"You said yourself you've been faithful to her, until, well, you know. So why not go for it and, in the process, make Alan super happy?"

A woman pushing a baby in a stroller passes by. The baby smiles at us, and we both wave. Christian says, "I don't know, Abbie."

"Sam ran to Alan, ratted us out. She wouldn't do that if she didn't care, if she didn't love you."

"Yeah, it's a fair point. Promise me one thing, though."

"What's that?"

"That you won't give up on our friendship. And you'll fight for your marriage if it comes to that."

"Only if you promise me you will fight for Sam."

"What am I supposed to do about my feelings for you?"

"It's time to let go, Christian. I can't tell you how or when. But I wonder whether your feelings have more to do with the idea of me, more so than the reality."

"What do you mean?"

"You thought we had all the time in the world to rekindle our relationship. But that didn't happen. My life got turned upside down. Do you feel as though you were cheated of a second chance?"

He doesn't say a word and, instead, looks down at his feet. I take his hand in mine and squeeze. "It's okay. I understand. But we should focus on the present. We made a mistake. It's time to face the consequences. Lucas wants you at his graduation, so you should still come, but after that, I have to confess to Ty. You and I will need to pull back. Not chat so often."

He nods. "It will be good for us," I quickly add. "It will give you time to focus on Sam and your future together and give me some space to convince Ty not to divorce me and split up our family."

My stomach churns. I keep talking to stop myself from giving in to the fear nipping at me. "It feels like we're breaking up, but we're not. We're still friends. Just at a distance, at least for a while."

That's what I tell myself, but the truth is if Ty gives me an ultimatum, I'll choose my marriage and my family.

Christian swallows repeatedly and then returns to biting his lips. Then he says, "It's the right thing to do, Abbie. Given the circumstances, we don't have a choice.

"It's fair to say that whatever respect or goodwill Ty had toward me will be obliterated once he finds out. That makes me sad too. I respect him; he's a good man."

"We were two consenting adults who must now face the adult consequences of our actions. I'm sorry it came to this."

"So am I."

"It's not goodbye, though. It's more like see you later."

"Yeah," he says his voice cracking.

"Will you let me know if Sam accepts your proposal?" I ask.

"I will. Since she involved my father, it may take me a while to convince her to give me another chance."

"Yikes. That can't be easy."

"I think Dad will keep a lid on our secret, but Sam is a loose cannon. She's angry at us both, and that's not a recipe for keeping quiet."

"Alan will protect you. Perhaps he can convince Sam to simmer down?"

CHAPTER 47

KRISTINA

HAVE A SEAT, Kristina. This won't take long." Cheryl's expression oscillated between fury and disappointment. When Kristina received the call to meet Cheryl in her office, Kristina couldn't fathom what the meeting could be about. As far as Kristina knew, her boss was happy with her work, despite being on the job only a few weeks.

Sitting across from Cheryl, a rail-thin, average-looking woman in her late forties, Kristina made a show of shuffling her notebook to a fresh page, her pen at the ready.

"What's this about, Cheryl? Is everything okay?"

"No, everything is not okay. Let me cut to the chase. I received a disturbing text message a couple of days ago from someone claiming that you never graduated from Oxford, that your resume is falsified. These are serious allegations, grounds for immediate termination."

Cold silence floated in the air. Resentment and frustration inflated inside Kristina. She couldn't afford any issues at work. She needed everything to run smoothly so she could focus her energy on winning Ty back from Abbie.

"Well?" Cheryl asked. A flash of irritation streaked across her face.

"That's just outrageous, Cheryl. Someone is obviously out of their mind to come up with such a blatant lie."

Kristina didn't know how she managed to get the words out, considering she felt as though someone just poured ten bags of scorching-hot desert sand into her brain.

"That's all you have to say, that it's outrageous?" Cheryl looked at her through skeptical eyes, as though Kristina's denial was dubious at best.

"What I mean is, whoever made the accusation is mistaken. I left America for the sole purpose of attending Oxford. After I completed my degrees at Yale, I could have gone on to graduate school here in the States. I had been accepted to Stanford, Princeton, and Harvard, among others. But I chose Oxford."

Cheryl drummed her fingers on the desk. "Okay, Kristina. I hired you. Your references were impeccable. You've made a big contribution to the team in the short time you've been here. I'll give you the benefit of the doubt. You have one week to produce your diploma from Oxford. The original, not a copy."

Back in her office, Kristina placed a quick phone call to a friend at Oxford. After she ended the call, she stood, and paced the office, doing her breathing exercises. At least Cheryl hadn't threatened to call Oxford to verify Kristina's credentials, but Kristina couldn't leave it to chance. She had to cover all her bases.

Kristina pounded her fists on the desk in frustration. Cheryl didn't say who the texter was. She didn't have to. It was Abbie. That seemingly generic comment about displaying her diplomas on the wall was a warning. *How many times do you need to be told to never underestimate Abbie?*

It was the end of the workday anyway, and Kristina left the office in a foul mood but not before setting up an appointment for later in the evening. She got home, took a shower, and dressed in an elegant, embroidered top with a scalloped lace neckline in dark red, adding black jeans.

In bed, she propped the laptop against her knees and dialed into her video conference call.

"Wow, you dressed up for me? I'm flattered," he said.

"Don't be. I need another favor."

"So soon?"

Ian Taylor was the younger brother of Kristina's friend Poppy. Ian considered himself an artist, an artist of the shady arts, as Kristina liked to say. She was in desperate need of his talent, however.

Ian created documents that could fool even the most seasoned experts. It didn't matter what the document was: phony drivers licenses, passports, official correspondence from any entity, including the government and private sectors.

With dark and spiky hair, a nose ring, and tattoos all over his arms and chest, Ian was only twenty-seven but had carved out a lucrative side hustle serving the financially well-heeled who could afford his ridiculous fees.

"Put the other project on hold for a bit. I need a diploma from Oxford with my name on it."

Kristina explained her predicament, that her new boss in Boston wanted proof and she had one week to produce it.

"Ah, a challenge," Ian said, rubbing his hands together. "My favorite kind of job. It's going to run you more than the current project."

"How much more?"

Kristina would rather pay whatever exorbitant fee Ian threw at her. One of the unfortunate downsides of dealing with Ian was that he'd been trying to make a move on her for years, despite the eight-year age gap. No amount of insults, hints, or the fact that she was married to Callum deterred Ian.

Ian said, "Twenty thousand."

"You want twenty thousand pounds?" Kristina eyes went wide. "You're being ridiculous."

"Okay. I'm a reasonable guy. I can knock the price down to fifteen, but you have to do me a favor in return."

"No thanks," Kristina said. "Twenty will do."

"You didn't give me a chance to ask the favor."

"Don't need to hear it. Can you deliver the diploma in a week? It has to be a hard copy and look as old as the graduation year."

"The timeline is a bit tight, honestly. Not sure I can pull it off, but I'll give it a shot."

"I need assurances, Ian. The diploma has to be in my hands in one week, no room for deviation. Understood? I'll wire the finds first thing in the morning."

She logged out of the call and went to the kitchen to make dinner. *Damn Abbie,* she thought. Was coming to the States a mistake? Was her plan more trouble than it was worth?

Kristina shook her head as she opened the refrigerator door. She had a plan and would stick to it no matter what obstacles Abbie placed in her path.

She would not stop until Ty was hers, as he should have been all along.

CHAPTER 48

ABBIE

THE HOUSE IS festive, overflowing with balloons, congratulations banners, and a plethora of decorations. Laughter and music float in from the backyard patio. Lucas officially graduated from middle school a few hours ago.

This milestone celebration brought the family out in full force: my parents, Ty's parents, my brother Lee and his family, my brother Miles, Layla, and BFF Callie, plus a few neighbors and friends. Christian is here too, and I've been avoiding him like spoiled milk.

I should be brimming with pride. Lucas graduated with high honors, racked up multiple awards, and got accepted into Branson Academy—a highly selective private school in Concord with a twelve percent admit rate and impressive price tag.

Lucas wanted to attend Branson not only because of its academic rigor, but also because of their winning soccer team, which has several national and regional championships to their credit.

My Lucas is a great kid: smart, kind, athletic, fiercely protective of his siblings, and if I'm being honest, quite handsome. Girls already clamor for his attention. I pretend I don't notice because he's still my baby and I'm not ready to deal with this phase of teenage life.

Despite all the reasons for celebration, to let my hair down, enjoy the moment, I can't. Dread slices through my skin like poisonous blades. I've been barely able to breathe freely since Christian told me Sam and Alan are in on our secret.

"Are you going to tell me what's going on?"

A voice startles me out of my gloomy thoughts. It's a good thing I wasn't holding the bowl of fruit salad I came to the kitchen to grab. I turn around and come face-to-face with Callie.

"What are you talking about?"

"Come on, Abbie. How long have we been friends? It's Lucas's big day, and you're walking around like you're about to burst out of your skin. And why are you and Christian going out of your way to avoid each other?"

"We are?" I ask, feigning innocence. "There are a lot of people here, Callie. Christian is like family. I don't need to babysit him."

"Family. Exactly, which makes this weird distance between the two of you even more obvious."

Callie removes a paper plate from the stack on the kitchen island, picks up the stainless-steel basting spoon, and piles fruit salad unto the plate. She pops a slice of honeydew into her mouth.

"I like your hair long," I say, deflecting. "It frames your face and brings out your eyes."

Callie's gaze lingers on me, trying to work out what's going on, why I'm behaving strangely. I was sincere about the compliment and wanted her to know. I believe in complimenting people when appropriate, especially women. Except if your name is Kristina Haywood Saxena. Callie usually wears her hair short. She's going for a new look, and I like it.

"Follow me," she says, abandoning her fruit salad on the kitchen island.

"Let me take the fruit salad out to the patio first."

"There's tons of food out there already. Trust me, no one is going to die of starvation if they wait a little longer for fruit salad."

Callie grabs me by the hand and follows the path to my office. Once inside, she shuts the door behind her and leans up against the edge of the desk where I join her.

"What's going on, Abbie? And don't say nothing. I saw you out on the patio, and though you had that sweet, everything-is-great smile embossed on your face, I could tell you're a wreck. Why is that?"

How do I explain to my best friend that my life is about to erupt like a volcano, that I can't celebrate my son because my actions one year ago could have consequences for him and his siblings? The kids will want to know why things changed. Of course, running worst-case scenarios is only adding to my stress. But I also know Ty. He will react strongly, and there's no telling what he will do.

Without thinking, I say, "This party may be the last few hours of happiness I'll have for a long while."

"What?" Callie's puzzled expression makes me want to fall to the ground and bawl my eyes out in an epic pity party. But I won't. If my marriage is going to be over, I need to be strong, for myself, for the kids.

I gesture for Callie to follow me to the two-seat leather sofa. For this conversation, we need to be sitting on something comfortable.

"I messed up, Callie." My voice is low in case someone comes looking for me and decides to eavesdrop on our conversation.

"Messed up how?"

"With Christian."

"I don't get it. What happened?"

I can't bring myself to tell her, say the words out loud.

Although I know she won't judge me, she'll be disappointed. Ordinarily, I wouldn't contemplate sharing with Callie before I've had a chance to confess to Ty. But she's in a unique position because she knows the players in this sordid, well, I don't know what to call it. Certainly not love triangle. I'm crystal clear on who my heart belongs to.

"We were both in a bad place." I explain to Callie what transpired last year at Christian's penthouse. I end with Christian's girlfriend finding my missing earring and how she went to Alan.

"Goodness, Abbie. I don't know what to say. You're right, you really messed up. And I can't believe Christian would put you in that position. When do you plan on telling Ty?" she asks, her attention anchored on a photo on my desk. The kids and Ty at a cricket match.

"After the celebration. I wanted Lucas to have good memories of today. I don't know what Ty will do. I must prepare for the possibility he might leave me."

I make retching sounds. The tears spill, snaking their way down my face. "I'm really scared, Callie. I don't want to do this, but I have to. If Ty finds out some other way, it will blindside him and make things ten times worse."

"So that's why you and Christian are avoiding each other? Won't that behavior raise red flags? It did with me."

"We agreed to take a step back, not communicate so often. Lucas wanted him here today, so he came, but I don't think he plans to stick around."

"And Ty doesn't suspect anything?"

"No. He said Christian should find a therapist in New York. Then we had an argument about me having lunch with Christian and forgetting to mention it. Kristina told him she saw us, obviously to score points with Ty."

"What about you, Abbie? Tell me the truth. Did this happen because you *do* still have feelings for Christian?"

"I'll always care for Christian. But I love my husband."

"Christian was your first. And he's been in your life ever since. That proximity makes it nearly impossible to dismiss your feelings. No matter what the rational part of your brain tells you." Then she adds, "Tell me this, why Christian?"

"What do you mean?

"You could have had a moment of weakness with any other man, but you didn't. It was Christian. Why?"

"I don't have an answer, Callie."

CHAPTER 49

ABBIE

C ALLIE HEADS OUT to the patio to mingle, and I stop in the kitchen to pick up that fruit salad. Lucas bounds in with Blake on his heels.

"Guess what, Mom?"

"What?"

"Uncle Christian got me the coolest graduation present: tickets to next year's European Football Championship. Blake and I will get to meet Kylian Mbappé. Isn't that awesome?"

"Wow! That is awesome. What a great graduation present, and you get to share it with your brother."

"We can't wait," Blake says. "It's like a birthday and graduation gift for Lucas wrapped into one."

The tickets were a generous gift. My boys are obsessed with soccer. Yes, I'm a soccer mom in the truest sense of the word. Soccer is not simply an extracurricular activity in our family. Blake and Lucas have been playing since they were five and six years old respectively.

They follow the European League and the World Cup. Both played in middle school. I have no doubt Lucas will easily make Branson's varsity team, even though he'll only be a freshman. He's that good.

Lucas and Blake exchange a look and then both fall silent. Something other than a graduation gift brought them to the kitchen.

Blake says, "Mom, I can take the fruit salad to the patio. You're always saying we need to help out more, right?" Blake's nervous grin sets my senses on high alert.

"Sure, sweetie. Thanks." I hand him the bowl, my gaze drifting from him to Lucas and back again. Blake scurries out of the kitchen. Lucas wrings his hands.

"What is it, Lucas? You can tell me anything."

The pained expression scrawled across Lucas's face makes my heart thud in my chest. He digs his hands into the pockets of his shorts and leans up against the kitchen island. I ease in next to him and give him an encouraging smile. Why is he so nervous?

"Are you and Dad getting a divorce?" Lucas blurts out.

It takes me a second to process the question. Where would he get such an idea? I haven't even told Ty the truth yet.

"What makes you think that Lucas?"

His eyes are downcast, staring at his sandals. But I need to drag the rest of the story out of him, so I shove my concern and fear deep down.

"Come on. Tell me. Why do you think your dad and I are splitting up?"

He looks up at me. "We heard you and Dad arguing about Mrs. Saxena."

My puzzled frown confuses him, so he adds, "That night when you sent Alexis to her room for asking about Mrs. Saxena coming to our house for dinner. After Alexis went upstairs and you and Dad went into your office, Blake and I followed."

I stay silent, giving him the opportunity to get everything out without interruption before he loses his nerve. "I know we weren't supposed to eavesdrop, but I've never seen you so upset. I never liked Mrs. Saxena since we met in London. When you and Dad argued about her, I knew for sure she was bad news."

"Oh, Lucas." I pull him into my arms and hug him tight. What he fears is a real possibility. But I must reassure my boy. I suspect all three of my kids are in on this little fact-finding mission. Since Lucas is the eldest, he was nominated to take the lead. I adore the fact that my kids are close, but them wondering whether their world is about so fall apart is hard to swallow.

I say, "Yes, your dad and I had a disagreement about Mrs. Saxena, but it's nothing for you or your siblings to worry about. It was a misunderstanding, and your dad and I worked it out."

"Alexis said Mrs. Saxena has a thing for Dad. She was totally crushing on him."

Having precocious kids was both a blessing and a curse. I imagine they all sat around in Lucas's room one day discussing this very topic at nauseum. Running into Kristina in London. The eavesdropping and what they heard through the door. Alexis riling up her brothers, convincing them Kristina is a bad person. All three kids sharing their fears about possible divorce.

"Your dad and I are great," I say, releasing him from the hug. "Tell your brother and sister they don't need to worry about Mrs. Saxena. She is a non-issue." I promised myself I wouldn't lie to my boy, yet here I am. Lying.

"Are you sure, or are you just saying that so we don't freak out?" Lucas's cool gaze bores into me. It's as if he can see into my soul and has deduced that I can't offer guarantees of any kind.

The sound of laughter from the patio drifts into the kitchen. My mother appears, saving me from telling more lies.

"Everything okay in here?" Mom asks, looking from Lucas to me.

"Yes, everything is fine. Lucas just had a question." Lucas picks up on his queue to leave and joins his siblings and cousins on the patio.

My mother says, "So, what's really going on?"

"Nothing is going on, Mom."

"Then why did my grandbaby just walk out of here like his world is falling apart?"

"You know Lucas is intense. Everything with him is either right or wrong, black or white. He doesn't play well in the gray areas."

"Care to enlighten me on these *gray areas?*"

I sigh. "Lucas wanted to know if Ty and I are okay because he and Blake overheard us discussing Kristina. I assured him everything is fine, and hopefully, he'll relay the news to his siblings."

"Is that true?"

"Is what true?"

"Are you and Ty okay?"

"Why wouldn't we be?"

"You're evading. I picked up on some weird vibes just now on the patio."

"What do you mean?"

"Christian and Ty. There's an undercurrent of tension I've never seen before. They get along, but something's changed. They're careful to stay at opposite sides of the backyard, away from each other."

Christian can't look Ty in the face after what we've done, and my husband's suspicion radar is shouting a code red at him.

"I wouldn't read too much into it. Being on opposite sides of the backyard is not evidence that something is wrong. As for the tension, you know Ty is under a lot of pressure to make a go of the start-up.

"Christian has his own drama with his father, Levitron-Blair, and his girlfriend, who isn't speaking to him. Just your everyday stress."

"What did Christian do? Why is his girlfriend not speaking to him?"

Interesting that Mom picks up on this one detail. Despite the fact that I'm an adult with children of my own, my mother's instincts when it comes to me are still razor-sharp.

"Mom, all relationships have ups and downs. They've been together a while, and Christian hasn't proposed. Sam is getting impatient. I don't blame her."

"Why do you think that is?"

"What?"

"Why hasn't he proposed to Sam? You and Christian are close, so he must have said something."

"I don't pry into the man's private life, Mom. I got my own issues. It's his business whether or not he wants to propose. It has nothing to do with me or our friendship."

Mom crosses the space between us, gets right in my face, and says, "You're playing with fire, Abbie. The family you and Ty created together is precious and worth protecting, no matter what."

"Mom, what are you—"

She cuts me off. "I always suspected you and Christian Wheeler had unfinished business. I hope for your sake, your family's sake, that I'm dead wrong."

CHAPTER 50

TY

W HERE DID COOPER disappear to? Ty grabbed an ice-cold, bottled water from the cooler, twisted off the cap, and took a long gulp. What a perfect day to celebrate Lucas. It was the end of June, the brilliant afternoon sun caressing every inch of the backyard, making the space glow.

A light breeze fluttered the leaves on the trees and the blooms of the abundant flowers Cooper had so lovingly tended to. The air was resonant with the laughter and the chatter of family and friends, feasting and socializing.

Lucas, Blake, Alexis, their cousins, and friends were caught up in the old schoolyard game of T-A-P-S. One of the boys was doing pushups. His team lost. Yet, despite the glowing portrait of domestic perfection, an icy chill seeped through Ty.

Perhaps he should get rid of the cold bottle. He kept his eyes peeled on the door that led from the kitchen to the patio. It wasn't like Cooper to leave her guests for long stretches, especially on such an exciting day for the Rambally family.

The icy chill returned when Ty spotted Christian talking to Cooper. Their body language was off. Their facial expressions were off. Cooper took two steps backward as though she didn't want to be near Christian.

Christian's hands were at his sides, balled into nervous fists. Cooper said something, and Christian snapped his gaze away. Then Christian moved past her and disappeared from view. Cooper looked shaken.

Ty began moving in Cooper's direction to find out what was going on, but his mother-in-law intercepted him.

"What's going on between you, Abbie, and Christian?" Shelby asked, her voice low. "Christian just left in a hurry. Abbie looks like her world is about to collapse. I asked her earlier how things were, and she said fine. What I'm witnessing is the exact opposite of fine. What's going on around here, Ty?"

"I'd like the answer to that question myself."

Shelby had always been an intuitive woman, and if she was picking up on the weird vibes too, something was afoot, Ty reasoned.

Cooper had been acting strange ever since they returned from Jamaica. Well, before that, when she had a meltdown during their vow renewal, a meltdown that still bothered him.

After they returned home, Ty told her to leave it alone, her interest in the investigation into Savannah Davis Patterson's death. Knowing Cooper, she probably did some more research and tried to keep up with the investigation. Despite knowing this, her recent behavior was a distress signal Ty could no longer ignore.

"Looks like you and Abbie need to sit down for a heart-to-heart," Shelby said.

Ty's phone chimed with an incoming text. Saved by the bell.

Grabbing the phone from his shirt pocket, he said, "Excuse me," and turned away from Shelby to look at the message.

Unknown

You deserve better than a cheating wife, don't you agree?

213

Followed by a photo of Cooper and Christian on a park bench, holding hands.

CHAPTER 51

TY

S HOCK AND DISBELIEF exploded in his chest, robbing him of breath. His legs became shaky twigs that could snap under his weight. Ty stared blankly at the screen, but the image was still there, his wife and Christian.

"Ty, what is it?" Shelby asked. She sounded distant. A scream sliced through the fog in his brain but never made it out of his mouth.

He snapped out of the daze when Alexis said, "What's wrong, Daddy? Is it bad news?"

Ty didn't know how he made it to his home office. He must have made some excuse to his stunned daughter and mother-in-law. Once he checked that the door was securely locked, he collapsed against it.

It took several minutes to get his racing heart and labored breathing under control. Only then did he stand, testing out his legs to see whether they could support him.

After he walked over to his desk, he placed the phone down and picked up the three gray ball bearings. Ty rolled them over in his hand repeatedly, a ritual to calm his raw, aching nerves that had just been yanked from their rightful place.

The text explained everything, why Cooper and Christian

were so distant with each other. Why Cooper had been nervous over the past weeks, why she freaked out during the vows in Jamaica. She knew she had betrayed him with Christian.

Ty plopped down into the black leather swivel chair, lost in a sea of grief and incredulity. How could the love of this life do this to him? The woman he pledged his forever to. The woman who stood next to him in Montego Bay and recited similar vows. How could she, knowing what she had done?

It didn't sound like *his* Cooper at all. His Cooper was not a deceitful woman, a liar, a cheater. That was one of the things he'd loved best about her from the very beginning. She was straightforward, honest, no games, no agenda.

What had he missed? How long had the affair been going on? When did it start?

When Ty thought about Christian Wheeler's hands all over his Cooper's body, he retched and then forced the image to dissolve from his mind's eye.

Who sent him the text and why? How did the sender know Cooper was unfaithful, found proof, yet Ty was clueless? Sure, he suspected Christian still had feelings for Cooper and didn't want her so entangled in his life, but never did he think they were having an affair.

Was this his fault? Should he have insisted Cooper cut all ties with Christian after he and Cooper were married? But at the time of their marriage, there was no reason to worry, no reason to insist that she cut ties with Christian.

Obviously, that was a mistake. How could he have known he needed to explicitly verbalize there was a line that neither Cooper nor Cristian should cross? He thought it was understood. Blinding rage took over once more. Ty didn't know who he should blame. How could Cooper jeopardize their marriage? How could she have been so weak?

What drove her to do this? Ty had a million questions and no answers. The text came from an unknown sender. At first, he thought Kristina sent the incriminating text. But Kristina would take any opportunity to diminish Cooper, make the case that Ty married the wrong woman. No, Kristina wouldn't hide. She would flaunt what she had discovered to Ty's face, not cower behind an anonymous text.

So who then? Who dropped a bomb on his marriage?

Ty was in no state of mind to learn the grisly details, get answers, but he didn't care. Cooper would answer to him that very night.

CHAPTER 52

ABBIE

HE KNOWS. TY stands in the corner of our bedroom, near the window, hands shoved into his pockets. Dressed in the blue jeans and the white, long-sleeved linen shirt he wore earlier, he glares at me without blinking. A cold darkness crosses over his usually luminous eyes, as though someone turned off the lights.

The graduation party was a success. Lucas is at his friend Liam's house for a sleepover. The twins, Blake and Alexis, went home with my brother Lee and his family. The eerie silence of the room frightens me. It's time to face the music—no buffer, no place to hide, no one to interrupt.

"How long have you and Christian been making a fool of me, Cooper?" he asks, blinking, finally.

I could play dumb, give him a chance to get more specific so I know what I'm dealing with, but I can't. It's bad enough what I did; there's no point in antagonizing or disrespecting him any further. On the other hand, I don't want him to think that I knew this could come out eventually but had never said a word, never confessed.

"Make a fool of you how, Ty?" My voice is but a squeak. I stand, leaning up against the dresser for support. I'm thankful for

218

the massive size of our bedroom, which provides some distance from his wrath.

He follows up with another question. "Were you ever going to tell me?"

Complicated question. It happened a year ago, and I said nothing. If I now claim I planned to tell him, he'll know it's a bald-faced lie.

"I told myself it was one mistake, a moment of weakness. One lapse in judgment in almost fifteen years of marriage, never to be repeated. When I weighed my mistake against what I stood to lose, I chose my family and tried to pretend it never happened."

"And how did you pretend it never happened when you were still communicating with him regularly?"

"That was part of the pretense, I suppose. Pretending we were just friends, the way it had been before."

"So when did this one-time lapse in judgment, roll in the hay, occur?" he asks. His tone drips with venom.

"Last year, at his apartment."

"Last year when?"

"The night before I flew home from the International Cognitive Neuroscience Conference. He invited me to dinner."

"Were all the restaurants in New York closed that night?"

"No. I didn't want to deal with the hassle of a busy New York restaurant after an exhausting few days at the conference. So I accepted the invitation when it was extended."

Ty begins pacing, arms folded, his cold gaze never leaving my face.

"Hmm. You were so exhausted from the conference, yet you found the time and energy to head to Christian's penthouse, eat dinner, and have sex with him? Seems that you weren't as exhausted as you thought."

I could just die now. I cringe at his words as humiliation washes over me. I hang my head, unable to meet his accusing glare. Silence spools out over the room as neither one of us says anything. But I must face his unblinking judgment if I am to pick up the pieces and stitch my marriage back together again.

"It wasn't like that at all."

"Then tell me, Cooper. What was it like?"

"We didn't plan—"

Ty holds up a hand, interrupting me. "Don't say it. Please don't say it just happened because we both know that's a lie. An opportunity presented itself, and you both acted on it. I warned you, Cooper."

He jabs a finger in my direction. "I told you Christian still had feelings for you. We fought about his impromptu lunch visit, a visit you deliberately failed to mention."

The pain of my betrayal is stamped all over his face, but he keeps firing. I don't bother to deflect the bullets coming at me.

"You offered reassurances that you were being a supportive friend, nothing more. Was it worth it, Cooper?" he asks. "Did you finally scratch the Christian itch that had been following you around for years? Is it out of your system now, or do you wish Yale never happened and you had married him instead of me?"

Silence envelopes us once more, the air in our bedroom bloated with pain and anger. What a grotesque thing to say. It's not even close to the truth. How could he think such a thing? Yale sped up the inevitable. There was never a doubt in my mind that Ty and I would end up together eventually.

"How dare you say that to me, Ty?" I croak. My eyes are now slick with tears, silently beseeching him to take it all back, every ugly, heinous syllable. His expression is haunted, lost, as though he doesn't understand what he just said or its impact.

"Because I made one mistake, all of a sudden, you devalue

what we've built, what we mean to each other?"

I'm in a full-on meltdown now, and strangely, I'm rambling without pausing to catch my breath. "For all the storms that raged against us, the battles that almost took us down, yet somehow, we're still standing. That means nothing to you?

"Because I was weak, and stupid, and overwhelmed. I didn't think anyone understood, I didn't have the right to complain, I didn't want to burden you, I was losing my mind, and I didn't know how to stop myself from crashing…"

I'm breathing too fast, and my heart beats wildly in my chest. Lightheadedness kicks in, and I'm convinced I'm going to black out. I land on the floor like a ton of bricks because I don't have the strength to do it gracefully.

Ty crosses the space and comes to kneel in front of me.

"Breathe through pursed lips, Cooper. Pretend you're whistling," he says, his voice strangled. My head rests against the edge of the dresser.

"That's good," he says after several seconds. "Now slow down your breathing. Take one breath every five seconds. I'll count."

He does, and my breathing slowly returns to normal. "I'm sorry, Ty. More than you will ever know. I regret hurting you. Keeping it a secret was my way of protecting us, self-serving as it sounds. I thought if I confessed, it would be the end of us."

I remind myself to breathe in and out. Round two of my meltdown is circling, but I need to speak from the heart, clearly and honestly.

"You have every right to be furious and ask uncomfortable, inconvenient questions. I can even take your wrath or whatever revenge scheme you concoct. But what I cannot take, what I won't accept, is the end of us."

He glares at me as he stands. "You don't get to tell me how to feel or influence my decision in any way, Cooper. You were the one who betrayed us. And now I must live with the image of Christian Wheeler's hands all over you. I can't express how wretched that makes me feel.

"Christian came to our wedding, socialized with us. He's been to our home numerous times. I thought he respected me enough to know my wife was off limits."

"I was the one who violated my marriage vows, not him."

"Even now you're protecting him?"

The sound of disgust in his tone makes me want to curl up into a ball and stay that way permanently. "No Ty. I exchanged vows with you, not Christian."

"How noble of you to take the blame, but I don't see it that way."

"What do you mean?"

"Christian took advantage of you. He recognized your defenses were down and, like a predator, moved in for the kill. And this is the guy you say is a friend. That's not a friend, Cooper. That's a man who took what he wanted, regardless of consequences."

A spike of shame pulls me into a vice grip, a deep burning in my bones. Before I can respond, Ty says, "I have to get out of here. I need time to think."

I shouldn't ask, but I can't help myself. "Where are you going?"

"I don't know, Cooper. Just away from here."

He means away from me.

I add, "How did you find out?"

"Anonymous text message that included a photo of you and Christian on a park bench. Holding hands."

With those words, my husband exits our bedroom and slams the door behind him.

CHAPTER 53

June 30

It pains me to write this. I still can't believe what I saw. At first, it was incredulous. I thought I had gone raving mad, that even my eyes had failed me because it couldn't be true. But there she was, with another man.

You deserve much better, a thousand times better, a million. I'm still angry if you want to know the truth. How is it possible that you gave Abbie everything a woman could want: a kind, loving husband dedicated to his family and his profession of serving others; three healthy, wonderful children; and a beautiful home, and still it's not enough?

She's a selfish, greedy, unappreciative woman who takes what she has for granted. Well then, she should lose it all. I'm going to make sure that she does.

I'm going to make sure she never hurts you again. That is my solemn promise.

CHAPTER 54

TY

T Y MADE THE twenty-minute drive to his parents' home in fifteen. He hadn't planned on driving to Wellesley after he shut the door and left Cooper alone in their Lexington home. But it was as if his Mercedes S class sedan knew where he needed to be and the powerful v8 engine went to work, ensuring he arrived at his destination as quickly as possible.

He pulled into the driveway and killed the engine as a memory sailed into his brain. The car had been Cooper's idea, and she picked it out. When he protested it was too expensive, she told him he worked hard, deserved a nice car, and they could afford it, so she didn't want to hear any more objections.

Swatting away the memory, Ty focused on a plan. A plan that required speaking to his father, telling him that his only child could end up in prison because he made a deal with a man he had no business making deals with.

Ty took a few moments to compose himself, chiefly because he didn't want his mother to worry. He couldn't stroll into the house looking like the broken man he was. For this, he needed his dad's wise counsel, not that he could admit to either of his parents that Cooper cheated on him. It would diminish her in their eyes, and he didn't want that.

Cooper wasn't the only one who had kept a secret, however. Ty couldn't tell her the truth. It was the reason Christian felt so emboldened, that he could take what didn't belong to him, and there wasn't much Ty could do about it if he wanted to stay out of jail.

"Tyler, what a pleasant surprise," his mother Jenny said, embracing him as he stepped into the foyer.

"Just thought I'd drop by for no reason."

"Really?" His mother raised a perfectly arched brow, her skepticism obvious.

"Come on, Mom. Can't a son drop by to see his parents? Am I that bad?"

"No, of course not. You're the perfect son, and I love you to pieces. Stop by any time." She dropped a kiss on his cheek. Ty trailed her to the family room where his dad was nursing a drink, his eyes on the TV screen. Ty had obviously interrupted their program.

His father turned when they came into the room. "Hi, Dad. What are you watching?"

"Hey, son. Come sit next to me. I need protection from your mother who's been grumbling and critiquing the movie since it started. I've lost track of the plot."

Ty chuckled and took a seat next to his dad on the plush leather sofa, even as a wave of sadness washed over him. This was what he wanted for himself and Cooper. His parents had been happily married for thirty-seven years. Like any other couple, they had their ups and downs, but they made it work.

Jenny Antoinette Whistler, a former Miss Bahamas who finished in the top ten at the Miss Universe pageant and won the Ms. Photogenic award, met Bobby Rambally when they were both second-year residents at a New York Hospital.

Ty's father claimed that his mother played hard to get. Mom said she was too focused on her career ambition to waste her time on Dad's pathetic attempts at wooing her, including showing up at the church she attended.

But his mother had revealed to Ty that her secret fear was his father's Indo-Guyanese family who might have a problem with her being black.

In her typical Caribbean, no-nonsense manner, she had said, "If just one of them had so much as looked at me sideways, Tyler, I would have suggested they go play in traffic."

Turned out his mother had nothing to worry about. His father's family fully embraced her, and Ty's aunt Alana was one of his mother's closest friends.

Dad paused the movie while Mom disappeared into the kitchen. Ty said, "Before Mom gets back in here, we need to talk."

"Oh. What's going on? Is everything okay at home with Abbie, the kids?"

Ty hesitated for a brief moment and then caught himself. "Yeah, everything is fine. Lucas was pleased with his graduation celebration."

"Good. Then what is this about?"

"Let's go to your study."

His mother chose that moment to reappear, balancing a tray with snacks and ice-cold glasses of guava nectar. She placed the tray down on the mahogany coffee table.

Ty said, "Mom, there was so much food at the party. I can't drink or eat anything right now."

He couldn't tell his mother that his stomach was balled up into knots and he probably wouldn't eat for days because he was in so much pain over what Cooper had done to him, to them.

"Then take it with you into your dad's study. You look like you'll need it."

"Why do you say that?"

"Come on, Tyler. I'm your mother. I know when something is weighing heavily on you. You didn't drive over here to check on us. We just came from Lucas's graduation party. You came because you want to speak to your dad in person."

"Oh," Ty said. "Well, um..."

"You don't have to say a word," she said, squeezing his shoulder. "I'm no longer jealous of the fact that you confide in your father and not me. It used to bother me. But now I see it as a blessing that the two of you share this special bond."

"Thanks for understanding, Mom," Ty said.

"I'll just get the details from Shelby," she said, a wicked gleam in her eyes. Then his mother exited the room, leaving both men slack-jawed at her retreating frame, as she chuckled to herself.

"What is it, son?" his father asked.

They'd had many man-to-man talks over the years in this office with its dark-blue walls, burgundy furniture, potted plants, and brass chandelier. The large mahogany desk and leather swivel chair dominated the room.

Father and son sat across from each other in two wicker chairs, a small table off to the side.

"I did something years ago for a good reason, but it was a bad thing, and now, it may come back to haunt me."

"Sounds serious."

Ty wet his lips. He should have rehearsed on the drive over what he would say, but his brain was otherwise occupied. The thought of keeping quiet and not confronting Christian for sleeping with his wife made Ty want to spit bullets.

The secret between him and Christian was an ugly stain that had preempted Ty from taking any action against Christian, although Ty hadn't yet figured out how he was supposed to exact revenge for the betrayal.

"What is it, Tyler?" his father asked. "Your face. I've never seen you look so wretchedly unhappy."

So he told his father everything, how he asked Christian to help him neutralize Zachary Rossdale after the failed kidnapping attempt. That Christian was eager to help and set the whole thing in motion. How Zach's death wasn't some random prison mele that got out of hand; it was a set-up. *Murder.*

Ty also revealed that Christian paid the warden a six-figure sum to keep quiet and look the other way, which the warden had no problem doing because Zach had been blackmailing him. Afterward, Ty and Christian made a pact that they would never tell another living soul. Not even Cooper.

The confession sucked all the air out of the room. Ty couldn't get an accurate read on his father. His dad was a kind, understanding man who consistently supported his only child, a father who never failed to offer comfort and wise counsel in the face of difficult circumstances.

Did his father see Ty as less than, his opinion of him diminished? Would his father tell his mother, or would he shield her from the disgraceful actions of their son?

Would Dad disown Ty, tell him to turn himself into the authorities? The rational part of Ty's brain said no, but fear had taken over and was running the show. He didn't know anything for sure anymore. Ty thought his marriage was solid and look what happened. His world no longer made sense.

Dad raked back his thick, graying hair back and held that position for long seconds. Then his hands dropped to his sides. He stood and began pacing, reminding Ty where he picked up the habit.

"Are you sure no one else knows?" he asked.

"Unless the warden said something, which I doubt, it was just the three of us."

Turning to Ty, his father said, "If this story gets out, it will be the end of your career and your freedom."

CHAPTER 55

TY

TY'S FATHER CONTINUED his pacing, shaking his head, trying to grasp the implications of Ty's revelation.

"Are you afraid Christian will reveal the secret? The incident happened three years ago. What's changed? Why are you afraid now?"

Christian is a treacherous snake, and I no longer trust him. I want to pound his face into a bloody pulp for sleeping with my wife, but I'm afraid he'll rat me out for spite and hide behind his multi-billion-dollar family fortune. He's untouchable. Me, I'll be ruined.

"Christian is getting too close to Cooper. I don't like it. What if he tells her the truth, convinces her I instigated and orchestrated the whole incident? What if he tells the hospital?"

"Do you really think he would sink that low?" His dad picked up a red leather cricket ball autographed by Virat Kohli from his desk and absently toyed with it. "Christian has always struck me as a man of integrity."

Men of integrity don't sleep with other men's wives. He had us both fooled.

"I don't know what he would do, and I'm not sure I want to find out," Ty said.

"Have you told Abbie about the pact you made with

229

Christian?"

A wave of exhaustion engulfed Ty, invading every bone, cell, nerve, and even his thoughts. He didn't want to talk about this anymore and began to question his sanity when he decided to come over and talk to his dad. It was not as if his father had the solution to Ty's predicament.

The smoking-gun text message followed by the conversation with Cooper in their bedroom earlier had knocked the wind out of Ty. Perhaps it was making him act irrationally.

Christian's words from Ty's impromptu visit to his New York office came roaring back. *I'm not the enemy here. But I can be.* Shivers went up Ty's spine as he recalled the menacing expression on Christian's face, how his eyes had grown cold and antagonistic. All of this after he knew full well he'd slept with Cooper the year before.

No, Ty didn't want to make an enemy of Christian Wheeler. Not because he was afraid of him, but because he was unpredictable and Ty had a wife—although he wasn't sure whether that would be the case in the long run —and three kids to consider.

Ty also had a career he worked hard for and sacrificed for to protect. He didn't have a massive family fortune or powerful, influential friends to back him if things went sideways.

"Cooper says they're friends; she just wants to support him and that's it."

"We have to find a way to neutralize this mess," his dad said. "Consider telling Abbie the truth."

"What would that accomplish, Dad?"

"You're right. It would only complicate matters further. But no threats have been made, neither from Christian nor this warden who was part of the plot. So maybe you have nothing to worry about."

His dad added, "Christian's family may be wealthy and powerful, but don't underestimate the damage this could do to his family, the company. He has as much to lose as you do."

"I hope you're right, Dad."

"Let's table this discussion until we can think more clearly. But I'm glad you confided in me, albeit three years too late."

"How could I tell you something like this?"

"You did now. But I suspect only because you're afraid the truth could come out. I don't condone what you did, Tyler. I'm disappointed in you. You took the Hippocratic Oath: First, do no harm."

"I wasn't thinking like a doctor when I asked for Christian's help. I was operating under a different rule. Kill or be killed. Zach Rossdale came for my kid, and he had his sights set on my wife next."

"Why did you ask for Christian's help?"

"What do you mean?"

"You could have gone to the warden yourself. Zach's history of murder and violence was well documented. So why Christian?"

How could Ty admit the truth to his father, admit that he knew what he was walking into and did it anyway?

Ty had the nauseating thought he brought this all on himself. He wanted to stand and pace like his father had earlier, to shake off the feeling. But the weakness in Ty's knees prevented him from roaming the space.

"What are you thinking? It can't be worse than what you've already told me."

"It is, Dad. It is."

His father came and stood in front of him. In a quiet tone, he said, "Tell me."

In a calm unflustered voice, Ty said, "I went to Christian

because I knew he would say yes without hesitation. I exploited his feelings for Cooper to get him to act, get rid of a problem I should have handled myself. Your son is a loser. And now, I may have lost my wife…"

As he said the words, the temptation to break down in front of his dad was overwhelming.

Christian had taken advantage of Cooper the way Ty had taken advantage of Christian. Saw a vulnerability, a weak spot and exploited it. This truism was a bitter pill that would take a long time to swallow and digest. Christian Wheeler and Ty were the same—opportunists.

His dad touched Ty's shoulder. "Tyler, I didn't raise a loser. We had a complicated situation on our hands. Perhaps you were operating out of fear, but I can't judge you for the decision. During that time, nobody knew how to stop Zach."

His dad paused to catch his breath. The he added, "You thought Zach would continue to torment your family and wouldn't stop until something tragic and irreversible happened. Is that how you interpreted the situation?"

"Yes, Dad. You're exactly right. Are you going to tell Mom what I did?"

"Don't worry about that for now. What did you mean that you may have lost your wife? You said Abbie doesn't know about this secret deal you made with Christian."

"I'm exhausted, Dad. I need to get home. Thank you for listening."

His dad reached out and hugged him. "I love you, Tyler."

"I love you too, Dad."

CHAPTER 56

KRISTINA

W HEN SHE SAW him sitting in the stairwell, shoulders hunched, his head in his hands, she didn't know what to think. Still in surgical scrubs, it was an odd place for him to show up. Shouldn't he be in surgery? With her coffee in hand, Kristina slowly eased her way down the stairs so as to not startle him.

"Ty," she said softly.

He didn't look up. Whatever was going on, Ty was in another space mentally. She tried again, placing a gentle hand on his shoulder as she sat next to him.

"Ty, are you okay?" Kristina placed the coffee next to her.

Ty slowly lifted his head and looked at her. Definitely not okay. His eyes were red and puffy, like he hadn't slept in days. More accurately, to Kristina's dismay, Ty looked like he had been crying.

What happened to the man she had been pining for all these years, and most importantly, who or what brought him to this sad state? As if she didn't already know.

He just stared at her, as though he couldn't see her and didn't know who he was or where he was. Kristina tried to get him to speak.

"Ty, you don't look so good. Do you want me to call someone? Abbie, your boss, your mom or dad? Can I get you anything?"

He shook his head and then broke off his gaze.

"Okay. Do you mind if I just sit here with you? You don't have to say anything."

More silence. Kristina handed him the unopened coffee she brought with her. Ty took the paper cup from her and just held it.

"It can't be all that bad, can it?" She tried to break the ice once more with a nervous, humorless chuckle. "You can fix it."

As though the fog finally lifted, Ty looked at her, his gaze connecting with hers. "Hello, Kristina."

Relief washed over her. There was no anger, disdain, or contempt in his tone. He seemed almost happy to see her. Kristina's heart soared. She gave him an encouraging smile.

Kristina said, "Hello, you. Tough morning?"

"You could say that."

"Surgery didn't go well?"

"It didn't go at all. At least not while I was there."

"How do you mean?"

"I bailed. Asked a resident to take over and walked out of the operating room."

"What? That doesn't sound like you, Ty. Won't you get in trouble?" She was genuinely concerned for him.

"Don't worry. He's a senior resident, and an attending is in there now."

"Why would you do something like that?" She really wanted to know. It was imperative that she know.

"I was having a bad day. It would be reckless of me to stay in the OR. I couldn't put my patient at risk."

Kristina frowned. "Doctors have bad days all the time."

"Okay. I was having a really, really, really bad day." Just a hint of a smile tugged at his lips, captivating Kristina.

"Is that your way of telling me to piss off? That it's none of my business why a world-renowned surgeon is sitting in the back stairwell of the hospital after having walked out of his own procedure?"

He really smiled this time. A big, wide, perfect grin that lit up his eyes and transformed his face, almost stopping her heart. It was as though she had stepped back in time, to the day when he "accidentally" bumped into her outside their ethics class at Yale.

He had said, "So sorry. I guess I should pay more attention to my surroundings."

"Maybe you should," she had said, as fellow students piled out through the doors, heading to their next class. "But I forgive you because you're wearing my favorite color."

Ty had sported a Nike sweatshirt in a gorgeous shade of royal blue and a pair of dark-blue relaxed-fit jeans. Kristina had appraised him in mere seconds and liked what she saw.

Before she knew it, they were having coffee at a downtown New Haven café, discussing their post-graduation hopes and dreams, their families, and so on. She had been intrigued by him. Kristina fell in love with his big brain, big heart, his wit, intelligence, and ambition.

Ty was a true match for her in every sense that mattered. And to be honest, the sexual chemistry had been electric. He was the whole package. Until he wasn't. Until Abbie Cooper swooped in like some opportunistic bird of prey and snatched him away.

The thought soured Kristina's stroll down memory lane. She returned to the present to find Ty's curious gaze on her.

"You checked out for a minute. Looks like I'm not the only one who doesn't have their act together today."

"Nonsense," she said, waving off his observation. "I've never known you to not have your act together. Whatever has got you down, you'll get through it."

"How do you know that? You don't even know what the issue is."

"But I know you. At least I used to. You're a problem-solver. The guy who always knows how to make the puzzle pieces fit when everyone else is banging their heads against the wall."

"You give me too much credit, Kristina."

"And another thing. The humility. Sometimes you have to put that aside and admit that you're absolutely brilliant. And not just in the OR. You're great at fatherhood too. Look how amazing your kids turned out.

"I could tell from the brief encounter in London how much they adore and respect you. I always knew you would make a great dad, Ty."

She turned away from him to get a grip on her emotions. Sitting with Ty in such close proximity had dredged up painful memories of what could have been. Kristina and Ty would share a teenager, had she not suffered a miscarriage.

How was it possible to grieve the loss of something she hadn't known she had until it was too late or to conjure up the little person they had created together countless times over the years? When the aching and longing seemed unbearable, Kristina purchased one of those apps that showed what your baby would look like, using a photo of herself and the one of Ty she had kept from their time at Yale. Somehow, the image staring back at her brought her peace. Gave her the will to move on.

Ty rested a hand on her shoulder. "I'm sorry, Kristina. I can't erase the miscarriage, but please believe me when I say I'm sorry for the pain I caused you."

Acting on pure impulse, Kristina leaned over and kissed Ty with all the pent-up passion and frustration she'd been feeling, catching him off guard. When he regained his equilibrium, she burned hot with shame.

He eased away from her. "No, Kristina. You shouldn't have done that."

"Why not?" she asked brazenly.

"For one thing, we're both married. Secondly, I don't go around kissing women who aren't my wife because I'm a basket case."

Kristina smoothed out her skirt. Then she said, "You're too good for her, you know. Do you suppose your wife would kiss another man given the opportunity, say a similar situation to ours where they knew each other in the past?"

He glanced at her sharply. "What are you getting at?"

"Nothing. Forget I said anything. It's just hard, rejection."

"What do you mean?"

"I don't know why I do this to myself, fall in love with men who can't love me back. Men who always pick someone else. Why am I never enough?"

She was not one for tears, yet she found herself whimpering in front of the man who had used her and discarded her the minute he got the woman he really wanted, leaving Kristina vulnerable, raw, and rejected. *Just like Mom.*

"I shouldn't have said anything." She stood and started walking up the stairs.

"Kristina, wait!" She stopped in her tracks. "Thanks for the company. Thanks for the encouragement. And… anyway, I'm sure you have a million things to do, so I'll let you get to it."

Kristina swallowed her disappointment and sadness. But perhaps she read it all wrong. Ty didn't dismiss her, look at his watch, or cut her with his words. He was kind; he listened. When he apologized for the past, Kristina believed he was sincere. Sure, the one-sided kiss was awkward, but she had startled him. Ty Rambally could be nice to her, and that was the biggest slice of hope she'd had in a long time.

CHAPTER 57

---◆◇◆---

CHRISTIAN

S AM STILL HATED him. When Christian denied cheating on her with Abbie, he saw the struggle play out across Sam's face. She wanted to believe him but couldn't bring herself to do it.

Christian tried to make things right, but Sam wouldn't return his calls. She pulled the too-busy card when he texted her suggesting they meet up for dinner or a show. Eventually, she texted him saying they needed time apart to decide what they both wanted, once and for all.

Courtney buzzed his line. "Your father is here," she said and then hung up.

Whenever Dad showed up to the office unannounced, trouble usually followed in the form of a verbal dressing down, wild accusations, or nit-picking the way Christian handled his role as chief operating officer.

Alan barged into his office without knocking. Christian stood, and his father said, "Don't bother getting up."

After both men were seated, Christian picked up his favorite pen from his desk and twirled it, waiting for his father to speak. In his late sixties, Alan Martin Wheeler was still an imposing figure—tall, elegant, with a head full of blond-gray hair, and attired in a tailored Brioni suit.

His father said, "You're getting sloppy, careless."

"I don't know what you mean."

"Are you and Samantha over? Because that would be a grave mistake."

"Why is that, Dad?"

"You're not a boy anymore. It's time you stopped acting like it."

Christian leaned forward and steepled his hands together. "Spit it out, Dad. I'm not a mind reader."

Alan repositioned his body in the plush leather chair across from Christian. He said, "Listen. You know what's expected of you. It's time to do the right thing."

"Which is?"

"Marry Samantha, start a family. Secure the line of succession for Levitron-Blair. Marrying her will be good for you and LB. The match makes sense. So what's the hold up?"

"Sure, the match makes sense. You approve of Sam because she checks all the right boxes: she's white, comes from a wealthy family, and her dad is as powerful and influential as you are. Maybe more so. Yeah, it's a perfect match." Christian's tone reeked of sarcasm.

"You think this is a game? That your future and the future of this company, my legacy and that of your grandfather's, is a game?" Alan leaned forward, eyes blazing with anger.

Pointing at Christian, Alan said, "You will damn well get your act together, you hear me? I will not have my only son embarrass me and put this company in jeopardy."

"Well, Dad, you have to make up your mind. You can't have it both ways. Am I an embarrassment or the future of Levitron-Blair or the father to your future grandchildren? Which do you want me to be?"

"That's a ridiculous question." Alan looked out the window,

a pensive look etched on his face.

"How exactly have I embarrassed you? I've done everything you've asked of me. I learned the business from the ground up and didn't cut corners or ask for special treatment. I sat in the room with you during dozens of negotiations. I learned not just from you but other executives at the company.

"I studied the LB playbook, studied our competitors, and learned to identify and exploit their weaknesses to our advantage. I hired a leadership coach to help me polish the areas I needed polishing. Not once did I complain. Not once did I let you down. So what's this visit really about?"

"Samantha came to see me."

"And?"

"What are you doing?"

Christian sighed dramatically, his brain already exhausted from the few minutes his father had been sitting across from him.

"You'll have to be more specific. We've already established I don't read minds. But I'm sure you'll find a way to add it to my extensive and growing list of shortcomings."

"So that's how you want to handle the situation? Play games? Mouth off?"

Tossing his favorite pen across the room, Christian said, "Since you can't be bothered to clue me in as to why you're here, let me make it easy for you. What did Sam say to you?"

"Finally, we're getting somewhere," his father said. "How could you gamble with your future like that? You've always had a reckless streak, but son, this is dangerous and could have disastrous consequences."

"I'm not the first guy to have a disagreement with his girlfriend. Stop blowing things out of proportion."

"Sam told me the reason you two are having problems is

because there's another woman in the picture."

"Sam can tell you whatever she wants, and she obviously has. What does that have to do with me gambling with my future, as you put it? We had a fight, so what?"

Alan leaned in close and looked him dead in the face. "When my son, who is next in line to assume the leadership of this company, sleeps with another man's wife and his girlfriend comes crying to me, it becomes my business."

Christian didn't react. His father continued, "That kind of behavior speaks to a lack of judgment, lack of control, and a weak moral compass. That combination is fatal in a leader."

A strong undercurrent of guilt battered Christian's conscience, but he wouldn't allow his father's tirade to go unchallenged.

"You of all people are going to sit there and talk to me about a moral compass—the man who had an affair with a married woman who worked for him, fathered two children by her, and then paid her off to buy her silence?"

"That's in the past. I regret my mistake," Alan shot back.

"It doesn't change the fact that it happened. It ended in a shit storm. Lives were forever altered, including mine."

His dad gave him a withering look. "Is that how you justify sleeping with Abbie? Throwing my past mistakes in my face to avoid accountability for your actions? Your obsession with her is bad for Levitron-Blair and bad for your personal life. Why won't you see that? Why won't you let go of her, Christian?"

Alan's booming voiced bounced off the walls in the room and landed in an icy silence at their feet. Christian was right. Sam didn't believe his denial.

Christian said, "I have very few friends. You're the reason why. How many times have you warned me that everybody I come into contact with has a hidden agenda? That being your son makes me a target?

"The one true friend I've had for the past seventeen years is suddenly a problem because Sam is jealous and fed you her suspicions?"

"Don't lie to my face," Alan said. "It's insulting. Look, I get that Abbie is special and the two of you are close. She's always been there to talk sense into you and offer advice and comfort when you needed it. But what you did was wrong."

"I know, I screwed up, okay?"

Alan leaned back in his chair with a somber look of reflection, as though his son admitting the truth set the universe back in balance.

"That's a good first step. Who else knows about this? It can't go any further. I warned Sam not to say anything. I told her I would speak to you and smooth things out."

Christian said, "If this gets out any further, Abbie's life will go down in flames because of one mistake."

"Haven't you heard a single word I just said, Christian? Your girlfriend came to me about your resistance to committing to her, yet you had no problem sleeping with a woman you claim is just a friend. And even now, all you can think about is protecting her? Don't you think you have your loyalties confused?"

Without hesitation, he said, "No, I do not. I made a promise to Abbie, and no matter how this plays out, if her husband gives her an ultimatum, I can walk away knowing I kept my word."

Alan ignored his comment. "How do you plan to win back Sam?"

"It's not up to me. If she doesn't want me, that's her prerogative. I reached out to try and patch things up. She wants space, so I'm giving her space."

"In other words, you don't love her enough to fight for her.

Yet, here you are fighting for a woman who isn't yours."

"I'm being a loyal friend to a woman who has been loyal to me for almost twenty years. A woman who never judged me and always saw my potential. Even when my own father was busy taking cheap shots at me."

"But she chose someone else."

"No thanks to you, Dad. Now I'll never know how things would have played out."

Alan's phone rang. He pulled it from his jacket pocket and looked at the screen. With his fingers tapping away at the screen, he said, "Get your head in the game. Patch things up with Samantha. You have six months to make her your wife. Your future as Chairman and CEO of Leviton-Blair depends on it."

CHAPTER 58

CHRISTIAN

ALAN'S WORDS LANDED like a sledgehammer. His father had always been a forceful, decisive man, never one for mincing words or backing down. But this was next level. Christian didn't know how to put this latest bombshell into words. *Blackmail.* There was no other interpretation. For the rest of his life, he would never forget those words. Nor forgive.

"Is this how low your opinion of me has sunk? You think I would cower to your blackmail and bullying?"

Pocketing his phone, Alan said, "Take your responsibilities seriously; then I won't have to resort to threats."

Christian had always been an obedient son. Even when he rebelled, deep down, he understood his father's wishes would win out eventually.

But not anymore. How could he insert his will into Christian's personal life, trying to dictate who he should marry? Did Alan not know what century this was?

Despite Christian's past reputation with women, he took marriage seriously, not that his father was a good example. Quite the opposite. Alan Wheeler's philandering was legendary. The hypocrisy almost made Christian gag with fury.

"I do take my responsibilities seriously. Let me remind

you again. I've done everything you've asked of me and proven myself to be a highly competent executive. I deserve an award for achieving the success I have despite you trying to control and undermine me at every turn."

Shifting about in his seat, Alan said, "There's a bigger issue at stake. If it's not handled properly, it will bring down Levitron-Blair and land you in prison."

Was this another attempt at controlling him by getting dramatic about LB again?

Tapping his fingers on the desk, Christian asked, "What are you talking about?"

"Your involvement in your brother's murder."

A shell-shocked Christian gaped at his father. Alan just dropped the bombshell as casually as though he was ordering coffee at his favorite café.

Christian needed a minute to breathe properly and slow down his heart rate. How should he respond? It depended on how much his father knew. Who provided the information? A denial would be the easiest thing. The simplest thing, but that would make a bad situation worse. Alan wouldn't have brought up the subject if he didn't have solid proof.

Swallowing hard, Christian said, "Why would you ask me something like that?"

Alan didn't answer the question. Instead, he added, "You covered your tracks well. But imagine my surprise when I received a call from Donald Wilkins, the retired warden of the prison where Zach was serving his sentence. He had a lot to say about why and how your half-brother died."

Christian didn't say anything for a full minute. Alan sat in silence, waiting. Christian had buried that part of his past deep down somewhere, and whenever the guilt threatened to consume him, he found ways to cope—weed, painting, and even drinking to excess at times.

"There were extenuating circumstances, and I didn't murder the man."

"You may not have bashed his skull in during the scuffle, but you helped set things in motion."

Christian hated when his father looked at him like that. Judgmental, disappointed, lording his mistakes over him.

Zach Rossdale was a stone-cold killer, a monster. When Ty Rambally came to Christian and asked for his help to neutralize Zach, Christian hadn't hesitated. Ty had come to him out of desperation, a last resort. Christian knew that. In fact, Christian was the one who suggested that Zach had to go.

Christian had worked overtime to convince Ty that he and Abbie and their family would have no peace as long as Zach was alive. It would only be a matter of time before Zach came for Abbie or one of the kids again.

"Why would the warden call you after three years? Zach was blackmailing him. I assumed he was relieved Zach was no longer a problem."

"Well, he's our issue now. He wants money to keep quiet about your involvement."

"Nobody honors a deal anymore," Christian grumbled. "How much is he asking for, and how can we guarantee he won't ask for more?"

"That's not important. I'll take care of it."

"How?"

"Don't ask questions you don't want to know the answer to. You obviously weren't thinking at all when you came up with the idea."

"I had no choice. When..." Christian stopped. He was about to blurt out that a desperate and petrified Ty had come to him for help, but he didn't see the point in dragging Ty into it.

They made a pact, Christian and Ty, that Abbie would never find out how they made the Zach Rossdale problem go away.

"Zach was a murderous psychopath. Look, Dad, I'm not proud of what I did, but there was no other way. Zach was not a person you could reason with."

"I understand you exercised what you thought was your only option at the time, but the implications are much bigger than you. Now LB might be in jeopardy, as well as your freedom. We don't know if the warden mentioned the plot to anyone. Tell me, is she worth going to prison for?"

Someone needed to clear Dad of his delusions of superior morality.

Christian said, "This bears repeating since you're eager to forget the facts. You never acknowledged Zach and Spencer were yours. They wanted to correct what they saw as a grave injustice and targeted Abbie as a way to get to us, to you."

"Spencer and Abbie paid dearly for your mistake. Abbie paid when Zach raped her and changed the trajectory of her life. Don't get me wrong, I'm glad Lucas came into the world, but getting pregnant at nineteen as a result of a violent assault was never Abbie's plan."

Christian shook his head in disbelief, as though he still grappled with the dark and perverse circumstances of the past.

He added, "She would have been a brilliant surgeon. Zach stripped her of the chance to make that dream come true."

"And you missed your shot at her because Ty Rambally was in the right place at the right time. Isn't that what's really bugging you about this entire situation, the reason you can't seem to settle down with any woman?

"You feel cheated and haven't been able to get over it since. I suggest you do. For all our sakes."

The self-satisfied smirk made Christian want to punch his father in the throat.

Christian had been thousands of miles away at the University of Texas, Austin, when things went sideways for Abbie at Yale. After her release from the hospital, still suffering from the injuries Zach had inflicted on her, Ty stepped up to care for her.

The attraction that had always simmered between them, just beneath the surface, exploded. The next thing Christian knew, he was sitting across from a tearful Abbie at a café in Bethesda, Maryland, listening to her tell him she was spoken for. She then removed her gloves and showed him Ty's wedding ring on her finger.

Blindsided by the news, he almost cried right there in front of Abbie. Only three months prior, he had met up with her in New York.

At the time, she had been an unattached, carefree college student who still made his heart race. Abbie had maintained her sense of humor, even when he shamelessly flirted with her. And just like that, everything changed forever.

For weeks afterward, Christian grieved privately and had himself a good man cry. It didn't matter whether he and Abbie would have worked out as a couple. What mattered was he never got the chance to find out.

"We can't help who we're drawn to, Dad. And although I struggle with my feelings for Abbie, I've been totally above board in all my actions and interactions with her and her family. What happened last year won't be repeated."

"How can you be sure?"

"Because as much as I hate to admit it, you're right. It's time I took steps to bury those feelings. I need to look forward, not backward. Callie told me as much.

"But if you're hoping I'll end my friendship with Abbie, that won't happen. Not in this lifetime."

CHAPTER 59

KRISTINA

RETURNING FROM CHERYL Bradshaw's office put Kristina in a fantastic mood. She leaned back in her chair, legs up on her desk, with a wide, satisfied grin on her face. She had more than one reason to overflow with confidence.

Ian came through by producing the diploma, irrefutable proof that she had indeed graduated from University of Oxford (Kellogg College). When she unboxed the thick, cream- colored paper with the gold Oxford seal and saw her name, Kristina Navi Haywood, with a MSc in Global Health Science and Epidemiology, she couldn't help but break out in a happy dance.

Cheryl had a family emergency, something to do with her daughter, and would be out for several days. Kristina delivered the diploma to HR and made certain neither HR nor Cheryl had any reason to call Oxford to verify anything.

By the time her boss returned to the office, she would be so distracted by her family situation that taking issue with Kristina's authentic, could-fool-the-experts diploma would be the last thing on Cheryl's mind.

Kristina removed her feet from the desk, planted them on the ground, and reached for a pack of grapes she brought in for a snack. She popped a grape into her mouth. A wave of anticipation surged through her.

The unanimous text she sent had worked its magic. Abbie had so broken Ty with her infidelity that he was falling apart at work. Kristina would pick him up, dust him off, and turn him back into the strong, capable, amazing man she knew. Abbie's affair with Christian Wheeler was a gift Kristina would be forever thankful for.

Her flash of inspiration to have Abbie followed came when Kristina discovered Seamus had taken out the wrong woman. It took a few days, but Henry Dalton, Kristina's private investigator, hit the jackpot the day he followed Abbie to Boston Common.

Henry was worth every cent Kristina was paying him. The fantastic photos of Abbie and Christian during what appeared to be an intense conversation, according to Henry, was proof.

Now that Ty knew the so-called love of his life was a lying, cheating tramp, the time had come to drive the final nail into Abbie's coffin. For that, she needed a fool-proof insurance policy in place. Couples reconciled all the time, and Kristina couldn't afford to risk the possibility that Abbie could charm Ty back into her cheating arms.

Everything Kristina had ever wanted was within her grasp. It was her game to win or lose, and Kristina refused to be the loser this time around.

The queen was exposed and vulnerable. It was time to capture the king.

PART V
THE ART OF WAR

CHAPTER 60

KRISTINA

S TANDING AT THE entrance of MCI-Framingham—a prison for female offenders—Kristina's pulse raced. This was it, the final play. The red brick structure loomed before her. Nausea roiled in her stomach. Kristina had never been to a prison before, but she reasoned it was the same as being locked up in a psychiatric ward.

People told you what to do, when to eat and sleep, and in her case, forced a ritual of pumping her full of medication. She would never forgive Callum for using his money and influence to force Kristina to check into a facility against her will.

The doctor he paid off was a well-respected London psychiatrist. No one believed Kristina's protests that she wasn't crazy and the incident with Sita Kapoor was just a simple misunderstanding.

After Kristina went through layers of security, signed the visitor's log, and stored her ID, keys, and purse in the lockers provided per prison rules, Brynn Rossdale Harper appeared in the visitors' room, grabbed a plastic chair from the stack, and then sat across from Kristina.

Kristina was unsure how to proceed. With dark hair pulled back in a ponytail, Brynn was thin with piercing brown eyes that produced an aura that made Kristina want to run—hostile and mistrusting yet curious.

"Thank you for agreeing to meet with me," Kristina began.

Brynn said, "I admit I'm curious. And the only reason I agreed to this visit is because you said it had something to do with Abbie. As the mother of my nephew, my only living relative, everything about her interests me. So what brings you to this palace," she said, gesturing around the room.

Kristina decided to butter up Brynn first. It would be easier to extract details from her if she was relaxed.

"I was friendly with your brother Spencer. We were at Yale together. I left for London after the tragedy and have only been back in the States for the past few weeks."

Brynn sat up straighter in her chair and leaned in. "Really? Did you know Zach too?"

"I met him twice. Very intense, if I remember correctly."

"Yes, Zach and Spencer were polar opposites. I'll never forgive Abbie. Both my brothers are dead because of her."

"You mean because of the accusations she made against them?"

"Yes. That self-righteous snob ruined our family. My mother never recovered from losing the twins. She died a few years after Spencer. A broken heart, everyone said."

"So sorry, Brynn. That must have been hard."

"How did you run into Abbie anyway?" Brynn asked.

"London, actually. Is Lucas your nephew?"

"Yes." Brynn's eyes lit up. "How is he?"

"I detected a resemblance between him and your brothers. He's a lovely boy, very handsome. I don't think he cared for me much."

Brynn chuckled. "He's intense like his father was, takes himself too seriously."

Kristina silently congratulated herself for taking this route. Brynn blamed Abbie for her loss, although Kristina didn't grasp the logic in Brynn's way of thinking. Zach shot Spencer. After Zach raped Abbie, she wound up pregnant. Lucas was proof.

But Brynn didn't see it that way. It wasn't Kristina's place to point out the woman's flawed thinking. Kristina would do and say whatever she had to get what she came for.

"Does Lucas know Zach was his biological father?" Kristina asked.

"How is that any of your business?" Anger inched across Brynn's face. Though Kristina had struck a chord, she needed Brynn's cooperation. It was best to cozy up to Brynn like two girlfriends sharing confidences over a glass of wine.

"Let's just say that during my interactions with Abbie, beginning with our time at Yale, I found her to be a conniving, manipulative, and untrustworthy person. Who knows what lies she told that precious nephew of yours about his father and your side of the family?"

Brynn splayed her palms flat against the table. Her features relaxed. In a subdued tone, she said, "You're right. Abbie never told Lucas that Zach was his father, and if she did eventually, I'm positive she made up a story that cast my brother in a negative light."

"How do you know Abbie never told Lucas about Zach?"

"Because when Lucas and I spent time together, he had no idea who I was. He believed Ty Rambally was his father."

Don't you mean when you kidnapped the boy?

"Oh. I'm sure he asked questions and Abbie lied to him."

"What do you mean?"

"Well, Lucas looks nothing like his siblings. So Abbie had to explain the situation somehow. I think you're right."

Brynn leaned back into her chair and assessed Kristina, as

though scanning her thoughts.

She said, "Why are you curious about Lucas and my brothers? What did Abbie do to you?"

"She stole something from me and caused me great pain. I lost my baby because of her. I'm here to see that she never takes anything from me again."

"Good for you," Brynn said, filled with enthusiasm. Brynn's gaze swept across the visitor's room. The room was near empty; only two other inmates were present with their visitors. One of them got up from the table and headed to the soda machine against the wall.

Brynn leaned in closer to Kristina and whispered, "I think Abbie had something to do with Zach's death, but I could never prove it."

"What?" Kristina's question came out like a yell, and she quickly covered her mouth when the officer in charge of the visiting room shot her a look. "What makes you say that?" she asked, her tone quieter.

"The story about a fight breaking out at the prison and Zach getting beaten, his skull bashed in by another inmate, never sat right with me."

Kristina folded her arms and could barely contain herself. She wanted to whoop and holler and break out in a dance right there. Was Brynn about to deliver the piece de résistance to Kristina's plan?

"If it was a fight, how do you figure Abbie's involvement?" she probed.

"The whole thing was staged," Brynn said, conviction ringing in her voice. "It was a set-up so my brother would be murdered and they could make it look like a tragic accident. But I know better. I'll never get justice for my brother stuck in here."

"What made you suspect foul play, Brynn?"

"The stonewalling. Everyone was tight-lipped when I started poking around. They were quick to close the case and rule it an accident. The conspiracy of silence went all the way to the top, including the warden. I asked for an investigation into Zach's death and was told his death was ruled an accident. That the ruling was final."

Brynn stopped to catch her breath. The pain was still raw as far as Kristina could tell. Brynn continued, "I suspect Abbie used her connections to get rid of my brother and made sure no one listened to me because I was accused of...anyway, Abbie is awful is all I'm saying."

Shock whiplashed through Kristina like a tidal wave. Her pulse pounded between her ears. *Abbie involved in a murder?*

When Kristina could breathe again, she said, "Wow, Brynn. That's truly awful. I had no idea Abbie was capable of something so heinous."

"She is. You pegged her right. Abbie is scheming and manipulative. Don't let up, and don't, under any circumstances, underestimate her."

Brynn leaned in and whispered, "She's relentless, and if you don't watch your back, she will take you down."

CHAPTER 61

ABBIE

A RE YOU TAKING the kids to camp like you promised?"
I ask.

"I can't. Something came up. I'll be gone for a few days."

"Where?"

Ty hurriedly grabs clothes from our bedroom closet and shoves them into a suitcase on the bed. I usually pack for him when he travels, but apparently my services are not needed right now. He'll arrive at his destination and realize he's missing several important items. I watch him scurry around trying to figure out what to bring and in what quantities.

"Santa Clara."

"Oh, California. The kids were looking forward to you driving them up to New Hampshire."

"I can't, Cooper. Parham Capital wants to go over the growth strategy one more time before they sign off on Series A funding. I can't miss that meeting."

"That's great news. It's what you, Stan, and Daniel have been working toward all his time. Looks like things are about to take off."

He ignores me and continues opening and shutting drawers, grabbing items from the bathroom, and then lets out a frustrated groan when he can't find what he's looking for. I most likely know what he needs, but he won't ask for my help and I'm not volunteering information. Call me petty. I just have no desire to act like an adult right now.

"So this is how it's going to be? Us not talking, you pretending I don't exist?"

Ty stops riffling through a drawer and turns to look at me. "What do you want from me, Cooper? To pretend it never happened? To pretend that the only woman who ever had my heart, my queen, defiled what we share?"

His words burn like acid through my veins. *Defiled.* I don't know why, but the phrase makes what I did a million times worse. It's one thing to cheat and, as bad as that is, *defiled* is next level. Our marriage was sacred to him. My betrayal equated to sacrilege—a large, ugly stain on something beautiful and perfect.

Ty slowly walks toward me and then stops inches from me, the closest we've been since he learned the truth. He had moved out of our bedroom and took up residence in the guest bedroom. He hasn't touched me either. I'm surprised he can look me in the face.

"Christian isn't who you think he is, Cooper. He's not some poor misunderstood soul, a victim of his father or his family name. Nor is he harmless."

My hands rest at my sides, but they're trembling. What bombshell is Ty about to drop on me?

Ty's jaw ticks, his expression hard. He continues, "Christian is ruthless. A persistent manipulator who knows how to get what he wants, a shark who can swim with the best of them."

Through the disjointed thoughts and lacerating emotions, I manage to ask, "What do you mean?"

"The good guy act was just for you. Christian knew exactly how and when to pull you into his orbit and how to keep you there. You were too blind to see it. Or maybe you didn't want to, despite the warnings."

"Why won't you be honest with me, Ty? I'm not the only one holding on to a secret."

"What's that supposed to mean? I don't keep secrets from you."

"Don't you? Your hatred for Christian goes beyond what we did. There is an underlying distrust you've been nursing for years. It came roaring to the surface once you discovered I cheated with him. What are the two of you hiding?"

Ty shuffles backward, widening the distance between us. With a raised brow, he says, "Is this how you justify cheating on me, coming up with some ridiculous idea that I'm keeping something about Christian from you?"

"If the shoe fits. I watched the two of you at my graduation party, the day I earned my Ph.D. from BU. You and Christian were holed up in a corner of the backyard talking about something serious."

Ty opens his mouth to speak. I hold up a palm, halting his protest. "Don't bother denying it. The way you gripped each other's hands, like you were making a pact or a promise. When I asked you about it, you said it was nothing, you were talking about how amazing I was. That story was a pile of bull, Ty. I knew it then, and I know it now."

Under the laser heat of his glare, I add, "You and Christian were always cordial. Though you were never close friends, you got along. Something happened that day in May three years ago. You've been keeping it a secret ever since, so don't you stand here and judge me with your annoying air of superiority."

There's no acknowledgement of what I've laid out. With bored detachment, he says, "I have to finish packing for my trip."

"Best of luck on the trip. I know this start-up has been a

dream of yours for a while. Let me know if I can help you in any way."

I leave the room and slam the door behind me. Standing in the hallway, trying to catch my breath, I realize with certainty that Ty lied. He is keeping a secret from me. A big one.

CHAPTER 62

TY

C HRISTIAN SHOULD WAIT. That was what Ty decided when he took his sweet time arriving at the hotel in Boston's Seaport District—a stretch of the South Boston Waterfront lined with sleek restaurants, bars, and hotels. He imagined Christian seated, looking at his watch every few seconds, and then at the entrance of the restaurant they agreed to meet, wondering whether Ty would show.

The thought had occurred to him to blow off the meeting and head straight to Logan, but Ty preferred to tackle his problems head on. He timed the meeting to coincide with his flight out to California on purpose. A reminder that he had a flight to catch would ensure the meeting ended quickly.

Ty had sent a text that simply said: We need to talk. Christian happened to be heading to Boston yet again, and Ty agreed to meet him at a restaurant inside the hotel at eleven a.m.

It was eighteen minutes past eleven when Ty strolled into the restaurant and spotted Christian staring out the massive window at views of the Boston skyline. There were only two other patrons in the restaurant, which made sense.

The establishment opened at eleven, and Ty wanted to be out of there before the lunch crowd came out in full force.

"Who else knows about what happened three years ago besides you and me?" Ty asked, taking a seat and startling Christian who hadn't seen him approach.

"That's what you wanted to talk to me about?" Christian asked, facing Ty.

"If the secret is going to come out, if you're about to break the pact we made, I need to prepare."

Christian's confused expression only irritated Ty further. "You betrayed me by sleeping with my wife. I can only assume that sooner or later you will squeal about my involvement with the Zach situation."

"I get that you're angry, and I'm sorry—"

"Save it, Christian," Ty said. "You're only sorry the truth came out. It came from neither you nor Cooper, although she admitted it when I confronted her."

Christian swallowed hard and then went silent. Bile burned in Ty's stomach. All sorts of blundering thoughts pummeled his brain, thoughts that reinfected the wound of infidelity.

Where did Christian and Cooper make love, Ty wondered? Christian's bed, which Ty suspected was already a high-traffic area? The thought made him retch. Or was it the living room? The sofa? What did they say to each other after it was over? Cooper said it only happened once, but Ty had no way of knowing whether that was true.

How many times had Christian flown up to Boston for business and Cooper failed to mention it? Did they sneak off to his hotel?

Christian said, "I regret hurting Abbie. And I'm man enough to admit I crossed a line I shouldn't have."

"Too little, too late," Ty said. "Your apology is meaningless to me. You claim to care about Cooper, yet you compromised her in the worst way possible. Your actions could cost her everything."

"What do you mean by that?"

Ty really wanted to hurt Christian. The desire was primal and rested on Ty's chest like a large boulder about to suffocate him. He thought about several medical scenarios that could cause Christian's death, most of which centered around how to stop his heart.

Ty knew exactly what would bring about such an outcome, including drug combinations, but he knew such dark, ugly thoughts were his pain talking.

Pain brought on by the man who sat there in his perfectly tailored suit, the pompous air of wealth and privilege clinging to him like a second skin. It wasn't the wealth or privilege that bothered Ty though. It was the ruthless and predatory way Christian had pursued Cooper. Christian knew she was vulnerable and weak. Instead of helping her as a friend would, he used her. Dishonored her.

"You're the last person on Earth I would discuss the state of my marriage with. I came here to determine whether my collusion with you, a giant mistake in hindsight, is about to ruin my life, my family. You owe me the truth on that at the very least."

Clearing his throat, Christian said, "My father found out because the warden, since retired, wanted more money to keep quiet and went directly to Dad instead of coming to me."

Anxiety swirled in Ty's brain. He took a deep gulp of air. When he asked for the meeting, he had no idea what to expect. This news was distressing.

Christian continued, "But Dad said he would take care of the warden. I don't know the details; he didn't share them with me."

Relief swept through Ty, not that he would admit such a thing to Christian. And as quickly as the relief swept through him, it seeped out of him, like air oozing out of a balloon.

If Alan Wheeler took care of the situation with the warden

to ensure this hideous situation went away permanently, it meant Ty would be back to square one—beholden to the Wheelers.

On the other hand, it meant Alan recognized the threat. If the story ever got out, it could cause damage to Levitron-Blair, not to mention the opening of old wounds that would heavily impact Cooper and Lucas.

"Are you sure you didn't instigate the conversation with your father?"

"Of course not." Christian had the nerve to look offended. "I kept my promise. I never told a soul, not even Abbie. Despite everything, I'm a man of my word, Ty."

"Oh, I get it now. Since I didn't make you swear you would never sleep with my wife, you took that to mean she was fair game?"

Christian pinched his nose repeatedly. He glanced out the window again at the view of the Boston skyline. Ty wanted him to feel uncomfortable, to be ashamed.

When Christian returned his gaze to the table, he said, "Are you and Abbie going to make it, or are you going to hold this one mistake against her for the rest of her life?"

"As I already stated, Christian, my family is none of your business. I'm not going to discuss my marriage with you."

"It is my business," Christian said defiantly. "Lucas is my nephew. However things end up between you and Abbie impacts him."

"You didn't care when you slept with his mother, so why the sudden concern?"

"Okay, Ty. Enough. I'm going to apologize one last time since you interrupted me when I tried before, and then I'm done. I won't take your insults anymore."

A waiter came by to ask about placing their orders. Ty said he would take a coffee to go, and Christian said he needed a few more minutes because he hadn't yet looked at the menu.

"What I did was wrong, and I'm deeply sorry. I thought I was protecting Abbie by not saying anything. I didn't want to be the cause of her losing her family, so I stayed silent."

"She just needed you to be her friend. Why couldn't you do that?" Ty asked. "Cooper was always there for you. No matter what was happening in her life, she never complained or told you she was too busy.

"She listened, encouraged, and offered her advice. She was a true friend, one of the few true friends you have. How could you take advantage of her because she was vulnerable and hurting?"

Ty wanted to cry as silly as it sounded to his aching brain. *Why can't you say no to him? Tell Christian to find a therapist in New York. Let him solve his own problems.* But Cooper hadn't listened. Christian was her friend, and she was going to stand by him, help him cope with his problems.

"I was trying to comfort her, and things got out of hand. That's the truth."

Ty didn't want to but part of him understood how easily things could get out of hand. He flashed back to the run-in with Kristina. She kissed him. Had he been in a different state of mind, who knows what could have happened? It still didn't excuse Christian, however.

"I have to go," Ty said, glancing at his watch. He stood and so did Christian.

Christian said, "Abbie loves you, Ty. She picked you years ago, not me. She married you, not me. I hope that counts for something when you decide how to move forward."

Ty said nothing and walked out of the restaurant.

CHAPTER 63

ABBIE

DRIVING TO WOLFEBORO, New Hampshire, to drop the kids off at summer camp was an exercise in both frustration and patience. It rained heavily during the two-hour drive up with poor visibility and traffic moving at a snail's pace. Fortunately, we arrived in one piece.

Taking a late afternoon flight to London required that I wake up early, get the kids ready, drive a total of four hours back and forth, and still leave enough time to get myself sorted out.

Having gone through Logan Airport security, I sit inside a chain seafood restaurant, picking at my salad, waiting for my order of a lobster roll and fries to arrive. The busy waitstaff navigates the tight space with ease. I pull out my cell phone from my purse and compose a text.

> Dropped the kids off at camp this morning. They're doing fine.

> Haven't heard from you. Did you make it to Santa Clara okay? Where are you staying?

Ty left for California early this morning, and it's not like him to keep me out of the loop regarding his movements, even though he's angry with me. The least he could do is inform me he arrived safely.

No response to my text. I call him and leave a terse message. *Please let me know that you made it safely and where you're staying. Don't be a jerk. You have a wife and children to consider. You can't fly halfway around the country and then ghost us.*

I hang up and place the phone down on the table. My server, Lara, arrives and places the lobster roll with fries in front of me. I thank her and ask for a refill on my drink. After she disappears, I root around in my bag for another phone, one of the two burner phones I recently purchased. Or rather, Layla purchased. There's a text message waiting for me.

Ryan

> Thought this might interest you before we chat.

The contact details for a Dr. Cressida Nelson, Psychiatrist appears on the screen.

Ryan

> She's willing to see you, but you may not get much out of her.

I respond to the text.

> That's fine. Just a few minutes face time with her might be enough.

Lara arrives with my drink and places it on the table. I take a long sip through the straw and move my neck from side to side, trying to work out the kinks and stress. My London trip is off to a great start, and I haven't even landed on British soil yet.

I'm halfway through my sandwich when my personal cell

vibrates on the table. I snatch it up and read an equally terse text from my husband.

Ty

> I arrived just fine. No need for name calling.

I'm tempted to press the question of where he's staying, but I don't.

Ninety minutes later, it's time to board. I'm traveling light, my luggage comprising of a small carry-on suitcase and my purse. The boarding queue is quite long, but that works for me. My burner phone vibrates. I grab it from my bag.

A photo of Kristina with three other people, two women and a man, pop up. The photo looks to be several years old. There's a red circle around the man's face.

Ryan

> Seamus Jones, former British Army sniper.

> He flew to Jamaica from Kenya during the timeframe we discussed.

> Will fill you in further upon arrival.

A bouquet of conflicting emotions rips through me. My chest tightens as though constricted by an unknown force. I swallow repeatedly as the truth comes into focus, the confirmation of what I had long suspected. Yet, my brain is unwilling to accept it.

If I accept what's staring back at me from the screen, I'll be forced to acknowledge there's a target on my back. Admit the Kristina threat level has been elevated from dangerous to *deadly*.

CHAPTER 64

CHRISTIAN

C ALLIE LOUNGED ON the sofa in his office, picking at her fingernails, painted a deep red that matched her lipstick. Dressed in a pair of ivory linen pants and linen blouse, her long dark hair cascading past her shoulders, he was unable to peel his gaze away from her stunning beauty.

What was that about? Christian had known Callie for years, and not so much as a hint of anything resembling a spark ever passed between them. A white Bottega Veneta ankle strap sandal in lambskin leather completed her sleek, elegant ensemble.

"It's bad, Christian," she said, turning her attention to him. He leaned up against the edge of his desk. Callie's visit had been unexpected, but he asked Courtney to move around his calendar for the day.

"What's bad?"

"Abbie's marriage to Ty is hanging on by a thread. How could you?" Her cobalt-blue eyes shot darts at him from across the room.

"Abbie told you." It was a statement not a question, and for a moment, he broke eye contact with her.

When he said nothing, Callie said, "Well? Explain yourself. Abbie is my best friend. All three of us have been tight since forever, and you just removed the pin from a grenade and blew up her life?"

"Abbie is not a child. It takes two."

Callie stared at him disdainfully. "Are you saying this is all her fault?"

"No. We weren't thinking, just went with the moment. Anyway, I protected our secret, but something I didn't anticipate popped up and changed everything."

"You mean Sam finding the earring and confronting you."

"Yes. And my father."

"What did Alan say?"

"That I had six months to marry Sam or my future as Chairman and CEO of Levitron-Blair would be in serious jeopardy."

"What? That's blackmail."

"Well, LB isn't the success it is because my dad played nice."

"What are you going to do?" Callie stood and approached him, sidling up next to him. "You've been groomed to take over LB since birth."

"Sam and I are over. It was a long-time coming. Finding out about Abbie and me was just the final straw. As for taking over LB, I've decided it no longer serves my interests, neither personally nor professionally."

Callie anchored her gaze on him as though spellbound, anxious to hear what came next. "What are you talking about? What are your plans?"

"I'll step down from LB and start my own company. I'm naming it after my mother, her maiden name, McLellan Plus Media."

"Christian, that's huge. Are you serious?"

"I've never been more serious about anything. It was all over the media when I tried to acquire Cushing Hill Productions and Dad overruled me, got the board to vote against the acquisition.

"In that moment, I realized he will never allow me to be my own man as long as LB is on the table. I'd be condemned to forever live in the shadow of Alan Wheeler. I refuse to do that."

Callie's eyes widened. He added, "McClellan Plus Media will compete directly with LB."

"Whoa, Christian. LB is a giant, billions in assets and resources. Not to mention its global reach."

"I'm not naïve. My strategy to compete is simple: smarter, faster, and more agile. Rather than take on LB as a whole, I'll focus on a handful of niches and dominate those spaces."

Admiration flared in Callie's eyes, and before long, they both got more comfortable, sitting next to each other on the sofa. Callie's rapt attention fanned Christian's flames of gratification as he outlined the blueprint for building his own empire.

"It's all about unique communities that challenge the narrative of popular culture."

"I'm listening."

"I don't want McClellan Plus to be just another run-of-the-mill media company jostling for an audience. I'm looking to transform the quality of life for millions of people around the world."

"Sounds ambitious."

"It is. I got the idea for one of the platforms from Abbie."

"What idea is that?"

"Well, it's what led to our indiscretion, and I'm hoping that something good will come out of it."

"Go on."

Christian explained what Abbie told him that fateful night last winter. Feeling overwhelmed, exhausted, like she was about to crash and couldn't express her feelings for fear of being judged. From the outside, it looked like she had it all and no right to complain.

"I did some research and couldn't believe the number of stories and articles about women all over the country who have felt the way Abbie did. Even female executives who were ashamed to admit they needed help balancing their high-powered jobs and family obligations.

"In many instances, a lot of the family responsibilities still fell on their shoulders. Those who did hire help kept it a dirty little secret."

"It doesn't surprise me," Callie said. "Our generation of women have been told for so long that we could have it all, but nobody told us what it would cost. Not in any honest, impactful way."

"Exactly. With this platform, I want to create a space where professional women can freely discuss their challenges. Members would be thoroughly vetted before joining the community. The five-figure annual subscription fee would provide access to unique content tailored just for them from experts at the top of their game."

Christian stood and walked around the room. He continued, "Career coaching, spiritual guidance, health and fitness advice, and a vetted list of services. Everything from housekeeping and childcare to landscaping and beyond.

"Each content provider would sign an NDA of course. They can't use the content they create for McClellan Media on any other platform or even discuss what they create for us."

"That's smart."

Turning to Callie, he said, "You can be a part of this too. I'm hoping."

"How?"

"As a content contributor from the perspective of a fashion icon and business mogul. You're in a position to speak authentically to our audience about the challenges of running a global business and balancing those obligations with a personal life. A good portion of the demographic we're targeting are already familiar with your brand."

"You've really thought this through. It's not just some pipe dream."

"No, it's not. I already hired a market intelligence and advisory firm. The business plan is in solid shape."

"What about start-up funding?"

"I'll dip into my inheritance, sell off some of my LB shares, and the rest I'll get from venture capital funding. I have a couple already showing serious interest. And in my final act of defiance, I'm taking a few LB executives with me."

"That's a gutsy move."

"It's smart business. They know the market, they understand what it takes to build successful online communities and media entities. So what do you say? Will you join me in this exciting new venture?"

"I'll give it some thought, but it sounds fascinating. I'm intrigued and will consider investing. I need to see your pitch deck though."

Christian returned to the sofa and gave her a look.

"What? Just because we're friends doesn't mean I should neglect my due diligence. I'm a businesswoman and need to see the plan, what you're presenting to potential investors."

Callie joined him on the sofa. "I believe you used the word *mogul* to describe my business success. Very much appropriated, thank you for recognizing my hard-earned status."

She laughed and then he did too, and soon they were both giggling like two kids who had cooked up a devious scheme. Callie was right though. Christian knew that House of Furi worldwide brand evaluation was in excess of four billion dollars.

"I would expect nothing less." Then, taking on a more serious tone, Christian said, "Who knows, maybe our collaboration could extend beyond business."

Callie waggled her eyebrows. "Christian Francis Wheeler, are you flirting with me?"

"What if I am? We're both single. We've been friends for a long time. We like and respect each other."

"What about Abbie?" she asked cautiously.

"What about her?"

"She's my best friend, and as far as I know, you still have feelings for her. Don't you think things could get awkward?"

"Here's the truth, Callie. Abbie was my first true love. Part of me will always love her. But the reality is, she loves Ty more than she ever loved me, and she chose to build a life with him.

"My father was a jerk during our last conversation, but he also made me realize it's time to stop living in the past and look forward to the future. I haven't given up on finding love with the right woman, getting married, and settling down. I do want a family of my own. Does that answer your question?"

"Perfectly. Thank you for being honest."

"The best thing I can do for Abbie right now is to stay away while she works things out with her husband."

"That's best for everyone," Callie concurred.

"You still haven't answered my question," Christian said. "Would you consider getting together outside of business?"

"What do you have in mind?"

"It's up to you."

"You're coming off a three-year relationship. And you have a reputation with women." Callie stared at him brazenly, daring him to contradict her.

"You sound like Abbie."

"Because it's true. I don't know, Christian. Ask me again in a few weeks. Convince me this is a good idea. Show me why I should consider a future with you."

"Fair enough. And Callie?"

"Yeah."

"Just so you know, when I'm in a committed relationship, I'm loyal and faithful. Sam and I had our problems, but she can attest to that fact."

"Really?"

"Okay, except for the lapse with Abbie."

They'd never been so open and candid with each other before. Callie had been a paradox to him, easygoing and laid back yet intense and driven. Her visit had brightened his day in the most unexpected ways.

Christian considered the timing of his exit from LB. His departure would happen after Callie signed on as an investor and the VC firm did as well. The goal was not to embarrass his father or create a leadership crisis at LB. The truth was far simpler: The time had come to grab the reins, seize control of *his* destiny.

Callie interrupted his musings when she said, "How do you plan to handle your dad?"

"What do you mean?"

"Alan Wheeler is going to flip out when he gets wind of your plans. He won't take this lying down, Christian. You have to be prepared. And to tell you the truth, I'm afraid of what he might do in retaliation."

Her concern warmed his heart. Christian had pondered the question over and over again, a relentless, never-ending cycle of paralyzing thoughts that pressed down on him but yielded no answers. He didn't see any scenario under which his plans would go over well with Alan. Part of him was resigned to that fate.

"I can't win with Dad, Callie. He'll be angry, lay on the guilt, and maybe even threaten to ruin me before I get this venture off the ground. But I can't live the rest of my life in fear of my father. That would make me a coward. I have no intention of cowering to Alan Wheeler or anyone else."

Admiration flared in Callie's eyes, and he couldn't deny it made him feel like he could walk on air.

She said, "Why don't we have dinner tonight and you can tell me more about your grand plans?"

CHAPTER 65

ABBIE

M Y FLIGHT LANDS at Heathrow just after six the next morning, giving me a little under three hours to make my nine o'clock appointment with Omega Global Investigators, the top-notch London firm I hired. It's my first face-to-face meeting with Ryan Aames, the investigator handling my case.

Standing in front of the bathroom mirror of my hotel room, I assess my appearance, wanting to strike the right balance between confident and *please do whatever it takes to stop this woman from trying to kill me—a second time.*

I select a deep, azure-blue A-line dress with a bow applique at the neckline and slightly ruffled hemline, flaring out just above the knees.

With a pair of strappy leather stiletto sandals and a matching Callie Furi bag, I'm ready to face what comes next.

A massive sign with the firm's logo greets me at the reception area. I give my name to the receptionist and ask for Ryan. She dials an extension and lets him know his nine o'clock has arrived. She offers me a seat and asks if I want tea or coffee, which I decline.

Sporting a white dress shirt and dark dress pants, Ryan appears to be in his forties, average height, with tussled brown hair and a lean physique. He greets me with a big enthusiastic smile.

"Dr. Rambally, welcome. It's a pleasure to meet you."

"Please call me Abbie, Ryan."

"Will do," he says, ushering me past a series of cubes with employees involved in various tasks and into his office.

"Everything we have so far is in this file," he says, pushing a brown manila folder across the desk toward me.

"Thank you. Tell me more about Seamus Jones."

When Ryan tells me Seamus has a history as a mercenary, the horror of what Kristina did flickers through my mind. Savannah Davis Patterson, in a cruel twist of fate, found herself at the end of Seamus's sniper rifle. Based on my latest research, Jamaican authorities still have no suspects and the case remains unsolved.

I've thought of reaching out to Savannah's family numerous times but always backed out at the last minute. What would that accomplish other than to exacerbate their grief? Seamus's real target was alive and Savannah was dead.

Ryan says, "We can put him at the place of the crime; we just can't prove he pulled the trigger."

We don't need to prove he did, I think but then realize Savannah's family may never get justice. And who should deliver justice? They have no idea I exist and was the intended target. But the bigger looming question is how to make Kristina pay for her crime.

Would British authorities extradite Seamus to Jamaica since his crime took place on Jamaican soil? Would he give up Kristina and provide evidence she orchestrated the murder? There were too many unanswered questions and complexities.

Both Seamus and Kristina had different nationalities, and their crime occurred on foreign soil. Kristina, an American, sent

Seamus, a British citizen, to take out an American in Jamaica. I empty my head of the distressing thoughts before I go down a rabbit hole from which I may never return.

Returning to the matter at hand, I say, "I understand. Do you have the records and the audio recording of Seamus's voice?"

"They were emailed via an encrypted file. The password is in your folder."

"Does Callum Saxena know that Kristina dropped out of Oxford and has been falsifying her resume?" I ask.

"There's no evidence to support that idea. There was a four-year gap between Kristina's departure from Oxford and her marriage to Callum."

"So she could have fooled him too?"

"It's possible."

"What about a financial trail? Any proof of payment to Seamus Jones?"

"We're still working that angle. I'm sure Kristina took precautions. She wouldn't deposit payment into a standard account in Seamus's name. Too risky."

"Fair point. Any luck with Sita Kapoor?"

"No. She doesn't want to discuss what happened with anyone. At the mention of Kristina's name, Ms. Kapoor got agitated and hung up."

"Can't say that I blame her. Is her career truly over because of what Kristina allegedly did, order a vicious attack on her?"

"It would appear so. Ms. Kapoor hasn't had an acting role since the attack."

"Is Sita still involved with Callum?" I ask.

Ryan says, "Hard to say. If she is, they're keeping a low profile. Very hush, hush."

He added, "What do you plan to do with the information you have so far?"

"Prepare. He who exercises no forethought but makes light of his opponent is sure to be captured by them."

Ryan leans back in his chair grinning. "What a delight you are, Abbie. Pulling a page from Sun Tzu's *The Art of War* is very clever."

"You're familiar with the book?"

"Yes. I've had several clients who used the advice to make power plays against their rivals."

"When the stakes are high, you learn from the master."

"Couldn't agree more," Ryan says.

CHAPTER 66

—◦—

ABBIE

FTER MY MEETING with Ryan, I hop in the rental car and set the navigation for the fifteen-minute drive to Chelsea. A posh London neighborhood known for its charm and high-end boutiques and restaurants, the central London suburb is also well known for its wealthy residents, many of them famous.

It would have been easier to take the train, or the tube as the Brits call it, to Sloane Station, but I felt more comfortable driving, despite my lack of experience driving on the left side of the road.

I squeeze into a parking space on a quiet side street with gorgeous Georgian houses, slip on my sunglasses, and exit the car for the walk. Perhaps wearing high-heeled sandals was not the greatest idea, but it should be a brief walk to the restaurant.

Taking in the hustle and bustle of King Road brings a smile to my face. I recognize several American department stores on my walk, including J. Crew and Anthroplogie. A red double-decker bus filled with passengers passes by. People hop in and out of stores, restaurants, and cafes while others fancy a bike ride.

I arrive at the outdoor terrace for Blue Bird, the restaurant where we agreed to meet. I'm taken in by the stylish atmosphere, but I'm hot from walking and would love to cool down in the air-conditioned interior.

After explaining to the hostess that I'm meeting a friend, I'm ushered to the table where Frances is already waiting. She stands, and we give each other a great big hug. It's been five years since we've seen each other in person.

We sit down and beam at each other like two long-lost siblings separated by decades.

"You look fantastic!" I say. It's true. London agrees with her. Frances hasn't aged a bit since we left high school, and she's chic as ever, her shimmering black locks hanging straight. She's all sunshine in a yellow sleeveless dress, belted at her tiny waist.

"You're still tall and thin and flawless after three kids. I hate you so much."

"I still loathe going to the gym if that makes you feel any better," I tease.

Frances sighs theatrically and slumps her shoulders with a flourish. "No, it makes me feel worse." Then she adds, "So, dish. Tell me everything that's going on."

"Ever the curious journalist," I say, grinning. I tell her about the kids and how great they're doing, Lucas looking forward to high school, Miles and Layla's impending nuptials for which I still need to be fitted for my Matron of Honor dress, and such.

The server comes to take our drink order. I'm famished. I've had no time to eat since arriving this morning. I ask for a few extra minutes because I haven't looked at the menu and would prefer to order the appetizer and main course in one go.

Frances cocks her head to one side and says, "Come on, Abbie. You know I'm not buying this picture of perfect domestic contentment. What's really going on under the surface? At the very least, Kristina is stirring up trouble, so there's that."

"Yeah," I say, picking up the menu and glancing at it. "I think she put out a hit on me while Ty and I were in Jamaica."

I fill in a stunned Frances on what I suspect was a case of mistaken identity.

"How can you be so calm about this, Abbie? I knew the chick was psycho, but this is next level from her previous level," Frances says. "Unfortunately, her campaign of chaos just keeps going and going."

"What do you mean?"

"A reporter ambushed Callum Saxena, wanting to know how he felt about his divorce and whether he was dating anyone new."

"I thought you said he was resistant to the idea of divorce."

"Callum's signatures were on the divorce papers Kristina filed. But Callum never signed divorce papers."

"You must be joking, Frances. Are you saying Kristina forged her husband's signature to speed up the divorce, bypassing his objections?"

"That's what I'm saying, yes."

"Are your sources sure about this?" I ask, still incredulous.

"Absolutely. My source is part of Callum's inner circle. The papers were filed in a London court two weeks ago, but his solicitor knew nothing about it."

"Kristina actually believed she could get away with falsifying legal documents?"

"According to my source, the papers looked legit. It's further complicated by the fact that the documents contain Callum's actual signature. His lawyers are working to untangle the whole mess."

The server returns, and I order salad and roasted duck breast for the main course. Frances orders the same, and we top off the order with ginger beer for drinks.

After the server leaves, Frances's cell phone buzzes, and she picks it up from her purse. She looks at it and taps out a quick text.

She explains, "It's Hugh reminding me of our plans for tonight."

Ty won't even text me unless I leave him an acrimonious voice message.

"Tell Hugh I'm sorry I won't see him this time around. But honestly, I'll plan a special trip, just to hang out with the two of you. I want to get back home before Ty..." I trail off.

Frances folds her arms and gives me that look of hers that says, *I knew something was going on and you better spill it.*

"Ty and I are going through a rough patch. He barely speaks to me."

"Why?"

"I don't want to get into it, but I made a terrible mistake last year and it blew up in my face. I couldn't mention this trip or reveal I was coming to London to gather evidence on Kristina. So I need to conclude my business by early evening and fly home first thing in the morning."

"I'm sorry to hear that, Abbie." Frances gives me a comforting squeeze on the arm. "Whatever it is, you and Ty will fix it. Yours is a love story for the ages. And you know how much I hate that sappy stuff, so consider it a gift I uttered those words."

"I do, Frances. I do."

By the time we finish our meal, I'm feeling much more relaxed and ready to tackle the remaining items on my agenda.

"Promise me you and Ty will be okay," Frances says. "If the two of you can't make it work, what hope is there for the rest of us? Besides, I know you. If you and Ty split, you won't recover. So do whatever it takes to get Kristina off your back. That way you can focus on fixing whatever you did that blew up in your face."

"I'll try my best, Frances, but it's not all up to me."

"Don't give Ty all the power, Abbie. You have a lot more clout than you give yourself credit for. Use it. Ruthlessly. It's the only way to save your marriage, especially with Kristina breathing down your neck. She's an invading species who intends to take over your life. You must purge her from your life for good."

My friend's intense stare is ferocious, the brutal spotlight of the truth she just outlined blinding me. All my attempts to shut down Kristina had ended in dismal failures. The dinner ambush with Callum. Sending that anonymous text to her boss, letting Cheryl Barnes know that Kristina never graduated from Oxford.

Even bringing up the trip to Jamaica to gage her reaction, subtly hinting that I suspected something nefarious happened on that trip and she was involved. None of it deterred Kristina.

"You're right, Frances. I must be ruthless and purge Kristina from my life."

CHAPTER 67

KRISTINA

S HE WAS AT a cookout when her phone rang. Kristina excused herself from the group of cheerful colleagues who had gathered in the backyard of Ed Mills, another assistant director of development with whom she worked.

Finding a quiet spot along a retaining wall, Kristina answered the anonymous call.

"If it's bad news, I don't want to hear it," she said sharply. It was after ten at night London time.

"Hello to you too, Kristina. I wouldn't have called if it wasn't important."

"Make it quick. I'm at a work thing and don't want to raise suspicion."

"It's about Jamaica. I don't think we've heard the end of it."

"What do you mean? It's done. I'll deal with my problem another way."

"Good for you, but what about me?"

Kristina's patience was wearing thin. Seamus was the last person she wished to hear from. The Jamaica hit was a bust, and as far as Kristina was concerned, it was all in the past. A past she had no desire to revisit. So why was Seamus bringing it up again?

"What happened?" From the corner of her eye, she

observed a colleague heading in her direction. She held up her index finger to indicate she needed a minute, halting the approach.

"Someone outside my flat. A suspicious man."

"That's it? You called me all the way from London to tell me a suspicious man was outside your flat?"

"A suspicious man parked in front of my flat who followed me. I think he's a detective. I've seen him more than once, Kristina. This bloke is tracking my movements."

Anxiety swirled in Kristina's brain. She almost regretted answering the call. But how? And who? Who was following Seamus, and how would they know anything about Jamaica? Seamus had flown straight from Kenya to Montego Bay. Nobody knew he went there to do a job.

Don't panic. Breathe in and out. You're smart. Brilliant. You always have a plan.

"Stay calm, Seamus. Nobody but the two of us really knows what happened in Montego Bay. Don't let this man frighten you. He wants you to make a mistake, so stick to your routine and don't do anything stupid."

"Easy for you to say. You're not the one who killed the wrong target. Why couldn't you handle Abbie Rambally another way? Why did I listen to you, take on the job?"

"Shh," Kristina admonished. "Somebody could hear you."

"I'm home alone. I've been having nightmares. I can't stop looking at photos of Abbie and replaying the trip in my head over and over again, how many times I saw her, how the mistake could have happened."

"Will you stop being so weak and get yourself together? Everything is fine. Stop falling apart. The guy who is following you could have nothing to do with Abbie."

"I think it does," Seamus insisted. "I should have said no

when you asked me. Abbie didn't deserve that. I've been reading up on her."

"Abbie Cooper is a rotten, conniving, lying, cheating, manipulative, spoiled, entitled little witch, and she deserved to die. I don't feel bad about it, and neither should you. Ty would have been better off without her. You messed up and she's still breathing, so stop whining and spare me the burden of your growing conscience."

Kristina ended the call. She did several breathing exercises to calm herself down. She wouldn't spend time worrying about some random guy following Seamus around. That was his problem, not hers. If he had taken care of business the way he should have, then he wouldn't need to worry about being followed.

Seamus was on his own. Nothing could be traced back to Kristina.

CHAPTER 68

ABBIE

TY TOOK THE red-eye home from California two days after my return from London, arriving in the early morning hours. I'm already downstairs in the kitchen, brewing fresh coffee in the state-of-the-art machine that allows you to grind your own beans.

He comes into the kitchen via the garage, his eyes bloodshot, with a three-day stubble and rumpled clothes. I haven't seen him look this rough in a long time, not even when he worked endless hours as a resident and got little to no sleep.

"Hi," I say. "You look like you could use a cup of coffee."

"No, thanks."

He walks past me to head upstairs. I'm hurt by the dismissive gesture but convince myself that, from the looks of things, he's exhausted and needs to sleep.

Tonight is a big night for the hospital, a private fundraising gala hosted by a wealthy couple. Everyone from the hospital's top executives and surgeons to select members of the development staff will be present.

Ty and I usually attend together, but I won't hold my breath we will this time around. That's why I plan to borrow my dad's sleek, brand-new silver BMW. I can't show up to the valet station at such a prestigious event driving the family car, a Volvo SUV.

My insides quiver at the thought we won't attend the gala together, because I noticed something vital missing when Ty arrived in the kitchen. He isn't wearing his wedding ring.

Ty's wedding band is always on his finger, except when he's at work in the operating room. He's been away for several days on a business trip. Was the ring off the entirety of his trip, or did he remove it on the way home to make a statement?

What statement? That he no longer loves me? Unlikely. That he wants out of our marriage? Possibly. I take a sip of my coffee and quickly place the mug down on the kitchen island.

I need to keep my hands occupied. There's a lot to do today, and I want a big breakfast to carry me through. I'll make scrambled eggs and toast and a smoothie. Mostly to stop my thoughts from spiraling down some depressing rabbit hole.

Ty has been punishing me with the silent treatment, leaving me to live in limbo and a constant state of panic about our marriage. I understand he's angry, but I can only take this treatment for so long before resentment starts to build and makes things worse.

I spray the non-stick frying pan with butter-flavored cooking spray and then crack the eggs. My cell phone pings on the kitchen island. I quickly cross the space to scoop it up. It's a text from Callie.

With one hand tending to the eggs, I compose a response. Callie wants to know if we could chat. I wonder if it's about the dress?

I must look stunning tonight. Scratch that. I want to look out of this world, breathless, a bombshell. Callie created a one-of-a-kind gown she brought with her when she came to Lucas's graduation party two weeks ago. Ty hasn't seen it because I wanted to surprise him. Now that he isn't speaking to me, I'll let the dress do the talking.

I scroll through my favorites list and tap Callie's name. When she picks up, I say, "I'm making breakfast, so I'll have to put you on speaker."

"Are you alone?"

"Yes." Something in her voice makes my skin prickle. Callie's usually breezy confidence is tapered for some reason. I ease the phone down on the counter next to me and tap the speaker icon.

"What's up?" I ask, turning the stove off. I pour the eggs onto a plate and put two slices of bread into the toaster.

"I would rather discuss this in person, but I'm leaving for Paris tonight and don't want to put off telling you."

Alarm bells ring at the back of my head. "Is everything okay with you? Did something happen to your dad?"

"No, nothing like that. Abbie, I really hope what I'm about to say won't change our friendship. It would devastate me if I lost you as a friend."

The toast pops, signaling it's done. "Hang on, Callie."

After I remove the toast from the toaster, I head to my office and close the door behind me. Whatever Callie has to say is heavy. She wanted to know if I was alone.

"Go ahead. We've been friends forever. I can't imagine anything coming between us. Why don't you tell me what's bothering you. I got you."

She clears her throat and says, "It's about Christian."

Nervous knots unfurl in my stomach. "What about him?"

"Abbie, Christian and I are together."

I'm not sure I heard her correctly. All kinds of thoughts are blossoming in my head like a flower garden in springtime.

"Abbie, are you there?"

"Um…yes, I'm here. You caught me off guard. Last I heard, Christian was trying to win back Sam."

"They've been over for a while. I don't want things to get awkward between us, Abbie."

"Why would they?"

"Because of your history with Christian. Plus what happened last year, and now you and Ty are…" She trails off.

"Don't worry about Ty and me. How did this happen? I didn't see it coming."

I want to project the image of the enthusiastic, supportive best friend, bubbling with curiosity to find out how Callie and Christian ended up together. But I'm afraid my tone comes off accusatory, as though I'm putting Callie on trial. *You did tell her to look out for him, make sure he was okay.*

"Sorry, Callie, I didn't mean to make it sound like you did something wrong. I'm just shocked, that's all."

She gives off a nervous laugh. "No one is more shocked than me. We've been spending time together, talking a lot. We're going in on a business venture together."

"Oh? Tell me."

Callie explains that Christian is leaving Levitron-Blair to start his own media company, that she's an investor as well as a content contributor. She reveals that Christian told her I was the inspiration behind one of the communities he plans to launch.

It's a lot to take in all at once. Christian leaving LB, him and Callie as a couple. I work overtime to dispense with my shock. Callie has been single for so long, and though she always wanted to find that special someone, finding love always took a backseat to running her multi-billion-dollar business.

I think back to high school when Christian and I first got together. It was Callie who gave him my phone number when he first started chasing after me. I remember her saying she would pay to see him naked and we all giggled, as teenage girls do about such things.

Had Callie harbored secret feelings for Christian all these years and just never had the chance to act on them? What if those feelings were strong and present during our high school years and she buried them because Christian was pursuing me and Callie decided to be our cheerleader instead?

Tears prickle at the corner of my eyes as a memory burrows its way into my head. When Ty and I got engaged, I snapped a photo of the ring on my finger and texted Callie and Frances. Callie was the first to respond. *At last!*

I pull myself together and whisper into the phone, "At last!"

"You really mean it?" she asks, her voice wobbling.

"Yes. I should have seen it before, but I didn't. Sorry."

"Stop it." Callie is sobbing, and soon, we're two blubbering idiots. When we eventually catch our collective breaths, she says, "But we're keeping our relationship under wraps for now. We're not going public just yet."

"I get it. You want things private, get to know each other in this new way."

"Exactly."

"Katherine is going to love you. Do they know, Katherine and Alan? Have you told Nicholas?"

"Yes, I told my dad. He's happy. My mother is already making wedding plans and baby-shower plans. I told her to calm down. I don't know if this new relationship will go anywhere."

"Of course it will. Christian wants to settle down. You may be his last chance at happiness, Callie. Don't let him get away."

"Why do you say that?"

I hesitate and decide to just go with the truth. "You know how he is about trusting people. He likes the familiar; it makes him feel safe. You've known him forever, warts and all. And I'm willing to bet he made the first move."

"He did."

"I rest my case." Then I add, "I'm happy for you, Callie. And tell Christian I'm rooting for the two of you."

"What about you and Ty? I'm worried."

I sigh. "I don't know, Callie. My husband looks at me with contempt. He's still struggling to come to terms with my betrayal, if I'm being honest. Ty is a proud man. I don't know how long it will take him to come around, whether we can restore the trust between us. I'm willing to do whatever it takes to save our marriage."

"Do you think it can be saved?"

"Yes, I do. I won't give up, but if only one of us is fighting, it makes reconciling difficult."

"Don't give up. Knock his socks off at the gala tonight. I guarantee he won't be able to resist you in that dress."

"Ty is pretty stubborn."

"Ty will never stop loving you, Abbie. You can take that to the bank."

"But sometimes love isn't enough."

CHAPTER 69

---◆---

ABBIE

A FTER HANDING THE keys of the BMW 7 series to the valet, I sashay through the entrance of Alden Castle, an exquisite architectural jewel in the Boston suburb of Brookline.

The Tudor style façade gives way to enormous windows flooding with natural light and a soaring, gold fleur-delis ceiling. This opulent gala brings together some of the wealthiest men and women in the state who donate their time and open their deep wallets to fund research and programs at MGH, separate from the annual MGH employee fund campaign.

My goal tonight is a charm offensive. The room will be packed with surgeons and other doctors and hospital executives. Ty's boss, Dr. Paul Stevenson, head of cardiothoracic surgery, as well as the hospital's medical director, will be present.

Ultimately, I want Ty to take notice and to melt the block of ice surrounding his heart since my betrayal came to light. I want him to know that I'm worthy of forgiveness, and no matter what, I'm irreplaceable. That's what I tell myself anyway.

Callie's design is a floor-length strapless dress with gold sequins and an almost thigh-high split. The fabric hugs my curves in all the right places. I never show this much skin, but desperate times call for desperate measures. I'll just have to get used to the uncomfortable feeling that I'm exposed.

My eyes do a quick scan of the place already alive with the drinking and socializing of this elite crowd. Men in tuxedos, women in glamorous evening gowns, and servers floating around the room with trays of wine and champagne, dressed in white dress shirts and black slacks.

A string quartet plays classical music. The tables are elegantly appointed with crisp, white linen tablecloths, gold table settings, and massive bouquets comprised of pink and white Stargazer Lilies, cream Lisianthus, and pink roses. The full-back chairs are eight to a table.

Though I only drink occasionally, I sidle up to the bar and order a glass of white wine.

While I wait for the server to prepare the drink, Ty's boss approaches, a tall gangly man with sandy-brown hair and delicate features. He's about to place an order when he does a double take.

"Abbie?" It's a question, as though his eyes deceive him. He's seen me dozens of times, but I'm always buttoned up and professional, and even at formal events, I keep it classy. Not that this dress isn't. I told Callie I was going for classy and elegant with a dash of risqué thrown in, thus the thigh-high split. Now I'm beginning to wonder if it's too much, whether I made a mistake.

"Paul, good to see you. It's been a while. How are Sun-Young and the kids?"

"They're great. Sun-Young is around here somewhere," he says, scanning the room as if looking for his wife who gave him the slip. We chat about our kids, what they're up to, and I make sure to play up my kids accomplishments: Lucas's acceptance into Branson Academy, Alexis's stellar academic record and wanting to be a surgeon like her dad, and Blake's swimming trophies and baking prowess.

Stevenson says, "Wonderful to hear the kids are thriving. And you're no slouch either. Great work with the Center for NeuroTech and NeuroRecovery. Knock those donors dead tonight."

I thank him for the compliment. Paul looks at his watch. "I'll let you order that drink and get on with your evening," I say.

He gives me a thin smile and then says, "Abbie, I don't want you to worry about Ty. I had a chat with him about the incident in the OR and want you to know I've got his back. He's one of the best surgeons at MGH. We'll make sure he's okay, in and out of the OR."

I take a step backward without meaning to. There was an incident in the OR that I know nothing about? I coax an all-knowing expression onto my face to disguise my shock. Stevenson can't know I have no idea what he's talking about, or how distressed I am.

What happened in the OR?

"Thank you. I'm glad I can count on your support of Ty's career."

Stevenson inches closer to me and lightly touches my arm. He says, "I know marriage is tough, believe me, I've been there. But whatever is going on between you and Ty, fix it. I've told him the same thing. I need his head in the game. The hospital *needs* him."

And with that, Stevenson disappears into the crowd without ordering his drink, leaving me to pick up my jaw off the floor. I take a deep, long sip of my white wine and place the glass on the counter.

"A refill?" the bartender asks. I nod, incapable of speech as a series of disconcerting thoughts circle my brain.

Ty is so broken up about my betrayal that it's affecting his work? It got so bad that his boss had to intervene? Ty is composed, even-tempered, and patient. He's not one for giving into emotions or theatrics, especially when it comes to his job.

When police detectives interrogated him after the tragic death of our nanny, Olivia Stewart, and they were trying to see if they could rattle him, even then, Ty didn't fall apart or lose his calm.

It's all my fault. This is the outcome of my infidelity; my husband is so brokenhearted that he can't think straight. Can't do his job.

I take another long sip of the wine. I must find a quiet corner somewhere to get my thoughts together, compose myself. I haven't seen Ty yet, but I'm sure I will.

My plan to find a quiet space is thwarted by Kristina's approach. She looks beautiful in a shimmering black gown with spaghetti straps and a side slit.

Her hair is brushed away from her temples, landing in a cascade of curls at the back of her neck. Her appearance is that of a glamorous nineteen forties' movie star. The whole ensemble is rounded out with a dazzling diamond necklace and teardrop earrings.

Kristina's gaze flickers over me. I return the favor, appraising her.

She says, "Abbie. Wow! We're seeing a lot more of you this evening than we're used to, aren't we?"

First off, who is this *we* she's talking about? Secondly, I don't need to justify my wardrobe to the likes of Kristina. I'm desperately trying not to feel self-conscious as it is. I don't need her pecking away at my confidence. Besides, the only person whose opinion I care about has yet to grace us with his presence.

With a smile as sweet as cherry pie, I say, "You know what they say, Kristina. If you've got it, flaunt it."

I place my half-empty glass of wine on the counter and saunter off without a backward glance.

Wading through the crowd, I'm met with a series of hellos, waves, compliments about one thing or another, and hugs. I'm relieved to finally make it to the ladies' room.

Leaning up against the door of one of the stalls, I take a minute to calm my frayed nerves. Fix it. Fix us before Kristina takes advantage of Ty's vulnerability and sinks her viper fangs into him.

I can't allow our collective sacrifices, Ty's and mine, to flitter away on a cloud of betrayal, anger, and pain. A good sit-down is called for. Just the two of us, no interruption. Some place quiet, away from the house. Perhaps a picnic in the park. Stevenson's newsflash provided the perfect weapon to force Ty to have that conversation.

The conversation where he has to give me an answer about the future of our marriage, force him to fight for us, because I can't do it alone.

After exiting the stall, I wash my hands, refresh my makeup, and dab a small amount of the sweet, velvety designer fragrance I bought for this occasion onto my chest and wrist.

I want the sensual fragrance with notes of ginger zest, grapefruit, bergamot, and orange to be fresh on my skin when I run into Ty. Costing several hundred dollars, it was worth every penny.

Standing in a barely lit corner in a little alcove down from the ladies' room, I whip out my cell phone and text my mother, letting her know I have yet to see Ty at the gala.

> No sighting yet.

Mom

> The gala started over an hour ago, where could he be?

300

Don't know, Mom.
Ran into Kristina, though.

Mom

She's irrelevant right now. Focus on finding
your husband.

Mom has been egging me on to make things right with
Ty before it's too late. After I told her he'd only spoken two
words to me since returning from California, her concern and
fear went into overdrive.

I glance at the clock on the phone. Mom is right. It's been
an hour since the gala started and no sign of Ty. Should I be
concerned? Should I ask Stevenson if he's seen him? I throw the
phone into my clutch and then take a deep breath to calm my
racing heart.

As if I conjured him up from my frazzled mind, Ty stands
less than a foot away from me, clean-shaven and as gorgeous as
ever in a classic cut tuxedo, looking like a yummy treat my mouth
had been watering for. We lock eyes, and for long moments, we
say nothing, just taking each other in.

I can't tell whether he's pleased to see me or not. A giant
ball of worry takes root in the pit of my stomach.

CHAPTER 70

TY

T Y WAS STILL angry with her, so how dare she show up to the gala looking sexier than any woman had a right to look? He'd left Cooper at home without saying a word, not caring whether she attended the gala. Over the past few weeks, he had been cold, indifferent to her feelings, and ignored the look of hurt on her face, the tears in her eyes, when he treated her like she wasn't worth much.

She had wept hard into her pillow at night when she thought he was sound asleep. Listening to her muffled wails into the wee hours of the morning made him feel like a heartless toad, so he had moved into a guest bedroom.

Was she truly sorry? Everything in her demeanor and actions since he learned of her infidelity indicated she was remorseful. That it would never happen again. That she wanted to save their marriage more than anything. Ty hadn't given her the chance to make things right, cutting her with his words and actions.

Ty had never seen Cooper dress so seductively. He had to admit, despite himself, his wife was smoking hot. He was still angry, though. *Let's not get carried away.* But wow! She certainly had his attention. *She's trying. Won't you meet her halfway?*

Without thinking, he leaned into her and brought his lips down on hers in a hard, passionate kiss that temporarily stunned her. But then she responded and soon fireworks exploded in the little alcove, with panting and writhing and moaning and hands groping frantically. Ty emptied his brain of all thought except for one: how much he missed his Cooper and wanted her back.

A deep, baritone voice burst through the smoke. "Get a room."

They untangled themselves, and after Ty got his breathing under control, he said, "Let's go home."

CHAPTER 71

KRISTINA

AFTER THE VALET pulled up to the entrance of the venue with her Lexus, she didn't bother tipping him. She hopped into the car and sped off, tires screeching, leaving a cloud of bellowing smoke in her wake. The horror of what she had witnessed landed like a terrifying, deafening clap of thunder.

By the time she made it home after almost crashing twice, Kristina couldn't stop bawling, sitting in the middle of the floor of her living room, still dressed in her gala gown.

Just when she thought they were getting close, that she would have what she always wanted, Abbie swooped in yet again and ruined everything.

Kristina had gone to the ladies' room to freshen up. On her way back to the gala, a couple caught her eye. She couldn't see clearly at first, but as she approached, her eyes almost fell from their sockets.

They were so hot and bothered they didn't notice anyone. What made it even worse, Ty hadn't been wearing his wedding ring when Kristina ran into him earlier in the evening. He had been pleased to see her.

"You look beautiful," he had said.

Her heart soared, his words like magic dust to her ears.

No matter how hard she tried to be impervious to his charm, she melted whenever she was near him.

"Thank you. How many hearts did you set a flutter this evening? You look quite dashing in that tux. I think you're giving Bond a run for his money in the debonair Olympics."

He had given her that look that said, *Aren't you exaggerating just a bit?* The man was a top surgeon at one of the country's leading hospitals, yet he lacked the arrogance and self-importance she had witnessed in a few of his colleagues, some less talented than him.

Kristina had gotten a taste of what it would be like to be Ty's wife when, throughout the evening, streams of people came up to him and thanked him for all he was doing for the hospital, not only as a surgeon but through his research, humanitarian work, and the new start-up venture.

She was used to these kinds of events when she was married to Callum, but people sucked up to him not because they admired him, but because they wanted something from him.

With Ty, people genuinely respected and admired him. Between her non-profit and healthcare experience and his work, they would be an unstoppable force for good. They would be mentioned in the same breath as the world's leading philanthropists.

All the dreams she had for them as a couple were nothing more than a pile of rubbish fit for a bonfire.

Did this brilliant man fall for the tired and cliché, the femme fatale stunt Abbie pulled with that dress that straddled the line between tasteful and slutty? If Kristina had known it was that easy to get him breathing hot and heavy with his hands all over her, she would've purchased dozens of such outfits.

One thing was certain. Ty had lied, made her believe he wanted her with nice words and gestures. But all the while,

Kristina was simply a distraction until he and Abbie reconciled. History had repeated itself, and she had no one to blame but herself for allowing it to happen again, the same as when they were together at Yale.

Fresh tears sprang to Kristina's eyes as she recalled that Ty didn't have the decency to tell her he was engaged to Abbie. The blinding ring on Abbie's finger had sent shockwaves through Kristina; then a hot, searing rage had taken hold.

The same thing was happening to her again. But this time, Kristina would control the outcome.

It was clear that Ty would never be hers. So there was only one thing left to do.

CHAPTER 72

ABBIE

THE NEXT MORNING, Saturday, Ty and I lie in bed. A slight awkwardness hangs in the air as the pitiless summer sunlight filters through the curtains. After we left the gala last night, we exchanged not a single word. We communicated in other ways, and although I'm not certain we've officially made up, it's my hope we can take tentative steps toward repairing the damage to our marriage that I've caused.

Turning to me, Ty says, "We need to talk, Cooper."

Oh no. Is he going to tell me last night was a mistake, run back to the guest bedroom and ice me out once again? I couldn't take it. I can't take any more of his rejection, contempt, the scorn in his eyes that said I'd been downgraded from queen to peasant girl.

Or perhaps it's about the bombshell Stevenson dropped on me about Ty's OR incident and him needing to get his head straight. Either way, whatever Ty is about to say will have major repercussions for our life, our future.

"What is it?" I ask, with more calm than I feel.

He props himself up on one elbow and strokes my face. "I don't want there to be any more secrets between us. I want a clean slate, and that means it all needs to come out."

307

"What all needs to come out?"

"You were right. There is something I've been keeping from you. The trip to California gave me room to think."

"And what did you conclude?"

"That I'm a hypocrite. It's my fault you were vulnerable to Christian."

I pop up into a sitting position so fast I almost injure myself. "What are you talking about? I'm trying to take accountability for my mistake and saying it's your fault is not helping."

"Listen to me," he says, sitting up. "When you told me about you and Christian, it ripped my heart out. But I had to look at the big picture and fess up to my part in the whole debacle."

This is going to be far worse than I anticipated. From the look on Ty's face, he's about to crack wide open like eggs for a breakfast omelet.

"First off, I hope you will be kinder to me than I've been to you. It's a lot to ask, but the truth is, I don't want to do life without you, Cooper. It may sound dramatic," he pauses and takes my hand in his. "What I'm about to tell you…please don't leave me."

"What is it? You're scaring me."

He says, "Christian and I plotted to take out Zach Rossdale. His death wasn't a prison fight gone terribly wrong. We orchestrated the fight with the help of the warden."

An icy chill invades my veins, robbing me of thought and speech. My mouth moves soundlessly as I attempt to speak, but the words catch in my throat. I pull the duvet tightly around me to ward off the chill, to stop the tremors in my fingers.

Ty sits rigid, his eyes closed as though he can't look at me.

When I do speak, it doesn't sound like me. The weak, raspy voice sounds alien. "Why? Why did you and Christian do something so…"

I can't finish the thought. Because the other thought clamoring for my attention is too awful to let it take root. *My husband is a murderer.*

I watch as Ty slowly opens his eyes. "Zach's killing rampage didn't end in New Haven fifteen years ago. He was coming for you, Cooper. Out of desperation, I asked for Christian's help to neutralize him."

"Whose idea was it to kill Zach?" *Does it really matter whose idea it was?* Like a train wreck I can't look away from, I keep asking questions that may help me understand the indefensible.

"When Brynn said he wouldn't stop until you were finished, I panicked. I couldn't stand by and allow the man who had brutally assaulted you and left you for dead the opportunity to finish the job.

"I just didn't see a way out. As long as Zach was alive, you and our kids would never be safe. I'll hold that conviction until the day I die."

His shoulders sag, and Ty closes his eyes once more, as though wading through the pain, the burden of carrying this horrific secret, and perhaps wondering if one day it would come back to haunt us.

"Who else knows?" I ask.

"Christian, me, my dad. I'm so sorry, Cooper." He picks up my hand in his and holds on tight, as though he's afraid I might pull away.

"I save lives for a living, but like I told my dad, I was thinking like a husband and father, a protector, not a doctor. The idea was way out there when Christian proposed it, not something I would ever consider. But he left the decision up to me, whether to proceed. So I told him I was all in, one hundred percent."

Ty buries his head in my chest and repeatedly begs me to forgive him. As he does so, conflicting emotions overtake me.

How could they do something so ruthless, so vile, and stay silent for three long years?

On the other hand, their actions may have saved my life. In all honesty, Zach's death freed me. For ten long years, I lived in fear he would make a move against me and my family in retaliation for sending him to prison with my testimony. Those fears were confirmed when he sent people to take out Lucas.

It wasn't a matter of *if* he would try to kill me; it was a matter of *when* he would succeed. Am I glad he's dead? No tears from me, not a single one. Yet, the idea of Ty and Christian cooking up this scheme and keeping it from me will take some time to process.

"I could never condone what you and Christian did, Ty. But I don't know what would have happened had Zach lived. I could have ended up dead, gone from you and the kids, my parents. I hope telling me frees you from the burden of carrying the secret."

I add, "But I worry your actions will come back to haunt us in unforeseen ways."

"Christian said his father took care of it." Ty explains how the warden contacted Alan, demanding more money.

"Let's hope that he does." I know Alan well enough to recognize the decision to take care of the warden is not about protecting anyone but his son and his business empire. If Ty and I also benefit, it's a plus I'm willing to wholeheartedly embrace.

"Thank you for telling me," I say. "There's something else I want to discuss. What happened in the OR recently? Why did Stevenson tell you to get your head straight?"

"I walked out of a procedure." Ty explains that he was so wrecked by my betrayal that he couldn't concentrate.

"So where do we go from here?" I ask.

Ty says nothing for a while. He must have given the

subject some thought before I asked the question. What is there to think about now?

"Can you emphatically promise me that nothing like this will ever happen again, you and Christian?"

"I promise. Besides, Christian has moved on. I take it as a sign he understands my heart belongs to you exclusively."

"What do you mean he's moved on?"

"He and Callie are together."

Ty's forehead forms a pleat. "I didn't see that coming."

"Neither did I. But I'm happy for them. Are you okay with this turn of events? Callie and I are best friends, so we'll be seeing Christian."

"I can handle it if you can."

"So you worked through your hostility toward him?"

"My hostility toward Christian has significantly diminished with this news." He cracks a smile.

I'm a grown woman for goodness sakes, but my heart does a somersault. The love of my life smiled at me, after he had banished me to his version of the ice age for weeks.

Not wanting to reveal how thrilled I am, I say, "You didn't answer my question. Where do we go from here?"

Ty reaches over to the nightstand and pulls open the drawer. He retrieves an envelope and then closes the drawer.

"Our fifteenth wedding anniversary is this December, a few months from now. It would be fitting to return to the Alexandra Rose Inn and Spa. It was where we spent our first night as husband and wife, the first time we made love."

Handing me the envelope, he adds, "It's a photo of the room we stayed in during our visit. They've renovated it since. It's been reserved for us."

I take the envelope from him but don't bother looking at the photo. I'm touched beyond words at the gesture. During our first stay, our wedding night, so much tragedy surrounded us. The idea of returning fifteen years later, triumphant, that we had survived every obstacle placed before us, brings tears to my eyes.

To make this celebration truly special, though, I have a few things to take care of.

CHAPTER 73

———◆◆◆———

TY

STEVENSON'S TEXT CAME in at six forty-five on Wednesday morning.

> Meet me in my office now. It's urgent!

Ty didn't like the dread spreading through his insides like a contagion. His first surgery of the day wasn't until nine, but he had patients to check on, operative notes to finalize, and discharge paperwork to handle.

When he walked into Stevenson's office, he didn't like the vibe.

"Thanks for coming on such short notice. Have a seat," Stevenson said, gesturing to the empty chair. "I'll try not to take up too much time; you have a full schedule for the day."

As head of cardiothoracic surgery, Stevenson was always pressed for time and usually got to the point quickly. Whenever he got polite and started saying things like, "Thanks for coming on short notice," something bad was about to go down.

"What's going on?" Ty asked. "You said it was urgent."

"I'm afraid it is." Stevenson leaned forward on the desk, his elbow bumping up against a family photo. Ty detected tiny beads of sweat forming on his forehead. The usually confident and sometimes abrasive Stevenson was nervous. He rearranged the family photo and pinched his nose.

"Ty, you've been reported to human resources for sexual harassment. The head of HR will contact you, but I wanted to speak with you first. Obviously, the hospital takes any such accusation seriously. There will be an investigation. I suggest you hire an attorney to look after your interests."

Ty felt as though Stevenson had whipped out a knife and made grotesque stab wounds all over Ty's body, slowly draining the life out of him. He went dizzy, black spots dancing in front of his eyes. This must be what acute shock felt like. *Focus. Stay calm.*

"Who made the complaint? I don't get it; this doesn't make sense, Stevenson." His voice rose in volume, and he detected a small tremor. Ty took a deep breath and continued. "That's like somebody accusing me of overthrowing a foreign government. Impossible."

Stevenson's grave expression left no doubt that this was going to be a huge mess with major implications for his career, the hospital, his family.

Stevenson said, "I'm having trouble believing it as well."

"Because it isn't true. Someone is obviously screwing with me." The minute the phrase left his mouth, he realized it was a poor choice of words. "Sorry, it's a fantasy, Stevenson. I would never do such a thing, and I don't know who would hate me so much as to make up these sick accusations."

"I didn't want you blindsided. Like I said, HR will contact you and sit down with you to discuss the situation and how best to handle it. This is only the beginning."

"What does that mean?"

"It means the hospital board could suspend you until the investigation is completed. I'm not saying it will happen; you haven't been found guilty of any wrongdoing. I'm simply laying out worst-case scenarios so you and Abbie can prepare."

Ty stood and stuck his hands in his pockets. He didn't want Stevenson to hear his heart thudding in his chest, ready to burst out.

"Who? Who would make up such vicious lies and for what purpose? What have I done to deserve being the target of some sociopath and their sick game?"

Stevenson swallowed several times. "HR didn't want me to say anything until they've had a chance to speak with you. It's my understanding that Kristina Hayward Saxena from the development office filed the complaint."

"Kristina?" Ty's legs were about to collapse under him, so he retook his seat. "Kristina did this? Why?"

"HR didn't go into details. So you know her?"

"Yes. We dated briefly in college. Our history is complicated because I broke up with her and proposed to my wife. Kristina never got over it and to this day despises Cooper. Is this some kind of sick revenge scheme?"

"You tell me. As your supervisor, it's my job to comply with HR. I'm happy to be a character witness for you. Your work as a surgeon speaks for itself." Stevenson leaned in closer. "But Ty, things could get ugly. This is not something we can keep under wraps for too long. I'll do my best to keep a lid on it, but it will blow up."

"So she just launched a complaint with HR with no evidence and I could lose my career, my livelihood?"

"HR says they have evidence, incriminating voicemails, emails, and even proof that you sent her flowers."

Unease hung in the air like the stench of a rotting corpse. Suddenly, Ty wanted to be anywhere but here, in this office, facing his boss, a man whose respect he had earned, who had been his mentor and unfailing champion.

How did he get here? Kristina was the one who planted a kiss on him. A kiss that was neither invited nor appreciated. Was that it? Did she get angry when he didn't return the kiss and told her it shouldn't have happened?

Was she so angry that she decided to get even? That still didn't make sense, not enough to warrant something of this magnitude.

It wouldn't matter that they would eventually clear Ty of any wrongdoing. Once something like sexual harassment accusations were made, it stayed with you, followed you like a permanent albatross around your neck.

If Ty were to leave MGH, not that he wanted to, the accusation would pop up on the radar of every potential hospital or clinic considering him for a position. Or maybe not. An accusation was not proof of guilt.

What had he missed? In all his interactions with Kristina, she seemed normal. A little overly solicitous? Yes, but Ty didn't take it to heart, had no inkling that she would flip out and lose her mind.

"Whatever so-called evidence they have was fabricated by Kristina. I promise you that." Ty knew how bad things looked. He tapped into his memory, trying to recall how many times he was alone with Kristina.

In London. The back stairwell last week when he had been at one of the lowest points in his life. When he invited her to his house for the dinner party.

Ty recognized how Kristina could easily spin that narrative. Stevenson said something about evidence. The only written communication Ty had with Kristina was texting her to meet him so he could invite her to the dinner.

He was innocent, yet he could see how a case could be

made. How benign comments or actions could be misconstrued, twisted, and altered until the truth was no longer recognizable.

What did Kristina hope to gain? What was her end game? And why didn't he pick up on the signs that her pleasant demeanor when she interacted with him was a mask for the broken mind that lay beneath?

"I appreciate the heads up," Ty said, and stood. "I've worked too hard to let anyone ruin my career and reputation with malicious lies. If Kristina wants a fight, she's got it."

CHAPTER 74

ABBIE

MERE SECONDS IS all it takes for lives to irrevocably change. And in those fleeting seconds, you wish you could rewind time to avert disaster, change the trajectory of the incoming missile that would eventually strike, causing your life to explode in spectacular fashion.

Ty and I are in the kitchen dissecting the psychologically challenging puzzle that is Kristina, what sent her over the edge. What was her tipping point? Did she decide, like a petulant child who can't get her way, that she would take her marbles and go home, burn our lives to the ground in some metaphorical middle-finger gesture?

"Are you sure there's not a trace of evidence, nothing that could be misconstrued or misinterpreted or twisted into a narrative that could support Kristina's claims?" I pour coffee into Ty's mug on the kitchen island.

Anxiety is embedded in his expression. "What is it? If we're going to call Kristina's bluff, you need to lay everything out on the table. These are serious allegations, and these days, even a whiff of sexual misconduct is enough to ruin someone, never mind the legalities."

I take the seat across from Ty and reach over to squeeze

his hand. I serve up an encouraging smile despite the anxious thoughts swirling around in my head.

I know my husband. He would never do what he's being accused of. Not Ty, not the man who cared for me after my own gruesome brush with sexual assault. He knows the stakes. The damage it can cause, the no going back. The pre and the post. Because no one who endures that kind of human misery is ever the same afterward.

"There was one thing. I didn't think much of it at the time, but I can see how it could be twisted around, made to look like I had crossed a line."

I sit up straighter as though bracing for impact. Whatever he's about to say, I will handle it. Nothing is more important than shining the spotlight on Kristina's deceit and fabrication, exposing the ugly underbelly of her psychosis.

Ty sips his coffee and places the mug down. He splays his hands out on the table as though he has nothing to hide.

"It was the day I walked out of the procedure. Kristina showed up in the back stairwell. She was polite; we talked. It seemed like a different Kristina. Not the aggressive, brash version we're used to. This version of her was softer, lighter, humorous even."

"That little viper was setting you up so she could rip you to shreds with her fangs. It was all an act, and you were too vulnerable to recognize the ploy."

"Maybe. I wasn't thinking clearly that day. It took too much energy to put my guard up or to dissect her words. Anyway, when I wasn't looking, she planted a kiss on me."

"What?" I almost fall out of the chair, outrage prickling at every cell in my body. I calm myself down long enough to ask, "And what was your reaction?"

"She took me by surprise, so there was no reaction. I didn't kiss her back. I made it clear she shouldn't have kissed me because we were both married."

Is that what sent her over the edge? Her bold move stopped cold, rejected, and then the realization that Ty would never fall into her trap? All of that had sent her on a destructive path? Despite all I know about Kristina, both past and present, there's a part of me that's frightened for Ty, for us, our family.

Kristina filed a formal complaint with HR, so that's in writing. Then there's the power dynamic. How easy would it be for her to convince the hospital's leadership that Ty used his position as a surgeon to intimidate her, threaten her, exert power over her? She's already proven to be a gifted liar and manipulator.

What if she succeeds in taking him down? Does the truth even matter, or would it become a casualty of everyone ducking for cover? Would the heavy cloud of accusation hang over Ty forever?

"I believe you. A thousand percent." The words tumble out my mouth because they need to be said, an official stamp that he never has reason to doubt my loyalty again.

But what if I'm wrong? What if my betrayal clouded his judgment and he did something out of character or turned to Kristina in some subconscious effort to punish me and things got out of hand?

A mask of worry takes over Ty's face. "Thanks for saying that, Cooper. Did you ever doubt me, thought that I felt something for Kristina and behaved inappropriately?"

"No. Never." My response is swift.

This is a clear-cut case of a vindictive ex with a toxic obsession, like some massive wound left untreated and has now turned gangrenous.

Ty says, "I hope we never have to explain this to the kids. It would kill me. They're teenagers; we can't hide this from them if the situation escalates."

His words are like a powerful shot of brutal reality that makes me realize: if we are to diffuse this mess and kick Kristina out of our lives permanently, all the rules must go out the window.

"You need legal counsel. We don't know what's coming our way. The hospital, any hospital in this situation, will protect their interests above all else. They don't want to get sued if Kristina decides to expand on her empire of lies and fabrication."

He nods absently.

"What is it?" I ask.

"Parham capital is ready to sign off on the Series A funding. The offer might be off the table once they get wind of this accusation."

"So we'll make sure they don't. Kristina doesn't have a leg to stand on. You know, for someone with her track record, she shouldn't be causing this much trouble."

"What do you mean?"

"Savannah Davis's death was no accident, Ty."

"What? I haven't heard her name in a while. I asked you to stay clear of that investigation. It has nothing to do with us."

"Oh, but it does."

"What do you mean?"

"The killer got the wrong woman."

Confusion blooms on his face. "What are you saying, Cooper?"

Without hesitation, I say, "The bullet that killed Savannah Davis Patterson in Montego Bay was meant for me, compliments of Kristina. But because of the striking resemblance between Savannah and me, the killer shot the wrong woman."

Ty gapes at me for long seconds. His expression morphs from shock to horror and back again. "Cooper, that's crazy. Where would you get an idea like that?"

"Kristina has a friend by the name of Seamus Jones."

"What does that have to do with Montego Bay?"

"Seamus Jones was a sniper in the British army. He could make a kill shot at a distance of two-and-a-half miles."

Ty grabs his coffee and takes a long gulp. His hands tremble as he places the mug back on the counter.

He says, "How do you know this? What makes you think this Seamus guy has anything to do with what went down in Jamaica?"

I lay it all out, explaining the connection between Seamus and Kristina, the photo I found on social media, and the most compelling piece of evidence: that Seamus flew from Nairobi to Montego Bay within the timeframe of our second honeymoon, the same time both Savannah and I were there.

"Snipers of that caliber don't miss, and Seamus didn't. He thought he was seeing me, Abbie, through the scope of his rifle and had no way of knowing there was another guest at the resort who could be my identical twin. As for how I know this, I hired someone to dig into Kristina's past."

"And you did all this behind my back?"

"Well, you weren't in a talkative mood. When I found out from Frances that Kristina was capable of ordering an attack on another woman she considered her romantic rival, it clicked for me. It wasn't a stretch to imagine she would graduate to murder for hire."

Ty shakes his head, grappling with the enormity of the situation.

"Think about it, Ty. Kristina knew we were headed to Jamaica. She was humiliated that night of the dinner when her husband showed up and it was clear we set her up.

"Then I told her to go back to London. With that kind of rage and resentment simmering, is it so hard to believe she wanted me eliminated? I've worked up a psychological profile of her, and I'm telling you, she's capable."

I fail to mention that I have certain levers in place in case things go sideways or that my London investigator is looking into things I have no business looking into.

LATER THAT AFTERNOON, I retreat to my office to make some calls, check and return email messages, and go over every detail of the plan one last time. I can't afford to make mistakes in case the police ask questions.

Minutes into mapping out the plan on my version of a police crime board, my phone pings on the desk. Then it pings several more times. I abandon the board and scoop up the phone. My Google alerts are coming in fast and furious. They're alerts for Christian. I'd all but forgotten about them. I tap the screen to read the first one.

It takes me to an article from *Bloomberg News*.

LEVITRON-BLAIR COO STEPS DOWN

What it Means for the Media Giant

Levitron-Blair's chief Operating officer, Christian Wheeler, son of Chairman and CEO Alan Wheeler, has resigned his position to launch McClellan Plus Media, a direct competitor to Levitron-Blair.

A smile tugs at my lips. I'm so proud of Christian for stepping out from under the shadow of his father and LB to forge his own path. I check out a few additional alerts, including Yahoo Finance, *The Financial Times*, and a segment from Squawk Box.

All the stories are similar in tone: what this means for Levitron-Blair, will LB competitors interpret this move as dissent in the executive ranks, and is LB vulnerable.

Some of the articles discuss how Christian's start-up is well funded with a world-class leadership team already in place, including two former LB executives and a handful in the marketing, technology, and finance functions he recruited from the Fortune 1000 ranks as well as Silicon Valley.

The headline in an opinion piece makes me smile big and wide. THE RISE OF A NEW MEDIA TITAN? I screenshot the headline and compose a text.

> R-E-S-P-E-C-T

After a few seconds tick by, a response comes in—a meme of a guy in his car with arms flailing around in excitement. Another text follows.

Christian

> Thank you, Abbie. I'll be forever in your debt.

I leave it right there and return to my task: the plot to take down Kristina before it's too late.

CHAPTER 75

ABBIE

EVERYTHING IS FALLING apart. Not only is a full-on investigation into Kristina's allegations in progress, the meeting with HR to discuss said allegations was shocking. Now the hospital board is involved. Kristina produced "evidence" that Ty was pursuing her romantically and got angry when she rebuffed him.

So-called evidence included voice messages, emails, texts, and a letter from Ty in his handwriting declaring that Kristina is the love of his life. The letter also alleges that Ty made a mistake marrying me because I couldn't stay faithful. We're not allowed to have access to any of the documents at this point.

Ty and I are trying to contain the situation before it spreads all over the hospital and makes its way into the public domain.

We sit in the living room with Shannon Murphy, the lawyer we hired, an attractive, stylishly dressed woman in her forties. She places her briefcase on the floor next to her after she removes a file from it. Ty and I sit across from her.

"I don't care what so-called evidence Kristina has," I begin. "It's all fabricated. Do they honestly think that a man of Ty's intelligence, knowing how unstable Kristina is, would communicate with her in such a blatant fashion?

"A letter declaring his love for her? Please," I say, rolling my eyes. "It would be funny if it wasn't so pathetic."

"I don't have to tell you how serious the allegations are. It's complicated by the fact that Ty dated Kristina in the past," Shannon says.

Ty says, "The complaint cannot leave MGH. The last thing I need is for Kristina to contact the state medical board with her pack of lies. The letter is obviously a forgery. She's been to our home. I don't know whether she had a look around when no one was watching."

"First things first," Shannon says. "Let's nail down every single interaction you've had with Kristina: where, when, date and time, as well as the subject of discussion."

"I can do that," Ty says. "What else?"

"A handwriting sample to compare to the letter you allegedly wrote. The key to exposing the truth is to be transparent, so transparent that it's uncomfortable."

Shannon continues, "The good news is that you have an impeccable record, no complaints of any kind have been filed against you. Plus, colleagues, including Dr. Stevenson, will testify to your character."

"What about discrediting Kristina?" Ty asks.

"If we can demonstrate that Kristina has a history of questionable behavior, it could go a long way toward dismissing the complaint."

I ask, "What kind of information would qualify as questionable behavior, enough to discredit Kristina, prove she fabricated the whole thing for revenge?"

"A history of filing false complaints for example."

"So if we can prove Kristina has done this before, filed a sexual harassment complaint that was false, we can shut this whole thing down?"

"That would be a big help, go a long way toward clearing Dr. Rambally. But it's not necessarily a slam dunk."

"What about attempted murder?" I ask.

Ty almost catches a case of whiplash. He quickly turns his gaze away from Shannon to focus on me.

I put on my therapist voice for Shannon's benefit. "I've learned some disturbing details about Kristina that, as a trained clinical psychologist, really bother me. Her mental state is of grave concern. I suspect it has something to do with this ludicrous allegation."

"What do you mean, Abbie?" Shannon asks.

Ty and I exchange a look.

"I have information from a trusted source that Kristina may have ordered an attack on a romantic rival. I don't have any solid proof, we're not in the court of law right now, but it speaks to a disturbing psychological profile."

I briefly but carefully outline my history with Kristina and the Sita Kapoor acid attack, and then I end with my humble professional opinion that Kristina exhibits sociopathic tendencies and could also suffer from Narcissistic Personal Disorder.

Some of the information I gathered from Ryan's investigation is thrown in to bolster the narrative that Kristina has serious psychological problems and cannot be believed. For example, she falsely accused one of her Oxford professors of sexual harassment because he refused to change a bad grade she received on an important exam.

I end my tirade with the subtle hint that, in my experience, it's not uncommon for people with Kristina's background to be treated by a psychiatrist or even spend time at a psychiatric facility.

I know for a fact that Kristina was admitted to a psychiatric facility in London, part of the file detailing her medical history that Ryan put together based on his investigation. Kristina had been seeing Dr. Cressida Nelson, a prominent London psychiatrist with whom I met during my recent trip. Dr. Nelson couldn't tell me much because of patient confidentiality, but I accomplished what I set out to do with that meeting.

Not even Ty knows all the things I uncovered from that trip, thanks to Ryan and Frances. None of the information I uncovered can help Ty without exposing my own questionable actions. A catch twenty-two of epic proportions.

Shannon says, "It's a start but not enough to go on, Abbie. Since you've never treated Kristina, we can't get your assessment to stick."

"What if I were to give you a name, someone your office can contact discreetly? Someone who will confirm Kristina has a history of lying and making false claims?"

I provide Shannon with the contact in London who can offer irrefutable proof that Kristina never graduated from Oxford and lied on her resume when she applied for the job at MGH.

Only I can bring an end to this nightmare. After all, Kristina came for me. It's time to make my final move.

CHAPTER 76

ABBIE

Let your plans be as dark and impenetrable as night, and when you move, fall like a thunderbolt. —*Sun Tzu, The Art of War*

I DON'T CARE what legal counsel says. I'm not staying away. She's going to have to face me. I ambush Kristina in her office once more. She comes through the door with a white Styrofoam container and bottled water in hand. Looks like she just picked up lunch from the cafeteria. I'm seated at her desk, leaning back in the chair opposite hers. Kristina freezes when she sees me.

Then she slowly closes the door behind her, places the food on the desk, and says, "What do want? You're not supposed to be here; you and Ty are to stay away from me."

"Well, Kristina, last time I checked you didn't accuse me of sexually harassing you, so I see no reason we can't have a civilized conversation."

She remains standing, arms folded, her expression dark, lips curled into a sneer.

"Your husband is about to lose his career, reputation, everything. That fairy-tale life you've been living will come crashing down."

Funny how all of a sudden it's *your husband*. When she was throwing herself at him, it was always Ty. And she doesn't insist Ty is guilty. Only that our perfect life is about to come crashing down.

Kristina just confirmed what I suspected. She went with the nuclear option. *If I can't have him, no one can.*

I say, "It's just us girls here, Kristina. We know the allegations are nothing but toxic lies. Tell me, how did you pull it off, make your so-called evidence look and sound so convincing?"

I have a theory, but I want to see her squirm. It's not difficult to use technology these days if you know what you're doing. You can make a text or phone call or email look and sound like it came from anyone you choose. *I should know.* The so-called letter from Ty in his handwriting? It's a joke.

"I didn't have to do anything. You cheated on Ty, and he turned to me for comfort. I refused to be his second choice, the one he turned to after he couldn't have what he wanted. I refuse to fall into that trap again, the way he treated me at Yale when he dumped me for you."

"Who told you I cheated on Ty?"

"He did, of course. You broke the man's heart, but that wasn't my problem. He came on too strong, and I couldn't handle it anymore, the threats, the intimidation."

As I look at Kristina, I wonder how she can summon tears at the drop of a hat. Her face is the epitome of a broken, scared, victimized woman.

"No, Kristina. You sent Ty a photo of Christiana and me together. That's how he found out. Care to explain how the photo came into your possession?"

Shock creeps over her face, replacing the phony sadness of just moments ago. "I...I...don't know what you mean."

She turns away from me, unable to meet my gaze. Then

she faces me once more, defiance radiating off her.

She says, "What matters is your husband's campaign of increasingly hostile threats after I told him to back off, that I wasn't interested in being his backup girl or his mistress. He got aggressive with me."

"Do you even hear yourself? Weren't you telling me, not so long ago, how kind and gentle Ty was when you were together? Now, he turned aggressive on you? Imagine that."

I shake my head, still grappling with the nerve of this woman, how effortlessly the lies slide off her tongue, how easily she sticks to her story, her wicked lies.

I continue. "Just goes to show you can never really tell about people, huh, Kristina? The man whose child you were so devastated to lose turned on you just like that." I snap my fingers for emphasis.

Her eyes go big and wide. I don't give her a chance to speak. I continue, "You never suffered a miscarriage. You were never pregnant with Ty's child. In fact, you've never been pregnant in your life. Isn't that right, Kristina?"

My words land like a punch to her face. She visibly flinches and backs up slowly into the wall. "How could you be so cruel, Abbie? So callous about my suffering? I thought therapists were compassionate people."

I suspect Kristina may have suffered from Pseudocyesis, a psychological condition that causes a woman to believe she's pregnant, even though she isn't carrying a child.

The condition is further complicated by the fact that it mimics symptoms of real pregnancy. As for the miscarriage, with Kristina's fragile mental state, she most likely made up the scenario. Even back then.

"I am compassionate. But I'm also human, Kristina. It's hard to show compassion for someone who's determined to ruin my family. The miscarriage was a lie meant to gain sympathy from Ty, and drive a wedge in our marriage."

The determined gleam in her eyes says she won't give up this vendetta.

"So what? You and Ty thought you could make a fool of me, humiliate me. But you're paying attention now, aren't you? You'll both get what's coming to you. I'll finally have the last laugh. I realized too late what a manipulator your husband is."

Interesting tactic. I say, "And when did this life-changing realization hit you?"

"At the gala."

I frown, searching my brain for a connection that would make sense. What does the gala have to do with any of this? Then it hits me. *She saw us.* Ty and me, kissing in the little alcove down from the ladies' room. That's what set her off. I make a mental note. This tidbit could be important.

"The gala? Ty and I arrived separately, so I have no clue what you're talking about."

"Don't you?" she asks, her tone scornful. "Weren't you all over each other near the ladies' room? Two adults acting like teenagers who needed a cold shower?"

"Ohh," I say slowly, drawing out the word. "You saw that, and it made you lose what little was left of your sick mind. I get it now."

I glare at her, not saying anything for a while. The silence stretches out, awkward and convicting. Kristina can't look me in the eye. Her gaze lands on a spot on the desk.

I say, "Do you know how many women out there are victims of sexual harassment, many of them are unable to fight back for a variety of reasons? And here you are, making up lies, trying to ruin an innocent man because your little feelings got hurt."

"Prove it, Abbie. Prove that what I've said isn't true, that my evidence isn't real. You can't, can you?"

"Leave Boston and never come back!" I rush to my feet and lean over Kristina. I'm done trying to be civil or reasonable. "Or I'll tell the hospital you never graduated from Oxford. That you lied on your resume."

She doesn't flinch, doesn't move a muscle, as though what I've said has no effect. Then a diabolical smile lights up her face, but her eyes remain cold and cruel.

"I don't think so, Abbie. My diploma from Oxford was presented to the appropriate hospital personnel. You can go check for yourself. But I know your secret, the one you tried to bury, so you're in no position to make threats."

Is she seriously posturing right now? It wouldn't surprise me if that diploma is falsified, much like the divorce papers Callum never signed. The diploma was just my opening bid, however.

"My secret? Is that one fabricated also, much like the evidence you have against Ty?"

"No, Abbie. It's about Lucas and his biological father, how Zach Rossdale really died."

Kristina's icy gaze tears through me, daring me to respond. I retake a seat, unable to move or speak for what seems like eons, long enough for Kristina's icy stare to morph from hate to triumph.

Alan took care of the problem with the warden. Kristina can't prove squat.

CHAPTER 77

——◦◦◦——

ABBIE

WHY ARE YOU bringing up my son? You know nothing about our family."

"Quite the contrary, Abbie. Lucas doesn't know Zach Rossdale was his father and that he raped you."

"You know how to use a computer to look up information. Congratulations."

"There's more, Abbie. Your Jamaican nanny, Olivia Stewart, got caught up in the whole sordid mess, all part of Zach's plot to take Lucas from you.

"But what's really fascinating is how Zach Rossdale met his bloody, violent, end. What do you think would happen if the authorities found out that you and Ty had a hand in Zach's murder?"

My body goes rigid. I try to assume a façade of nonchalance, like Kristina has completely gone off the rails, but I can't quite pull it off.

"Is there no end to your capacity for lying and weaving fantastical tales?" I ask.

"I visited Brynn in prison. I got the feeling she didn't much care for you. She was concerned about Lucas. That you never told him the truth about his father. I wonder how he would

334

react if he found out his mommy had his daddy killed? That his poor daddy never got a chance to meet him?"

I say nothing, waiting her out. She continues, "Lucas would never forgive you, would he? He would never forgive you for lying to him his entire life about his dad. I bet you never showed the boy a single photo of Zach and you made up some story about why Ty was raising him. Such a shame. Lucas deserves the truth, don't you think?"

My emotions whiplash inside me: rage, fear, hate for the woman standing in the room with me, an uncontrollable desire to do her harm circling round and round in my head. It's one thing to come after Ty and me. But what kind of monster would lie to a child, tell him his mother had his father killed? What kind of deranged lunatic would risk a child finding out his biological father raped his mother?

A long time ago, Lucas, while I was in college, before you were born, I met a man. At first he seemed nice and we started dating, but it turns out he was only pretending to be nice…We got into a huge fight and I got hurt…he died before I could tell him we were expecting you…

Is that why I look different from Blake and Alexis? Because the mean man was my original father and you got me a nicer daddy?

That conversation three years ago nearly broke me. Having to explain to Lucas why Brynn took him and her relation to Zach. What did Brynn say to Kristina? She may not know that Ty and Christian cooked up the scheme, but she definitely knows Ty was involved. Did Brynn suspect Zach's death wasn't a tragic accident? That's the only explanation that makes sense, why Kristina would use it as a threat.

I must protect Lucas at all costs. If he ever found out the truth, it would destroy him. There's no amount of therapy in this world that could heal my child if a bomb like this dropped in his lap.

Kristina uses my shock and dismay to press her advantage. She says, "I will go to the police, file criminal charges against Ty, and play the victim up until the appropriate time. By then, Ty will be totally destroyed and you along with him.

"After the damage is done, I will return to London but not before I present Lucas with my parting gift: a photo of his dad and the truth about you and your role in Zach's death. I might even tell Lucas you cried rape to get Zach sent to prison. I haven't decided yet, but I'm giving it serious thought."

I want to throw up. I clutch my stomach and force down the bile climbing up my throat.

Kristina opens her bag and comes up with a white envelope. She pulls out a folded piece of paper.

She comes to stand directly in front of me, waving the envelope. "Do you know what this is?

I don't respond. She says, "It's a signed confession from Donald A. Wilkins, the warden of the prison where Zach was serving time, confessing he helped Ty and Christian Wheeler orchestrate the attack that killed Zach. Yeah, Abbie, I knew it was Ty and Christian all along."

I say nothing. That letter is a pile of nonsense meant to intimidate me. Most likely a fake, just like her so-called evidence against Ty. Her fake divorce papers. Not worth my energy, so I ignore the phony signed confession she holds as if it's some historic document of infinite value.

Kristina says, "You get in the way of my plans, and I will go to the police with this letter. I will make sure Lucas also receives a copy."

"What do you hope to gain?" I ask calmly. "Your vindictive, desperate actions won't change anything. Tell me, what have you gained since you left London to chase after my husband besides rejection and humiliation?"

The hatred and defiance that burned hot and bright moments ago seem to seep out of Kristina. Her eyes go dull and lifeless, face flushed with embarrassment.

I add, "You're a loser who doesn't know when to quit the game and go home so she can live to fight another day. Brashness, manipulation, and lies don't make you strong, Kristina. In fact, I think you're a weak woman. Weak in mind, spirit, and character."

She grits her teeth. Then she says, "I'm not a loser. This time around, I have the power to bury both you and Ty."

I sigh dramatically. "You got me, Kristina. I don't know what to say. But I also have a parting gift for you. Care to find out what it is?"

"It doesn't matter, but why not? Amuse me."

I extract my phone from my purse, place it on the desk between us, and tap the screen. A conversation fills the room.

Seamus: "You're not the one who killed the wrong target. Why couldn't you handle Abbie Rambally another way?"

Kristina: "Abbie Cooper is a rotten, conniving, lying, cheating, manipulative, spoiled, entitled little witch, and she deserved to die. I don't feel bad about it, and neither should you. Ty would have been better off without her. You messed up and she's still breathing, so stop whining and spare me the burden of your growing conscience."

Kristina's eyes go wide. Her mouth hangs open in horror. "How...how did you..."

"Like you, I have all kinds of tricks up my sleeves, Kristina. Tell the hospital you made up the sexual harassment allegations. Or you're going down for murder."

But I know Kristina won't do the right thing. It's against her nature to back down.

That's why I have a backup plan in place. One that Kristina won't see coming.

CHAPTER 78

CHRISTIAN

H IS FATHER BARRELED through the entrance of his penthouse at seven thirty in the morning, not bothering with greetings or pleasantries of any kind. Alan Wheeler was on the war path. Christian expected that reaction. It had been several days, less than a week since he announced his departure from LB to start his own company.

Dad hadn't uttered a single word to Christian since the announcement. All media requests for a reaction, statement, or sit-down interview with Alan Wheeler were rebuffed. The company's highly skilled PR team went into overdrive and put out a statement that was as ambiguous as it was bland.

Christian Wheeler was a valued member of the Leviton-Blair leadership team, and we wish him the best of luck in his future endeavors. Levitron-Blair continues to focus on executing its business strategy and vision with bold, innovative leadership that has made the company a dominant force in the media landscape.

"Why did you do it?" his father asked, sitting across from Christian in the living room space. Alan glowered at him. "Is that how I raised you, to betray your family?"

Christian said nothing for a beat, meeting his father's gaze. He wanted to craft his next words carefully—respectful, yet forceful, leaving no doubt in his father's mind that this was a different Christian. One who would no longer tolerate his father's overbearing attitude.

"I don't know what you mean, Dad. I've worked for LB since college. Fourteen years to be precise. I gave it my all. It was time to move on. I fail to see how this equates to betraying the family."

"You did it to hurt me. Don't bother denying it. You wanted to lash out to make a point."

"What are you complaining about? You told me to grow up and take life seriously. I thought that's what I was doing, but you didn't see it that way."

"You could have warned me, Christian. Instead, you blindsided me and made me look ridiculous. My own son. Quitting the family company without telling his father. To add insult to injury, you took two key LB executives with you. I will never forget that."

"Nor should you." Christian all but growled his response.

Alan shifted ever so slightly in his seat. "Watch your tone. I'm still your father."

"And I'm a grown man. I put in my time at the family business. I'm proud of the work I did during my tenure. You saw things differently. And the only reason you're upset is because you didn't think I had the guts to stand up to you. To walk away from LB and forge my own path."

Christian ignored the look of bewilderment on his father's face and continued. "You can't do it, can you, Dad? Even now, you can't look me in the face and say, 'Well done, Christian. Well played.' I proved you wrong, and you can't stand it."

It pained Christian to admit that a small part of him still wanted his father's approval. Christian didn't quit LB to prove a point, but it would have been nice for his father to acknowledge that Christian made a gutsy move.

Start-ups have a high failure rate, although Christian had no doubt he would succeed. Ultimately, he recognized he would never get Alan's approval, which was partially the reason he left Levitron-Blair.

Christian said, "Don't you have fires to put out, media interviews to give where you explain that my leaving LB is irrelevant and inconsequential? At least that's how I interpreted the press statement the PR team put out."

"I wouldn't say your leaving was irrelevant or inconsequential," a sullen Alan admitted.

"You wouldn't? That's how you treated me. As though my work never mattered to you or the company. You went so far as to try and control my private life, using LB as bait. That's how little respect you have for me, Dad."

"You and Callie Furi; it's so sudden," his dad said, changing the subject abruptly.

Without missing a beat, Christian said, "Callie and I have known each other for almost twenty years. We've been close friends for many of those years. She believes in me and is a major investor in McLellan Plus Media. We're planning a future together and don't care what anyone thinks."

He let the statement hang in the air. His father could interpret it any way he wanted. And frankly, Christian neither wanted nor needed Alan's approval about his son's private life. Starting a relationship with Callie had been a delightful surprise that had changed Christian's life in unexpected ways. There were so many facets to her, and he relished getting to know every single one of them.

"Well, I guess you have everything all figured out," Alan said wearily.

"No one has everything all figured out. But I'm excited about this new venture and new chapter in my life."

Christian stood and walked over to where his father sat, stopping directly in front to him. "It's a funny thing, Dad. The women in my life were the ones who really saw me. Christian. Not Alan Wheeler's son. Not an extension of you. Just Christian. Abbie, Callie, and especially Mom were my champions, my fiercest advocates. They never gave up on me."

Alan said nothing. The silence stretched out for what seemed like eons.

Then Christian said, "What happened with the warden?"

Alan's head jerked upright. "What?"

"The warden, Donald Wilkins, the guy who has been blackmailing you to keep quiet about my involvement in Zach's death."

Christian needed to know. He had confessed to Callie, and she wanted him to make sure the warden problem went away permanently. Since getting rid of Zach was Christian's idea to begin with, he felt obligated to make sure the situation was handled. If his father hadn't taken care of business as promised, Christian would do it himself.

"Why do you ask? I told you I would take care of it."

"I need details. Please. I'm entering a new chapter in my life and don't want this fiasco hanging over my head, especially since Callie and I are talking about a future family."

Alan's brow shot up. "Really? Is Callie pregnant?"

"No, she isn't. So, will Donald Wilkins become a recurring thorn in our collective side?"

"He won't. With any luck, he'll never set foot on American soil again."

"What does that mean?"

"Do you think aiding in your half-brother's death and covering it up was Wilkins's first or only crime?"

Alan detailed how Wilkins had a long history of involvement

341

GLEDÉ BROWNE KABONGO

in illegal activities, including embezzling funds, corruption, bribery, and murder. He paid Wilkins three million dollars and offered a one-way ticket to Costa Rica where Wilkins had always wanted to retire.

His father made it clear. If Wilkins attempted to extort more money from him or his family or ever set foot on American soil again, Alan would provide evidence of Wilkins's crimes to the proper authorities and ensure he spent what remained of his life rotting in prison.

Christian said, "It all sounds good, but I still don't trust the man. He and I had a deal, including the money I paid him to keep quiet. I never expected he would go back on his word. There's no guarantee he's going to remain in Costa Rica. He could sneak into the country without you knowing. And what about the evidence he has regarding my involvement?"

"I'm not naïve, nor am I an amateur," Alan said.

"Meaning what?"

"I've prepared for that eventuality. Donald Wilkins is living out his last days as a free man. The ticket to Costa Rica is useless. In a few days, he'll be arrested. The evidence is already in the hands of prosecutors."

"So you double-crossed him the way he double-crossed me?"

"It was the only move that made sense. As for the evidence of your involvement, it's handled. I had people keeping tabs on Wilkins from the moment he reached out to demand more money for his silence. Eventually, they figured out where he was keeping the evidence and retrieved it. It's all destroyed. I saw to it personally."

"Thanks for telling me," Christian said when his father finished. "That makes me breathe easier."

"No one messes with my family and gets away with it," Alan said.

Then he stood and quietly walked out of the apartment.

CHAPTER 79

---•◦•---

CALLUM

C ALLUM SAXENA WAS a man ready to take matters into his own hands.

Enough was enough. His wife had brought him enough trouble to last him a lifetime. It was time to move on. He wanted to bid her farewell, face-to-face.

It was getting late, past ten p.m. Kristina had left the door open for him, and when he arrived inside, he called out to her.

"I'm here." He drew out the phrase, almost playfully. All was quiet in the apartment. Where had she gone? She was expecting him, after all.

After a visit to the bedroom and every space he could think of came up empty, Callum retrieved his phone from his suit jacket. He didn't have to make the call. Kristina entered the apartment and closed the door behind her.

"I was worried and about to call you," he said.

"I'm fine. Went for a late swim. It helps me relax."

Her wet hair and plush terry robe offered proof of the late-night swim.

"Why don't you have a shower, and I'll make us some tea," Callum said, as she placed her key on the kitchen counter.

Kristina's brow shot up. "Aren't we chivalrous? No insults,

343

subtle or otherwise, no barbs or takedown? Who are you, and what have you done with Callum?"

He shrugged. "You were right. We gave it a good run, didn't we? But it's time to move on. You have and so should I."

When his wife returned from her shower, dressed in a pair of pink cotton pajama pants and matching camisole, Callum handed her a steaming cup of tea. He sat at the kitchen table and invited her to do the same.

After taking a sip of tea, Kristina asked, "Tell me the truth, Callum. Why the sudden change of heart, the willingness to end our marriage after I've been begging you for years?"

Callum held her gaze and said nothing for a while. It broke his heart that this was the end. There was no other way out.

"After you forged the divorce documents, I was angry and wanted to retaliate, hurt you in the worst way possible. Then I thought, is it worth hanging on to a woman who would employ such devious tactics to prove how much she doesn't want me?

"It was the ultimate insult, humiliating. My wife wanted rid of me so badly that she resorted to fraud. You smashed my ego into tiny pieces."

"I asked nicely, Callum, for years. It didn't have to be this way. You were always so stubborn."

Calum's gaze swept around the kitchen, around the apartment. "Where is the good doctor? I thought he would have left his family for you, given the lengths you went to break up his marriage."

Kristina suddenly found the tea extraordinarily fascinating. She gazed into the mug, patiently waiting for the ceramic piece to give up some profound response to Callum's question.

"It didn't work out the way you hoped, did it? Ty Rambally chose his wife."

Kristina continued gazing into the mug, not saying anything.

Callum said wearily. "No matter. I'll sign the divorce papers and agree to the settlement you wanted—twenty million pounds."

Her head shot up. "Are you pulling my leg? I'm not interested in your silly games, Callum."

"No game," he said softly.

Kristina pushed her mug away. "What's going on here? This unexpected generosity, what brought it on?"

"I won't be around much longer."

"What do you mean?" She leaned forward, her expression urgent, curious.

"Stage four lung cancer."

Her mouth popped wide with shock. "I'm sorry, Callum. Can't they do anything? You must be getting the best care, so there's hope, right?"

"It's spreading to other parts of my body."

After a long silence, she asked, "How long?"

"Four to six months at the most."

Then the most peculiar thing happened. Her eyes glistened with unshed tears. The woman who had treated him with nothing but contempt. She felt sorry for him. Callum didn't want her pity.

"Stop it. I don't want your tears. I've lived a fantastic life. And even though you deprived me of the children I so desperately wanted, I've come to terms with it."

He added, his expression somber, "I suppose you were saving your womb for *him*, to bear his children. But he's all set in that department, isn't he? And here we both are, with no children of our own while Ty Rambally has three to carry on his legacy."

Callum sniffled and then stood. "No time for regrets. Let's get to it, shall we?"

Kristina followed him to the living room sofa. They both sat. Callum unlocked a briefcase and pulled out several documents.

"I had my attorney draw up these, real divorce papers. The terms are very much the same as the phony ones you had made. That was a work of genius, by the way. My hat's off to your forger."

"Callum." Kristina hesitated. "Perhaps in light of recent revelations, we—"

He rudely cut her off. "Save your pity, darling. I'm putting my affairs in order, and that includes the divorce you've wanted for so long. I have no heirs. I'm offering you a twenty-million-pound payout, and that's that."

Fifteen minutes later, having acquired her signature on the appropriate documents, Callum placed the papers back into the briefcase, locked it, and stood.

"I suppose this is it then," Kristina said awkwardly, still sitting.

"I suppose it is, "Callum said.

He then reached into his waistband, pulled out a Glock 19, and leaned over Kristina.

"Goodbye, darling," he said and shot her in the temple.

CHAPTER 80

HENRY

H ENRY DALTON STRODE toward the deck of his Milton home to enjoy a beer and the summer evening breeze but stopped short. He pivoted, strode to the kitchen counter, and plunked down the bottle of beer. Henry was overcome by an inexplicable yet urgent need to turn on the television.

He wished he hadn't.

The news story made him grimace. His warning had come to pass. *She played with fire and got burned*, he thought.

Turning to the reporter outside a luxury apartment complex in Bedford, with the flashing lights of police cruisers in the background, the news anchor asked for more details.

The reporter said, "The victim, who moved to the States from England two months ago was found shot to death in her apartment. Police refuse to disclose her identity until the next of kin has been notified. Bedford police is actively investigating the death and so far have no leads or motive for the killing."

Henry's mind drifted back to their second meeting at a café in Bedford.

"I don't know the real reason you want all this background information on this couple, but as someone who spent fifteen years plus in law enforcement, I can tell when something doesn't

347

smell right."

It was a bold move for him to speak to a client that way, a client who had been paying him a fortune for his services.

"I'm not paying you to assess my motives," Kristina had snapped. "If this assignment is too difficult for you, I can find someone else to get the job done without offering their unsolicited opinions."

Henry held up both hands to indicate he meant no harm. "I'm giving you the benefit of my experience," he said. "It's why you hired me. Sometimes it's best to leave well enough alone. Digging into someone's life can have unintended consequences. I've seen the damage it can cause."

She was not amused by his honesty. "Thanks for the unwanted advice, but I know what I'm doing."

What Kristina didn't know was that Henry had done some digging of his own. When she asked him to have Abbie Rambally followed, he thought it was an odd request but wanted to see where things would lead.

Once he provided Kristina with the photos of Abbie and Christian Wheeler together at the park, she was delighted. Henry figured Kristina wanted evidence to bust up the Rambally marriage, and although that was a rotten thing to do in his humble opinion, he didn't call her out.

When Kristina circled back to the issue of court transcripts, Henry got really worried. "Can you use your contacts in the legal community to gain access to the trial transcripts for Brynn Rossdale Harper?" she had asked.

"Why? I already told you they're sealed."

"I know what you told me," she responded frostily. "I need to know what went on at that trial. If you are unable or unwilling to carry out the assignment, I'll find someone who can."

Henry couldn't resist trying to talk her out of whatever she was planning one more time. He knew the consequences would be disastrous.

"All I'm saying is one doesn't need to be a detective to know that you came to Boston with an agenda, a mission that involves Dr. Rambally and his wife. I've seen a lot of things in my day, Kristina. My gut tells me you're playing with fire."

What a waste, Henry thought as he returned his attention to the news story.

"Residents of this luxury complex are beyond shocked that a crime of this magnitude happened in their neighborhood," the reporter continued.

Cut to residents being interviewed.

"That kind of stuff just doesn't happen here."

"This is a nice neighborhood. Everyone in this complex is friendly, and security is top-notch. Just goes to show nowhere is safe."

"I hope the police catch the killer soon. Such a tragedy for that young lady and her family. God rest her soul."

Henry flopped down on his living room sofa. Could he have done more to stop Kristina before she reached the point of no return? He had stopped a countless number of individuals from doing things that could land them in prison or worse during his days with the Boston PD.

How soon would the investigation into her death end up at his front door? The police detectives assigned to the case would no doubt discover Kristina had hired him to look into the Ramballys. They would want to know why.

Kristina was determined, and no amount of reasoning or warning would deter her. Unbeknownst to Kristina, Henry had gone so far as to use his contacts in the legal community to locate a juror from Brynn's kidnapping trial who might be willing to talk to him.

Alice Holt, a retired high school principal, said she would never forget that trial as long as she lived.

"That poor woman, Abbie Rambally, Lucas's mother. Reliving the horror of what that monster Zach Rossdale did to her, having to explain to her son why Brynn kidnapped him, but she couldn't tell him the whole truth."

Tears had sprung to Alice's eyes as she recalled the testimony. "No mother should have to explain to a child that they only exist because of such a heinous crime.

"He wanted to kill his own son," Alice had continued, shaking her head in disbelief. "That's what Zach Rossdale sent Brynn and Brian Rogers to do. No one on that jury shed any tears when they heard Zach died before the trial had even begun."

Henry popped up into a sitting position. A thousand thoughts exploded in his head, and he desperately tried to reel them in, to make them fit together like a jigsaw puzzle. Kristina wanted to bust up the Rambally marriage, get Abbie out of the picture.

She wanted access to trial transcripts and visited Brynn in prison, Henry found out. Zach Rossdale was dead within a month of Lucas's kidnapping and safe return, long before Brynn's trial kicked off.

What did Kristina learn from Brynn, and why was Zach Rossdale conveniently dead due to a prison fight a month after his plot to kidnap and murder Lucas was uncovered? Why didn't prison guards break up the fight?

Something about this scenario stuck in his craw. And whatever it was, Kristina Hayward Saxena was up to her neck in it. It was what got her killed. Henry would bet his life on it.

CHAPTER 81

ABBIE

THE POLICE ARE here, just like I knew they would be. When news of Kristina's death broke a week ago, I knew it would only be a matter of time before they came knocking at our door as the investigation heated up.

Two detectives from the Bedford police department are in our living room, sitting across from Ty and me. A feeling of déjà vu overwhelms me. This exact scene played out a little over three years ago when the police were investigating the death of our nanny, Olivia Stewart.

Frank Conklin and Elizabeth Chaisson are the detectives leading the investigation.

Conklin gets straight to the point. "How do know the victim?" he asks Ty.

"We attended the same college."

"Where was that?"

"Yale."

"And that's it?"

The detectives know full well that's not it. They wouldn't be here talking to us if they thought that was it. Ty and I discussed the interview prior to their arrival and agreed to operate under the assumption the police know a lot more than they're saying.

While Kristina's death was a shock, I can't say I'm devasted. The vile things she threatened to do and the unnecessarily diabolical, hateful scheme she outlined to me during our final, contentious encounter resulted in many sleepless nights. Her words had a terrifying hold on me and now, no longer.

No longer will I look over my shoulder, live in fear of what she might do next. I'm not saying she got what she deserved, but I'm saying I can live in peace again. And truth be told, Kristina was a tortured soul. May death bring her the peace that alluded her in life.

Ty said, "Kristina and I dated for a couple of months. She left for England after graduation."

After answering a series of questions, we get to the heart of the matter, the reason the detectives came to see us.

"Why did the victim file a sexual harassment complaint against you, Dr. Rambally?" Conklin asks.

Ty and I had prepared for this question. The police aren't stupid. Our plan is to be transparent enough to ensure we don't become the investigators number-one suspects.

"Kristina wanted me to leave my wife for her. When I refused, she wanted payback, so she fabricated the complaint."

Chaisson asks, "Why would she do something like that? Were you having an affair with the deceased?"

"No, Detective." Ty explains running into Kristina in London, her move here, and everything that happened leading up to her death. Neither detective reacts.

Conklin asks, "When was the last time you both saw Mrs. Saxena?"

"At the hospital gala three weeks ago," Ty said.

"And you, Dr. Rambally?" Chaisson asks, her eyes focused on me.

"Same as my husband," I lie.

"Have either one of you ever been to her apartment?" Conklin asks.

We both shake our heads.

"When did you learn of Mrs. Saxena's death?" Chaisson asks Ty.

"Let's see. A week ago. The head of my department, Dr. Stevenson, called me into his office and told me Kristina was discovered dead in her apartment after she no-showed for work and her boss got worried."

"Is your supervisor in the habit of delivering news privately?"

"What do you mean?"

"Never mind," Chaisson says. Her next questions puts us on the defensive.

"So we have a victim who filed a sexual harassment complaint against you, Dr. Rambally, and two weeks later, she's dead. Care to comment?"

"There's nothing to comment about. As you probably know, my wife and I hired an attorney to protect our interests. If Kristina's lies had escalated, it could have been the end of my career."

"How so?" Conklin asks.

I jump in. "My husband is a prominent surgeon at a leading hospital. You don't have to be a detective to know the kind of damage an allegation like that can cause, long before an investigative outcome determines guilt or innocence."

Neither detective says anything. I add, "I'm sure you'll discover during the course of your investigation that Kristina was a disturbed individual with serious psychological problems."

"Is that your professional opinion?" Chaisson asks.

"Kristina was not a patient of mine. But it is my professional opinion, based on my interactions with her and observations of her actions, that she displayed characteristics of mental instability."

"Is that so?" Conklin asks. I can't determine whether he's skeptical or intrigued.

I dodge the question of Kristina's mental instability and lob a question of a different kind. "Do you have any leads on the killer or a motive?"

"It's still early in the investigation," Conklin says.

"How did Kristina die?" I ask. "I mean, we know from the news reports she was shot, but where?"

Chaisson leans in. "Why do you ask? Is there something you want to tell us?"

"No. I'm just wondering if Kristina could have survived. I don't know anything about guns, but wouldn't someone in the apartment next door hear the shot and call for help? That's all I'm saying."

Chaisson's gaze lingers on me a few seconds too long, as though she's not sure what to make of my curiosity. Then she says, "Mrs. Saxena was shot in the temple."

"Oh," I say and slink back into the sofa.

The detectives ask several more questions. When it's finally over, I breathe a sigh of relief. Soon, the police will have everything they need to wrap up their investigation, concluding that Kristina committed suicide.

CHAPTER 82

ABBIE

One Week Earlier

I LET MYSELF into the apartment. It was after ten at night. Kristina went out for a swim in the complex's Olympic-sized swimming pool fifteen minutes ago. She was expecting a visitor and left the door unlocked. I'd been following her movements and monitoring her electronic communication over the past several days.

When I left Kristina's office at MGH for the last time, I knew she wouldn't back down until she succeeding in destroying my family. I couldn't let that happen. I had to stop her.

I was in the middle of scoping out the perfect hiding spot when I heard a man whistling. The sound got closer and closer to the unlocked apartment door. My eyes scanned the space in a panic. *Where can I hide?* The closet in the hallway off the living room would have to do. I made it inside in the nick of time.

"I'm here," a male voice called out.

I recognized the voice. It was Callum Saxena. Dressed in a suit after ten at night. He dropped a briefcase on the sofa. The living room closet door had peep vents. The view was far from perfect, but I could make out movements.

Shortly thereafter, Kristina arrived. Callum said, "Why don't you go have a shower and I'll make us some tea?"

Callum headed to the kitchen out of my view, making tea, I assume. The closet was small, but I didn't dare breath or move. Fifteen minutes later, Kristina came back from her shower and stopped in the kitchen. I was sweating, my gloved hands making me even hotter.

It was difficult to hear clearly. I caught snatches of their conversation. It was a beautiful apartment, small enough that sound carried, but being stuck in a closet didn't help. After a while, they returned to the living room.

Good. I can hear better.

"I had my attorney draw up these. Real divorce papers. The terms are very much the same as the phony ones you had made. That was a work of genius, by the way. My hat's off to your forger."

"Callum." Kristina hesitates. "Perhaps in light of recent revelations, we—"

Callum cut her off. "Save your pity, darling. I'm putting my affairs in order, and that includes the divorce you've wanted for so long. I have no heirs. I'm offering you a twenty-million-pound payout, and that's that."

Whoa! I almost let out a *you gotta be kidding me*, but then I quickly realized I would give away my position. And knowing Kristina, she would have me arrested for trespassing.

Callum unlocked the briefcase and handed Kristina a bunch of papers, which she signed. Callum then took the papers from her and placed them back into his briefcase.

"I suppose this is it then," Kristina said.

"I suppose it is," Callum said and then stood.

Callum reached into his waistband, pulled out a gun, and shot Kristina in the temple. Then he calmly left the apartment, closing the door behind him.

It took me a minute to catch my breath. It happened so fast; there was no time to act.

Once I stopped shaking, I slowly exited the closet and went over to the sofa. Kristina lay lifeless, blood pooling onto her camisole.

I reached into my bag and pulled out the dark-blue journal I'd brought with me. I placed it under one of the sofa cushions and then exited the apartment.

EPILOGUE

ABBIE

Blue Heron Lake—One Year Later

FRANCES, CALLIE, AND I sit under an umbrella canopy protected from the August sun while enjoying spectacular views of Blue Heron Lake in upstate New York. Miles and Layla exchanged wedding vows a few hours ago in a sweet, intimate ceremony that brought us all to tears.

This celebratory occasion is mostly a family affair. The spectacular lakeside property, with its immaculate landscaping, windows all facing the lake, and separate boathouse and lake house, is the perfect place to celebrate family, according to Dad who made the purchase months ago. After the year we've had, we deserve the serenity and beauty of a place like this.

"Are you planning on moving back to the States so we can all live on the same continent?" I ask Frances. "Now that Callie is settling in New York again, it's time you come home to America. We can hang out like old times."

"I don't know if it's safe to come home, Abbie. Do you have any more psychos coming for you?" she asks cheekily. "Besides, Hugh is very British. I don't know if I could convince him to move here."

Frances glances at the massive lawn where her husband Hugh is chasing one of the kids in a game of tag, despite the fact they're still in formal wear and it's eighty-five degrees.

"You've spent your career convincing reluctant people to speak to you. You can convince Hugh," Callie says.

"Agreed," I say. "And to answer your question, I'm done with psychos. For good. So it's safe to come home."

The hospital cleared Ty of any wrongdoing when the blue notebook detailing Kristina's obsession with him was discovered by investigators. The hospital ruled her allegations false based on a desire for revenge against a man who had repeatedly rejected her.

Callum Saxena passed away three months after I saw him shoot Kristina in her apartment. To this day, no one knows I was there when it happened. I still wrestle with my guilt, but it's a small price to pay to keep the truth buried forever.

I knew Callum planned to kill Kristina and make it look like a suicide. When he approached me with the idea, knowing he didn't have long to live and could get away with it, I saw a way out of the unending nightmare Kristina had brought on my family.

Ty would have been exonerated eventually, but Kristina wouldn't give up so easily. She would find other ways to torment us, no matter how much information I dug up on her past.

Like Kristina, I dabbled in a bit of forgery to bring the nightmare to a conclusion. I typed out the various journal entries. Then, armed with a sample of Kristina's handwriting I swiped from her office, the highly competent forger I hired wrote each entry into the blue journal.

That insurance policy paid major dividends when investigators found it in Kristina's apartment, detailing her obsession with Ty, which supported the suicide conclusion.

Diabolical? Yes. Necessary? Yes. Do I regret it? No.

Police investigators also found on Kristina's phone a recorded conversation between Seamus Jones and Kristina discussing the botched attempt on my life in Jamaica.

Or was it a conversation between Kristina and me posing as Seamus in an attempt to get Kristina to admit her role in the fiasco? Voice-altering software had made that conversation possible.

I'm not proud of the things I did to protect my family, but I have zero regrets. I've spent years dodging dark forces that brought chaos and mayhem into my life. I'm exhausted. No more battles with sociopaths. I just want to watch my children grow and thrive. Grow old with my husband, hold our grandchildren. Make a difference in this crazy, messed-up world.

I step out of the past and focus on the present. Frances says, "It's going to take a lot to uproot my life in London to move back stateside."

"But it'll be worth it," I say. "You can help me spoil Callie's kid."

"Oh, no you don't," Callie says, wagging a finger at me. "You and Frances are not going to be those aunts who spoil their nieces and nephews rotten and then run away, leaving the parents to deal with the spoiled brats."

Frances and I exchange a look. "But of course we are, Callie," I say. "That's what aunties do, and we can't wait to spoil her."

I reach over and lovingly rub Callie's baby bump. She's five months along. Callie and Christian were married at the beginning of the year and decided to start a family right away. According to Callie, at almost thirty-five, she couldn't wait any longer.

"What are you ladies talking about?"

We hadn't seen Ty approach. Christian and Hugh trail behind him.

"Oh, this and that," I respond, as the men place drinks down on the table and take a seat. "We were just telling Callie how rotten we're going to spoil the baby. She's not too happy about it."

Christian kisses Callie on the cheek. He says, "Don't listen to them. No one but me gets to spoil our daughter rotten."

"Sorry to break it to you, dude, but we already started," Frances says.

We all burst out laughing. Next thing we know, the family descends on us. My parents, Ty's parents, Layal and Miles, Lee—with his wife Mavis and their daughters Zoe and Gabrielle—Layla's mom Zoya, and Grandma Naomi. The rest of the wedding guests are busting a move on the dance floor inside the reception tent.

The wedding photographer tells us to relax and pose however we want for this candid family shot. After he snaps several photos, he returns to the reception and the family does the same. Callie, Frances, and their husbands leave us alone too and head to the reception.

Only Ty and I remain with our children, now fourteen and fifteen. The twins will join Lucas at Branson Academy this fall. They're beyond thrilled to attend the same school once again.

The sun begins its descent over the horizon, its rays reflecting off the water the soft violet of twilight. The opening notes of "Endless Love" by Lionel Richie and Diana Ross float from the reception tent.

Ty turns to me and says, "May I have this dance, Mrs. Rambally?"

"You certainly may." I traipse to an open spot under a large tree. Ty and the kids follow.

We move to the slow, sensual rhythm of the classic ballad. And the funny thing is, our kids don't make fun of us or say we're being cheesy or embarrassing. They don't make any sarcastic, cutting remarks as teenagers sometimes do.

They just watch us, their faces beaming with joy, letting us know they approve.

I would do anything for my babies. And that means giving them the most precious gift in the world.

Family.

AUTHOR NOTE

Dear Reader,

Thank you for reading *Reign of Fear*, and if you've read the entire series, I'm humbled and grateful that you stuck with me and these characters. I've been living with Abbie for the past eight years and ending the series is bittersweet.

The idea to build a series around Abbie came from my novel *Fool Me Twice* (formerly called *Swan Deception*). Abbie was only fifteen in that novel and a point of view character. Even then, I knew she was special and something kept telling me I wasn't quite done with her.

Strange as it may sound, I didn't create a series Bible in the beginning nor did I decide how many books would be part of the series. I only knew the first book, *Game of Fear*, would pick up two years after *Fool Me Twice* ended. Each book spurred the idea for the next book in the series and so on—an organic approach which worked out well.

The Fearless Series went on to win multiple indie book awards including the IPPY, Eric Hoffer, Next Generation Indie and National Indie Excellence Book Awards.

I'm hard at work plotting my next novels, including the Rebel Squad YA thriller trilogy. And guess who will be the protagonists? Abbie's kids of course: Lucas, Blake and Alexis.

I invite you to sign up for my author newsletter at gledekabongo.com to get information on upcoming releases including the new series. As a thank you for signing up, **you'll receive a free copy of my novella, *The Inside Girl*.**

Thank you so much for your purchase(s) and hanging with Abbie and company. Please consider leaving a review.

Again, thank you for your support!
Gledé Browne Kabongo

ACKNOWLEDGMENTS

Thank you to my readers; a special thanks to my beta readers whose insights are always enlightening. To my family and friends, your love and support sustain me.

And last but not least, to my husband Donat Kabongo, my champion and first reader when the manuscript is just taking form. You always talk me off a ledge when I overthink the plot (it happens with every novel). But most importantly, thank you for giving me the space and peace to tell these stories. I love you.

ABOUT THE AUTHOR

Gledé Browne Kabongo writes gripping, unputdownable psychological thrillers. She is the Eric Hoffer, Next Generation Indie, IPPY and National Indie Excellence Award-winning author of the Fearless Series, *Our Wicked Lies, Fool Me Twice,* and *Conspiracy of Silence.*

Gledé holds a master's degree in communications and has spoken at multiple industry events including the Boston Book Festival and New England Crime Bake (Sisters in Crime). She lives outside Boston with her husband and two sons. For more information, visit www.gledekabongo.com.

CONNECT ONLINE
⊕ www.gledekabongo.com
✉ glede@gledekabongo.com
𝐟 gledekabongoauthor
◯ @authorgledekabongo

Made in the USA
Middletown, DE
21 July 2023